Sociological Progress in
Mission Lands

Sociological Progress in Mission Lands

By
EDWARD WARREN CAPEN, Ph. D.
*Secretary, Kennedy School of Missions, Hartford,
Conn.; Author of "The Historical Development of the Connecticut Poor-Law."*

Introduction by
JAMES A. KELSO, Ph. D., D. D.
*President Western Theological Seminary,
Pittsburgh, Pa.*

NEW YORK   CHICAGO   TORONTO
Fleming H. Revell Company
LONDON   AND   EDINBURGH

New York: 158 Fifth Avenue
Chicago: 125 North Wabash Ave.
Toronto: 25 Richmond Street, W.
London: 21 Paternoster Square
Edinburgh: 100 Princes Street

To my Father
Idol of my boyhood
Companion of my manhood
Always living in the spiritual world
Passionately devoted to the Kingdom of God
In advocacy of peace
In civic reform
In missionary leadership
Who went home from the firing-line

Introduction

By James A. Kelso, Ph. D., D. D.,
President Western Theological Seminary

ONLY a few interested observers are aware of the stupendous changes being wrought in heathen society by the leaven of Christianity. It is common enough for supporters of foreign missions to use the arithmetical test as an index of the progress and influence of their faith in pagan lands, but only the very thoughtful take into consideration the social revolution which the preaching of the Gospel has effected in the ancient civilizations of Asia and the rude tribes of Africa and the Islands of the Sea. A study of sociological progress in missionary lands constitutes a modern *apologia*, not only for foreign missions, but also for the social power of the Gospel. Our age has witnessed a singular spectacle—the denial of the social dynamic of Christianity, not only by the out-and-out socialist but also by those who are within the pale of the Church. It is not strange that Karl Marx and his followers wish to destroy the idea of God as the keystone of a perverted civilization and denounce Christianity as the bulwark of the present economic system. On the other hand, it is certainly startling to discover the defiant attitude of many earnest men and women, members of the Church or

standing in sympathetic relations with her, who are
working for the amelioration of social conditions
and the removal of the wrongs of our age.   Dis-
mayed by the apathy of the Church and a large
proportion of Christian people, this class have been
easily led to mistake this spirit of indifference to
the social implications of the Gospel for the typical
Christian attitude towards the problem of social
welfare.   Often in despair they claim that Christianity cares nothing for the ills of this existence but
is lost in dreams of other-worldliness, hence as they
face the inequalities and wrongs of the social order
they fling their taunt:

> "Ah but, Religion, did we wait for thee
> *   *   *   *   *   *
> .   .   .   .   we should wait indeed ! "

" Sociological Progress in Missionary Lands " not
only refutes the materialistic contentions of the
socialist, but also removes the misgivings and doubts
of thoughtful Christians when they consider the
failure of Christianity to remove many of the plague
spots of our own social order.   It is not necessary
to hark back to the early history of the Church to
learn that with the Christian religion was born a
new force of 'immeasurable social significance,' or
that the new religion, as Lecky puts it, aroused to a
' degree before unexampled in the world an en-
thusiastic devotion to corporate welfare.'   To
realize the truth of these assertions one has but to
turn to the annals of contemporary Christian mis-

sions all over the non-Christian world. The Christian missionary has gone to these lands to proclaim the evangel of redemption through Christ; to put it specifically—to save individual souls, and lo, there comes as a by-product, the infusion of a new leaven into the social order, which tends to remove evils that have been securely intrenched in heathen society not for centuries but for millenniums. We may cite a single example. The caste system of India has begun to fall before the social ethics of Christianity while Buddhism, which was to an extent a revolt against this feature of Hindu society, beat in vain against this adamantine rock.

In this volume Mr. Capen has dealt with this sociological by-product of Christian missions. He is adequately equipped for the performance of this task as he is a scientifically trained sociologist and has investigated by travel and observation the problems with which he deals. He possesses the combined resources of a scientific investigator and an eye-witness. On account of his equipment for the performance of this task, he was selected to deliver these lectures at the Western Theological Seminary of the Presbyterian Church, located at Pittsburgh, during the second semester of the academic year 1911–1912, in connection with the L. H. Severance Foundation.

This lectureship was endowed by the late Mr. Louis H. Severance, of Cleveland, Ohio, for the purpose of providing instruction on foreign missionary themes. No layman of the Presbyterian

Church was more deeply interested in or more thoroughly acquainted with the work and problems of evangelizing the heathen world, and his aim in making the gift which rendered this course of lectures possible was to awaken among the theological students an abiding and intelligent interest in the spread of the Gospel in pagan lands.

Preface

THIS book consists of six lectures, somewhat changed and enlarged, which were delivered in the winter of 1912 before the Western Theological Seminary of the Presbyterian Church in Pittsburgh, Pennsylvania. The theme was announced as Sociological Progress in Mission Lands. A fuller but too cumbersome phrasing would have been, An Examination of Sociological Progress in Mission Lands with Special Reference to the Influence of Christian Missions as a Factor in this Progress and with some Allusions to the Duty of the Church in the Face of these Mighty Social Movements. In many ways, it would be more satisfactory to speak of this book as a study of the sociological results of missions; but in that case it would be necessary to omit many interesting phenomena or to run the risk of claiming too much for the influence of the missionary.

As a matter of fact, the process of social development is too complex for one to claim that the changes have been due to the operation of any single cause, however influential that may have been. In the early days, the changes in countries like India and Hawaii were due chiefly to missionary influence, as the missionaries exercised almost the only reformatory force at work. Of late years, however, many other influences have coöperated with that of Christian missions in producing these changes and it would be folly to claim for Christianity a monopoly of the influence, except in the remote sense that these influences have come from the West and that the West has been largely moulded by Christianity. Again, many a reform which has been started by a missionary or native Christian has been adopted by others until the origin of the initial impulse has been forgotten, and any exclusive claim by Christians of the credit for the change might be regarded as insulting as well as false. Hence the book contents itself with the simpler task of sketching some of these social changes, the part the Christian missionary has played in their production, and the resulting challenge to the Church of Jesus Christ.

No worker in this field but is under the greatest obligation to Dr. James S. Dennis for the pioneer work which he has here done. His " Christian Missions and Social Progress " is a monumental work, which none but one possessed of ample resources and untiring patience could ever have produced. I have freely used the materials found in this thesaurus of information on social subjects, wherever my subject has concerned those sections which Dr. Dennis so thoroughly explored. I wish also to express my personal obligation to Dr. Dennis for assistance most willingly granted me in past years.

To those whose generosity made possible the personal investigations referred to in this book, I would at this time pay tribute ; and especially to him who would eagerly have read these pages, and who in the other world awaits the consummation of the task to which he gave his life. I am also under obligation to the friends in Pittsburgh and Boston who have taken a kindly interest in these lectures, have urged their publication, and suggested important improvements.

It has not seemed wise in a book of this character and size to give in foot-notes the authority for each statement of fact. Instead, references have been given for some of the more significant facts and for most of the quotations, and in an appendix are listed a few of the important works which have been used in collecting the material for these chapters.

E. W. C.

Hartford, Conn.

Contents

I.   The Problem   17

II.   Progress in the Removal of Ignorance, Inefficiency, and Poverty   .   .   47

III.   Progress in the Ideals of Family Life and the Position of Woman   .   .   95

IV.   Progress in Ethical Ideals   .   .   .   138

V.   Progress in Social Reconstruction   .   189

VI.   Christianizing Tendencies in Non-Christian Religions   .   .   .   232

Bibliography   280

Index   285

I

THE PROBLEM

BEFORE entering upon the discussion of the sociological progress that has been witnessed within the last hundred years in the countries where the Christian missionary has been labouring, it is necessary to set forth the problem. This includes an inquiry into the basis of social institutions and customs, the causes of social changes, and their limitations.

It needs no profound investigation to realize that individuals are to a very large extent the product of their environment, material and human. Children are born into a family, the form of which is prescribed by the state. The home in which they are brought up conforms to certain standards prescribed by custom, if not by law. The food people eat and the clothing they wear have been produced by others, and have come to them through complicated industrial channels, which ramify throughout the world. The content of education is the result of the strivings of men for knowledge throughout human history, and its provision and content are both prescribed by society. Even in the religious life, the truths which are taught have been battled over and been achieved at a great cost of energy and of life itself, and this religion centres in the Church, which is itself subject to human law and is a social institution.

Social control is about men constantly, and those who violate social customs have to suffer the consequences, either in social ostracism or in the penalties of statute law.   People are more or less consciously aware of their dependence upon those about them, less so of their dependence upon those who are more remotely serving them, and ordinarily city-dwellers are least of all conscious of their dependence upon nature.   It is only when a coal famine threatens, or the supply of food partially fails, and men have to pay more for what they eat, that they are brought face to face with the fundamental fact that everything of a material sort comes from nature.   On the other hand, those who are engaged in the primary occupations of agriculture and mining have no doubt regarding this fact, nor do the people in less highly developed civilizations than our own, where famines are of frequent occurrence, and millions never know what it is to have more than one meal a day, and even that barely sufficient to support life.   Through the past ages men have learned by bitter experience how to extract from nature the means of satisfying their bodily needs, and how to live and work together for their best interests.

Social institutions and customs are nothing more than the stereotyping of the adaptations to nature and to their fellow-men which men have found, or have thought they have found, to be conducive to their well-being, and which they therefore impose upon individuals in the interests of society. They thus embody the ideals which men have held up before themselves and prescribe the lines within which the individual must walk. Change these ideals, or introduce new knowledge or new factors into the relations of men to one another or to nature, and the social institutions and customs change inevitably, though usually slowly. Law and custom tend to lag behind and they often embody ideals that are passing away. They may, however, express an ideal which the leaders in thought have been able to put into force and to use as a lever for bringing the rest of the people up to a new level. Illustrations of both possibilities are seen in our American life to-day. The present statutes for regulating industrial combinations were framed to meet a situation which was passed a decade and more ago. On the other hand, leaders in tenement house reform endeavour to secure the enactment of building regulations which are in advance of the opinion of the majority and by sheer force of character and influence are able to get a lever by which they raise the whole housing standard of the community. Institutions and customs are thus not something mechanically imposed from without but are the embodiment of the experience and ideals of a group of men living together in a given environment and under given conditions.

The causes of social changes are the introduction

of new factors into these relationships. A natural calamity like the earthquake at Messina does more than throw down buildings; it dislocates institutions, breaks up customs, and may lead to profound social changes. Introduce into a country like Japan a new industrial system, and the customs, laws, and institutions which have served feudal Japan for centuries become almost as unsuited to meet the new situation as the old armour of the samurai would have been to protect the Japanese troops in their assaults upon Port Arthur. The life of England in every department has been profoundly affected by the introduction of a single invention, the steam-engine. This produced the industrial revolution of the eighteenth century, and led naturally to the profound social and governmental changes now in progress. Not that this has been the only factor, but it helped to set in operation the forces which are transforming aristocratic England into a democracy.

New relations to God and man are other factors that produce social changes. Nineteen centuries ago there appeared in Galilee a preacher of a new doctrine. The power of His divine personality, which impressed itself upon a group of obscure men, put before the world new ideals of life, and these at once began to transform a pagan world into a Christian world and to render obsolete, even hideous, institutions and customs which had embodied the lower ideals of the ancient civilization. Slavery was rendered unproductive by industrial changes, but the preaching of the brotherhood of man coöperated with this economic force in abolishing the sale of human beings as things. These two causes of change, material and spiritual, have in all ages worked side by side in guiding men into new experiences, with their resulting modifications of custom and institution.

At any single point in the process of social evolution, the possibilities of change are limited by the environment and the character of the people. The effect of climate upon the life and character of a community is not fully understood, but that it has a definite effect is not a matter of doubt. The intense heat of the tropics reduces the energy of the inhabitants, and encourages social customs and habits of life which are quite different from those that prevail where there is need of more protection from the weather. Extreme cold and long winters are also unfavourable to economic progress, except where a complicated system of industry has been introduced and has made man partially independent of surrounding conditions.

The health conditions are also of vital importance. A population which is being decimated by cholera, bubonic plague, or the sleeping sickness, or which has its vitality lowered by malaria or the hook-worm, is incapable of as high a development as one which enjoys a greater certainty of life and greater strength for its tasks. At this point of health, the climatic conditions are relatively flexible. Through the scientific control of disease, the enforcement of sanitary regulations, and the adoption of proper methods of living, a social and industrial development is made possible which would otherwise be out of the question. A comparison of a classification of the land surface of the globe according to its healthfulness to-day with a similar one of a few decades ago would reveal the fact that the margin within which life is possible has been pushed up many per cent. Thus, the ravages of sleeping sickness have been checked in Busoga, British East Africa, cholera has been stamped out in the Philippines, and the Panama Canal Zone has been changed from a pest-hole into a sanitarium.

The character and location of the soil also have a determining influence. They limit the density of population that may be supported on a given area, and condition the economic activities. These, in turn, affect the social life of the people. Here, too, science comes in to remove in part these limitations. By improvements in agriculture or by the utilization for other purposes of land which as grazing or as farming land could support but a small population on a relatively meagre scale, the number that can be supported on a given area may be greatly increased. The density of population upon Manhattan Island and upon the Rand in South Africa are typical illustrations of this fact.

Much has been made in the past of the so-called "aspect of nature." In those regions where the natural phenomena inspire awe and man seems helpless in his contest with nature, the effect of

environment upon character is different from what
it is where man is able as a rule to make nature his
servant. The great religions have originated in the
tropics, where man is forced to meditate upon the
cause of the phenomena about him. The hopeless-
ness of the struggle is typified in the pessimism
which breathes through Hinduism and Buddhism.
It is suggestive that the great religion of China,—
or, rather, its ethical and social system,—which
originated in the north, is agnostic. Confucius and
his followers did not concern themselves with the
other world, but left the people, who needed a
religion, to content themselves with the pessimism
that came with Buddhism from India, or with the
crude speculations and superstitions that originated
in their own primitive days when their command
over nature was relatively small.

Even in the aspect of nature there are possibilities of modifications from two sources. Science
can control, or at least can mitigate, the results of
natural phenomena or catastrophes, such as flood,
tempest, and earthquake, and it can lessen the
danger of famine. Japan's success in constructing
buildings that resist earthquake shocks severer than
those which ruined Messina ; the possibility of preventing by engineering works the famines that
follow the frequent floods of the Yellow River in
China, and the beneficent results of the irrigation
works in Egypt and India, indicate how science can
reduce to a minimum the evil social results of such
great natural catastrophes. Again, upon one who

sees behind nature a loving Father, the effect of all
such events will be radically different from what it
is upon one who sees in them the operation of evil
spirits, who hate men and rejoice in human suffering.

Finally, the present character and attainments
of the people themselves, however they were produced, limit the possibility of change. One cannot
expect that a people, who have been kept in utter
ignorance for generations, will at once rise to the
intellectual level of a country like the United States,
back of whose civilization are centuries of intellectual progress, and whose people are required to
receive mental training. Likewise, on the ethical
side, a people whose ancestors have for generations
had low standards of honesty, truthfulness, and
purity, cannot at once throw off this heredity.
Even the Spirit of God does not immediately and
forever overcome the influence of an evil ancestry
and a bad social environment. The records of
church discipline on the mission field bear mournful
testimony to this fact.

These are some of the factors which need to be
taken into consideration in the discussion of the
possibilities of social change and in an appraisal of
the worth of the changes which one sees on every
side in mission lands. The reformer needs to bear
in mind that the millennium will not come in a
day. It is a mistake to expect too much and so
become discouraged. It is easy to overshoot the
mark and be unduly disheartened because the

people are unwilling or unable to move rapidly enough.

It is not necessary in these days to refute the objection, formerly brought against the work of the missionary, namely, that it is worse than useless to introduce a new religion into the Orient, or to attempt to remove social abuses and modify social customs, for the reasons, forsooth, that the social organization and ideals of the East are better suited to the people than anything the West can offer, the people are satisfied to remain as they are, and any changes that occur must come exclusively from within and by a process of slow modification. The recent history of Japan is sufficient to answer this objection. This country, which centuries ago accepted Buddhism as one of its religions and took over from China the culture and much of the social organization bearing the name of Confucius, has within a few decades adopted the material civilization of the West. Still more recently, the world has seen how these different Asiatic peoples, in whose supposed interest the Church was commanded to keep " hands off," are themselves making changes which are profoundly influencing the future of the world. It is important, however, to analyze this process, see its need, and discover the missionary's relation to this movement.

This chapter cannot do more than outline these new factors and indicate their bearing. Five new factors may be mentioned as having entered into the social life of the East: Western influence, a new education, a new industry, new ethical and social ideals, and new political aspirations.

The first new factor is that of Western influence. In a sense, this includes all the others, for the changes along educational, industrial, ethical, and political lines may be traced to Western influence. However, as all these latter movements have been taken over by the people themselves, and have come to express their own desires and ideals, one may rightly treat Western influence as an independent factor, at the same time recognizing its genetic relation to the others. It has been shown that men are affected and moulded more or less directly through their social relations with all the individuals and groups of persons who touch them. The chief reasons for the differences in social development between the Orient and the Occident have been their isolation and the contrasts in their environments. Starting with different material surroundings and resources, and separated by natural barriers, the peoples of the East and West developed along independent lines. Until within a century or two the relations between East and West were so slight that their influence upon each other was negligible. In fact, it is within only a few decades that, through the improvement of transportation, Orient and Occident have been brought into intimate relations. The development of the transcontinental railway system unified the Atlantic and Pacific coasts of the United States. The railway development in China has helped to break down the provincial spirit and thus has contributed to the unity of purpose recently witnessed in that country's change of government.

So, on a larger scale, the whole world is becoming one. The men of the West carry their wares to the East. Even the introduction of so simple a product as a good quality of illuminating oil assists in the intellectual progress of the people of Asia. How many American youth would study even as hard as they now do, if the old tallow candle were their only means of illumination? The literature of America, England, France, and Germany is read by the educated youth of Asia, either in translation or in the original, and this literature often reflects the worst side of Western life. Students from India, China, and Japan study in Europe or the United States. They become acquainted with Western ideals and learn how the West regards their mother countries. At the same time, they often see more of the worst elements in Western life than of the best. They get a new idea of the world and return home either to advocate social changes or to be more tenacious than ever in clinging to their ancestral customs. Thus, the thought and life of Asia are affected by this influence emanating from the West.

Secondly, a new education is spreading all over mission lands, both that furnished by the missionary and, still more in certain countries, that provided by government. This means that peoples among whom the percentage of illiteracy has been nearly one hundred per cent. are becoming literate and intelligent. They are broadening their mental horizon, they are learning a new mastery over nature, they are becoming citizens of the world. No longer do the conditions that prevail around them satisfy the needs of their life.

A third new factor is the new industry which has entered Asia. The factory system has been introduced into Japan, China, and India. It is leading to a massing of population in cities, and to a growth of problems of housing, sanitation, hours of labour, and morals with which the old institutions are unfitted to cope. It is introducing abuses, the removal of which will tax the intelligence of the leaders of these countries. On the other hand, the new industry has in itself the promise of a higher standard of living and the removal of the burden of abject poverty. It teaches how nature can be induced to furnish the means whereby life can be enriched on its material side; it makes possible the development of public undertakings in the interests of justice, public health, and happiness; and it furnishes the basis upon which the process of social development can be carried on with greater efficiency and upon a higher plane.

Fourthly, new ethical and social ideals have been acquired. Men who have become familiar with the thought of the West and who have learned to regard the life about them from a new standpoint inevitably acquire new ideals and become reformers. The anti-opium movement in China, the various reform movements in India, which concern purity of worship and the position of woman, are instances of this new factor. These men become centres of influence which make for the uplift of their people and they use public opinion and law to enforce new standards.

New political aspirations are a fifth characteristic of the Orient to-day. The four factors already mentioned have united to produce this fifth, which is the desire to emerge from political servitude or political tutelage into political independence. The nationalistic movement in China has transformed the political institutions of that old empire, while in India the kindred movement has already secured reforms, the possibility of which would never have been dreamed of a generation ago.

These are some of the most obvious factors which are entering into the life of the East. They mean that the relations between men and their physical and human environments are changing, and that customs and institutions which were well adapted, it may be, to meet the needs of a former day are no longer satisfactory. Elements in the life about them that have been taken for granted in the past are now seen in their true light, and leaders are arising to give the lie to the assertion so frequently made in the past, that the life of the Orient is idyllic and should not be disturbed by the West.

What, now, are some of the evils which the reformers are seeking to remove, or should seek to remove ? Eight points may be mentioned at which there is need of improvement :

1. Ignorance. Up to within a comparatively recent period the great mass of the people of the world were ignorant. Education and culture were the monopoly of a few. What was true of all Europe until a not very remote past, what is true even now of certain backward Western countries or of some sections of more progressive nations, was equally true of Asia and Africa. What learning existed belonged to some one class, or perhaps to several classes, social or more usually religious. The mass of the people, including in most cases all the women, were denied direct access to the best thought of their nation. It was not only ignorance in this sense which marked the intellectual activities of the East, but to this should be added the ignorance of a narrow provincialism, both international and national, if one may use such terms. That is, the people of such countries as Japan and China believed their civilization to be the best in the world, and regarded all other peoples as barbarous. They were unwilling to make changes because they regarded their own institutions to be beyond reproach. This may be called international provincialism. Within the limits of most countries, likewise, there existed a national provincialism. The people were divided into sections by racial, linguistic, or religious barriers, which made impossible the free interchange of ideas and all united effort.

The first condition of progress is intelligence, and this must be supplemented by freedom of communication for persons, commodities, and ideas within the region in question. These conditions were absent in Asia until recently, and for the most part they are still wanting. Here is an obvious evil.

2. Physical suffering, due to ignorance of sanitation and medical science. No one but a medical man or woman can fully appreciate what this means to the people of the East. The foolish or disgusting medicines and the cruel practices of the medicine-men need not be dwelt upon. In large sections of the non-Christian world half the population has to suffer practically without hope of relief, and until women can be relieved of this unnecessary burden, there is a social benefit to be conferred. Apart, however, from the consequences to individuals, the lack of an understanding of the principles of sanitation, hygiene, and medicine seriously affects the progress of society. Premature death deprives society of the services of millions each year, while the results of disabling injuries and disease not only take from society possible contributors to its wealth but also impose upon it the burden of supporting a large class of dependents. Hence, in the interests of humanity and of social efficiency, this is another point at which progress is demanded.

3. A third closely related evil is that of economic inefficiency. There are countries where the population is not given to overmuch exertion and the

charge of laziness might be sustained. Even here good reasons might often be given for holding that much of this apparent unwillingness to work productively is traceable to their system of the division of labour, by which war and the chase are the proper occupations for men. Other contributing causes are the lack of the spur of necessity and uncertainty as to the enjoyment of the fruits of toil. The greatest peoples of the Orient, however, contain a body of labourers whose patience, persistence, and endurance are most admirable, far surpassing that of Western artisans. At the same time, the output of their toil is pitifully small. They have so little command over natural forces that their labour is unproductive, and even after their long hours they have little to show for their toil, measured either in cash or in goods. Missionaries in India declare that the half-dozen or more servants they have to employ are less efficient than a single good servant of the old type in an American home. To be sure, these workmen often possess much artistic ability and even technical skill, but their tools are so crude, if ingenious, that their output is small. Some Indian tools have been declared by an expert to combine ingenuity and stupidity. If a high degree of civilization is to be enjoyed by the mass of the people, it needs for its basis an economic efficiency far surpassing that which was prevalent in Africa or Asia before the advent of the present new industrial era.

4. As a result of these three evils, we have a fourth, the low standard of living. Nothing but

poverty, and poverty of an abject sort, can be expected under the conditions already indicated, and that is what one finds. It is probable that in the slums of London or New York may be found many cases of greater degradation, even of greater suffering, than exist in these great Eastern countries under normal conditions. At the same time, the poverty of the Orient must be seen and studied to be appreciated. A large percentage of the people of China and especially of India is never well nourished. A smaller percentage, but still a frightfully large one, is always on the verge of starvation, and needs only some calamity, like flood or famine, to put it in a starving condition. In India, competent authorities declare that from forty to sixty millions lie down hungry upon a mud floor every night, after but one or at most two scanty meals during the day. This is when famine conditions do not prevail. An Indian member of the British Parliament estimated that the average income per capita in India was only seven dollars a year; Lord Cromer's estimate was nine dollars; and the Hindu writer, Mr. R. C. Dutt, contrasts the average income in England of $210 a year with that in India of ten. In one district of South India the class of day labourers get but twenty dollars a year for themselves and their families.[1] Fifty-three per cent. of the population are dependents.

Even this is not all. In many of these Eastern

[1] Eddy, S., " India Awakening," p. 21. Cf. Jones, J. P., "India's Problem, Krishna or Christ," p. 19.

countries, even those who can manage to exist in a
fairly vigorous manner live in homes which are
inferior in many respects to the buildings in which
we house animals. This is not to say that a
tolerably rich and an entirely Christian life cannot
be lived with fewer creature comforts than are to
be found in the homes of the United States, or that
our people are not in danger of over-emphasis upon
the material side of life. It is, however, to maintain that, from the standpoint of humanity or of
Christianity, the standard of living of a great proportion of these people, often of a vast majority, is
below that which can in any way be satisfactory
to one who desires to see each child of God living
the abundant life which Christ came to give to men.
Privacy, decency, and something to minister to the
æsthetic and intellectual, as well as to the ethical
and spiritual side of man's nature, are elements in
the minimum with which any broad-minded Christian or social worker can be satisfied. Besides this,
men and women must cease to be used as beasts of
burden or mere machines and must have an occupation that is worthy of a human being.

5. Again, we find that the status of woman
constitutes another typical evil among these people.
There are great variations here, but in general the
women of Asia and Africa have been regarded as
inferior to men both in ability and in character.
They were denied the privilege of education on
the grounds of incapacity and social inexpediency.
They were often treated like chattels. Their chief

function was to satisfy the passions of men and bear children. They were too often the victims of cruelty and lust. It would be wrong to conclude from this that women were without influence. Ignorant and despised, they nevertheless were in many countries powerful factors in the life of society. The result was inevitable, for the higher degrees of civilization or culture are impossible when half of the population is kept in ignorance and denied the rights that belong to a humanity touched by the Spirit of God. From the disabilities of women have flowed consequences in the family life which are most serious from the social point of view.

6. Another evil was the low estimate put upon the individual. This was shown in the cheapness of human life. The individual counted for little. The killing of hundreds or even of thousands in constructing public works, in war, or as a consequence of some catastrophe or scourge, was regarded as an event of no importance. The callousness to human suffering that is so prevalent outside the domain of a vital Christianity is akin to this view of the value of life. Another aspect of the same evil is the lack of a sense of individual responsibility, and the denial to the individual of the opportunity for development. As a member of a family, a guild, a caste, a clan, or a tribe, the individual had his place and was cared for. As an individual, he counted for next to nothing. What his fathers had been for generations, he and his descendants had to remain. It was regarded as

impious for a man in India to attempt to change his social status. China, with its mixture of democracy and absolutism, did permit the man of ability to rise, but the value put upon the ordinary individual was low. This general position stunted the growth of individuality and prevented a full social development.

7. Another social evil, which was common, was that of the corruption and inefficiency of the government. Justice, in our meaning of the term, was practically unknown, its place being taken by the decision of the personal ruler, who often followed his caprice or whim, or decided in favour of the one who could offer the largest bribe. Life and property were both subject to his will, and the lack of security here hindered economic and social development. The theory of government was that of exploitation in the interests of the ruling class, and the well-being of the people was a matter of very minor importance.

8. Lastly, we may mention the low ethical standards. There is great danger of misrepresentation at this point; but in general it may be said that in such matters as purity, honesty, and truthfulness the conditions were far from satisfactory, except in certain isolated cases. Out of people whose life is honeycombed by lust, fraud, and duplicity cannot be formed a social life which shall make for the enrichment and uplift of human life.

In the light of these statements regarding the

need of social progress, its causes, and its limitations, what shall be said as to the question of the
relation of the missionary to this whole subject?

In general, the missionary has been the pioneer
social reformer in mission lands. Whether purposely or not is not the question, but as a matter of
fact the missionary has taken the lead. Of the five
new factors, just enumerated, which have entered
into the life of the Orient, three were introduced by
the missionary, and upon the remaining two his
work has had a distinct bearing.

In the matter of Western influence, the missionary was the pioneer. He was the first Westerner
who brought the Western point of view to these
mission lands. Usually the traders touched only a
few points on the coast, and their influence was not
continuous or usually in favour of higher ideals.
The missionary was the one who went into the in-
terior, who lived with and was trusted by the people, and whose point of view became known to
them. Even trade followed the missionary, and it
was in those regions where the missionary introduced Western wares for his own use, and accustomed the people to them, that the trader found a
market for his goods.

As to the new education, there is no disputing the
claim of the missionary to the credit for its introduction into most mission lands. Western schools
were introduced into China, India, Persia, Turkey,
Africa, and the other great fields of Christian work
by the missionary. Missionaries have done a no-

table educational work in Japan. In India and in China the best education is still in the hands of the missionaries, and in certain fields they have a practical or even an absolute monopoly.

A similar statement may be made regarding the new ethical and social ideals. It was the missionary who first inaugurated the agitation against foot-binding in China. It was the missionary who protested against the obscene elements in the Hindu religion, against *sati* and the evils connected with the marriage system. It was the missionary who inspired the Christian community with higher ethical and social ideals and thus set a new standard for the whole community.

In the matter of the new industry, the missionary was not in the same sense the pioneer, although early missionary efforts in some fields included training in agriculture and the mechanic arts. In India and in Africa the missionary has made a real contribution to the economic progress of the people through industrial and manual training classes and schools. Indirectly, through inspiring the people with new ideals and by making them dissatisfied with the plane upon which they had existed, he aroused the people to desire new and more rewarding industries.

The political movements towards national independence cannot be attributed directly to the missionary who is everywhere scrupulous in teaching loyalty to government. At the same time, it was through the education given by the missionary and through the information received from him regarding the conditions in Europe and America that the first steps were taken towards preparing the people to desire and to be fitted for a larger share in the government. A Christian college trained the leaders for the new Bulgaria. Members of the Young Turk party publicly declared that they would never have dared to strike the blow for liberty and constitutionalism had they not been sure of the intelligent and hearty support of the young men scattered throughout the country who had been trained in the Christian schools and colleges and had become firm believers in Western political institutions.

Again, take the eight typical evils enumerated above, and the result is even more interesting and conclusive. Missionaries have done much to remove the evil of ignorance. They have introduced into the East modern medicine and are treating yearly millions of patients who would otherwise be beyond the possibility of relief. Where the need is the greatest, they have undertaken to increase the industrial efficiency of the Christian community, and to prepare Christian leaders for the new industry. In various ways they have raised the standard of living among the native Christians and those who are under Christian influence. Under the impulse of Christianity, woman has been coming to her own. Education has been provided for her, and in Christian homes the wife is becoming the companion and helpmeet of her husband and the intelligent guide and teacher of her children. Christianity has emphasized the infinite worth of the individual before God, and the Christian has come to have a new sense of self-respect, and he stands before the community as a free man in Christ. The missionary has ever preached and exemplified new standards of justice, honour, truthfulness, and purity, and thus personally and through those whom he has influenced and trained he has helped to solve both the political and the ethical problems of the people among whom he has lived. The missionary body has been the mightiest single social force in the changes which are taking place to-day in Africa and Asia, even though other factors have now entered into the movements, and the missionary's own influence has become in some ways relatively less important than at first.

This is the inevitable result of missionary work. Even the missionary who is most conservative in his conception of the purpose of his undertaking, who would carry on a purely spiritual work, and who would keep clear of all that he would call outside and secular, cannot avoid setting in motion forces that will transform the social environment in which he works. Whether he will or not, he is introducing new factors into society, and this inevitably means changes in the structure and functions of the social group. Society, as already explained, is nothing more than the stereotyping of the experience of a people in adapting themselves to their environment, material, human, and divine. It is the embodiment of their ideals of life and relationship. The mere acceptance of the Christian view of God as a being of perfect holiness and of love, of the Christian view of man as a child of the loving heavenly Father, and of the Christian view of human relationships as those of brothers, makes at once impossible the toleration of customs and institutions which have been handed down from the past. Slavery must be abolished, justice must be done, and men must be permitted to live a self-respecting, decent life upon a higher plane.

The Christian will not willingly endure the oppression from which he has suffered and which he accepted when he believed that his nature was inferior to that of his ruler. Give a man knowledge of medicine and the old acceptance of sickness as inevitable, with its frequent result in callousness or indifference, ends and an efficient sympathy takes its place. Add education, and with it comes a greater power over nature and a greater industrial efficiency. The whole aspect of nature and of life is changed, the power of the old superstitions has been broken, the influence of the medicine-man and priestly class has been shattered, and inevitably a new day has dawned, a day which will witness profound social changes. And all this has been set in motion by the simple proclamation and acceptance of the Gospel.

Thus, the missionary cannot, if he would, escape being a social reformer, indirectly if not directly. At the same time, few missionary leaders to-day would limit the work of the missionary so narrowly.

There prevails now a broader conception of the aim of the missionary than was accepted a generation ago. It is an interesting fact that this is a return, though on a higher plane, to the purpose which actuated the great leaders of the movement of foreign missions a century ago. The instructions given to the first band of missionaries who sailed for Hawaii in 1827 declared that the people of the islands must be formed " into a reading, thinking, cultivated state of society with all its schools and seminaries, its arts and institutions." The social aim of Christian missions was not overlooked then, even though the interpretation of Christianity was individualistic, and the great motive urged was the salvation of individual souls.

The change in the emphasis at home is nowhere better exhibited than in the five-fold programme of the Men and Religion Forward Movement which swept the country in the winter of 1911–1912. The theology of the leaders was conservative ; so were their views of Biblical questions ; but the social note was marked. For almost the first time the men of the Church had brought home to their attention the facts that social service, missions, and work for boys cannot be separated from the duty of evangelism and Bible study, and that the effects of these last are not complete until the message of the Bible is applied to men in all their relations, or until the men who have been saved by the evangelistic message are set to the task of realizing in actual every-day life the principles of Jesus Christ. The Church has come to see that its duty does not end with changing the life of individuals; that, in fact, this result cannot be either perfect or permanent, so long as the environment is characterized by conditions which are out of harmony with the teachings of the Sermon on the Mount. Men now believe that saved individuals must in turn Christianize society and make sure that customs and institutions help men to attain to the likeness of Christ Himself.

This new social note in Christianity at home is only an echo of the social note which the foreign missionaries were long ago forced to sound because of the conditions around them. A recent writer has strikingly illustrated this change of emphasis by a figure which he himself admits is inaccurate in details. In the old days, he says, the world was likened to a sinking ship, and the work of the missionary was to rescue a few individuals and land them on the shore. The modern missionary, however, has gone on board the vessel, has sounded the water in the hold, and has decided that it is possible to bring the ship safely into port; besides which, the majority of the passengers resolutely refuse to leave the ship.

What, then, is the aim of the missionary? At the Student Volunteer Convention in 1906, one of the leading missionary secretaries declared in a public address that the missionary must preach and propagate the following ideas:—" The Gospel of physical cleanliness, . . of physical perfection, . . of industry, . . of a sane, safe and pure society, . . of brotherly love, . . of good works, . . of intellectual development, . . of justice, equality, and common rights, . . of human sin, . . and of redemption for the entire man."[1]   No gospel less comprehensive than this will satisfy the needs of the present day.   The Church has come to realize that the gospel has a message for man in all his relationships and is not satisfied until a man has realized all his divine possibilities.   This means that the great nations of the East must be thoroughly Christianized so that the social environment will coöperate with the Spirit of God in transforming men and women into the likeness of God. More specifically, the primary work of the missionary will always remain what it has always been, that of transforming individuals ; for no society exists apart from the individuals that compose it ; and a nation can be Christian only as the dominant influence in it is that of Christian men and women. But his work will not stop there.

Beyond this, the missionary seeks the naturalization of Christianity in each mission field.   This includes the making of Christians, their gathering into Christian churches, able to support, direct, and propagate themselves, and the planting of all the institutions which embody the spirit and perform the multiform work of Christ in that community. There must be a Christian educational system, a Christian home, an industrial system based upon

---

[1] Rev. J. L. Barton, D. D.   *Vid.* "Students and the Modern Missionary Crusade," p. 111 *et seq.*

the principles of Christ, a government that in all
its activities is in harmony with the same principles,
and a public opinion that will support every movement for the realization by each individual of the
ideals of Christ. To be sure, much of this is the
work of the Christian community more than of the
missionary as such, but it is for the missionary to
lay the foundations and to make all his work count
in this direction. The mission educational system
can be used to train Christians for leadership in
every phase of activity, educational, industrial,
ethical, even political. The missionary can stand
for Christian ideals at all times, and can inspire
and guide in the Christianizing of society without
neglecting his task of reaching individuals.

In all this he can have a realizing sense that,
apart from the influence of Christianity, all these
social movements will fail of their purpose. As
one examines more closely these new factors which
have entered into the development of the Orient,
one is struck by a lack. The Western influence,
apart from the missionary, is largely materialistic,
agnostic, or even anti-religious. The new education, except as it is Christian, is weaning the future
leaders of Japan, China, and India from their old
superstitious beliefs. They are losing their old
standards, the old sanctions of conduct, but they
are getting nothing in their place. Leaders of
Japan are alarmed at the moral tone of their country. The new industry is for the most part actuated by the spirit of materialism, and there is

danger that, without the restraints of a Christian public sentiment and the Christian sense of the value of the individual, the worst instances of exploitation the world has yet known will be witnessed. A godless industry may prove a curse to East and West alike.

Likewise, in the realm of social and political reform there are not enough leaders of absolute integrity and unselfishness, men of broad vision and utter devotion to the best interests of all the people and not of a single class or section. These nations are waiting for the appearance of a new type, a type which can be produced only by Christianity with its adequate doctrines of God, sin, and salvation; with Christ as the ideal of the new manhood of the East; and with the mightiest dynamic in the world, which can send men out into the service of others in the spirit of Jesus. Mere reform is not enough. Patriotism will never answer. The ethnic religions have had free reign for centuries and have produced or tolerated the evils from which relief is now sought. It is for the followers of Christ to prove that the religion of the Carpenter of Nazareth, of the risen and glorified Redeemer is able to cope with all these social evils and transform the nations of the East and the West alike into the Kingdom of His Father and their Father.

II

PROGRESS IN THE REMOVAL OF IGNO-RANCE, INEFFICIENCY, AND POVERTY

THE degree to which men have a command over the forces of nature determines the scale of their living, and to a large degree the possibilities of their social development. It is a truism to say that every material thing men possess they have obtained from nature. Men have never been able to create a particle of matter. They can do two things. They can make the matter more useful by changing its form, and they can induce nature to produce what they need in the way of food and clothing. Every one knows this, and yet men take it so much for granted that they tend to overlook its significance.

For instance, in these days of social and industrial betterment people are apt to assume the existence of unlimited wealth for improving conditions. Cities issue bonds in large amounts in payment for great public works and improvements, but they sometimes appear to forget that these must be paid for out of what men extract from nature or manufacture out of the materials which others extract or produce. Only a nation that is rich in the products of its soil or its toil can afford those luxuries or necessities which the apostles of social betterment demand. Likewise, labour leaders, in their attempt to secure a larger share of the products of their toil, cannot safely reduce the total output. Whenever they do, they forget that their income depends just as truly upon how much there is to divide as it does upon what proportions shall go to capital and labour. Real industrial progress is assured only when the amount of product per unit of labour is increasing.

Because of the natural richness of our soil and the efficiency of our machinery and labour, we in the United States are comparatively free from the restraints imposed upon a people by lack of a command over nature. Not so in most mission lands. Even a rich country like Japan finds itself almost staggering under the burdens it has assumed by entering fully into partnership with the great nations. The Japanese are unable to develop their school system fast enough to meet the increasing demand for higher education. In matters of sanitation, housing, and the like they are hampered by the fact that their present command over nature is not sufficient to make possible the realization of their schemes for social development.

India also illustrates the same point. The people cannot pay increased taxes because of their lack of industrial efficiency, which limits the product out of which they have to support their families and pay their taxes. With the present taxes, the government cannot put into effect those comprehensive schemes for universal, free, and com-

pulsory education in which the leaders see the hope
of realizing their dreams of self-government.

Again, take the Christian community in these
countries. All missionary leaders desire and work
for the day when the Christians shall be able to
support their churches and schools and all the
philanthropic institutions that go with a Christian
civilization. Even if all the Christians gave as
much as they could reasonably be expected to
give,—and in general they come nearer to this
standard than the Christians in the home-lands,—
it would yet be a long time in many of these
communities before they could be self-supporting
on any adequate scale. A few years ago a secretary of a great mission board was making his first
tour of the field. He was in India and was visiting a group of Christians who had been gathered
out of a community of outcastes. As he saw their
homes, their manner of life, and their crude industries, he exclaimed, "Now I understand why
there is not more self-support in this mission."
It was simply impossible for these men, with their
slight power over natural forces, to produce much
more than enough to keep soul and body together.
Only as their economic efficiency can be increased,
can they rise gradually to a greater measure of self-
support. The difficulty in such cases is not so much
moral as it is industrial.

These illustrations make clear the fact that the
realization of the social ideals which the Christian
desires for the peoples of mission lands must rest

upon a sound economic basis, and that apart from economic progress there can be relatively too little progress in the higher realms. Hence, progress in the removal of ignorance, inefficiency, and poverty is logically the first step towards an improvement of social conditions. This is not to maintain, however, that this economic progress must, in point of time, precede ethical and spiritual progress. It is often the case that, only as man's whole nature is touched by the Spirit of God, is he aroused to desire and to seek those material aids by which he can realize the Christian ideals for his daily life.

From this point of view one sees the significance of those elements in the situation confronting the missionary to which attention has already been called, namely, ignorance, inefficiency, and poverty.

Taking the mission field as a whole, the missionary, when he entered upon his work, found himself throwing in his lot with people who were extremely poor. Americans think they know something of poverty at home. People here and in England speak of "the submerged tenth" and there are other tenths of the population whose income is below what we regard as a proper minimum living wage. Abroad, however, in many a mission field one might more justly have spoken of the submerged nine-tenths, or even ninety-nine-one-hundredths, for the amount of wealth per capita was far below that of a progressive industrial country in the West, and the wealth that existed was in the hands of a very small fraction of the population.

Among the causes of this poverty may be specified ignorance, with its resulting inefficiency, and the lack of medical and sanitary science, which increased needlessly the burdens of sickness, physical incapacitation, and premature death. Among other contributing causes were unjust government, insecurity of life and property, and, in certain countries, the existence of a large class of dependents, who lived out of the offerings of the rest of the population, although most of these had not enough for their own support upon a proper standard of living. In India even to-day this class is numbered by the million.

What has the Christian missionary done to remove these evils? It is only fair to say that, except in the limited field of industrial training, he has not aimed to increase the people's command over nature. He has taken up medical work in order to relieve suffering and gain access for the Gospel. He has engaged in educational work, both for the sake of getting a hearing for the Gospel, and for the purpose of securing an intelligent Christian community, capable of reading and understanding the Bible. Other reasons have been largely incidental, but the result of the work has been to make a real contribution to social progress.

The modern missionary has been an educational pioneer. In most countries there was little education before the advent of the missionary, and this, except in China, was not usually open to the people as a whole, but was the prerogative of certain classes, social or religious. The content of the education had no relation to modern thought and did not prepare the scholar for leadership in the industrial sphere or fit him to guide his people in competition with the Western nations. There was no science and no history worthy of the name. The students became familiar with their religious books, or, in a country like China, with their classical literature. They cultivated a certain literary style. In its day this education was the best these peoples could devise and fitted the student for life, but it had no relation to present-day problems.

When William Carey entered India and opened the modern missionary epoch, one of his first thoughts was to begin the work of Christian education, and to-day there still stands at Serampore one of the most impressive educational buildings ever erected for the spreading of a knowledge of Christian truth. From that day to this, the missionary has been an educator, and as a rule the missions which have the greatest results to show for their work have made large use of the Christian school as a means of Christianizing the nations. The work of Christian education has grown from the humblest beginnings until to-day it numbers its pupils by the million, the grand total being more than 1,520,000. The sun never sets upon these students, Christian and non-Christian, boys and girls, children and adults, of all colours and social position, who study in a variety of buildings, ranging all the way from thatched-roof huts, with or without sides, or thatch stockades, up through simple native buildings to structures that are as impressive as most that our colleges and universities at home possess.

The grade of these schools ranges from kinder-gartens and the most elementary village schools up to colleges and advanced theological, medical, and technical institutions.   Even as a mere matter of statistics, the mission education makes an impress-ive showing.   The latest statistics, contained in the " World Atlas of Christian Missions," [1] give the following facts:

There are 86 universities or colleges, with 8,628 pupils in college classes.   While the grade of these classes is in most instances below that of our col-leges, yet it means that they are offering more than high school work and are relatively as ad-vanced as our colleges were a generation or so ago.

Of theological and normal schools and training classes there are 522, with 12,761 pupils, who are in training for immediate leadership in the work of the Church and the Christian community.

There are 1,714 boarding and high schools, with an enrollment of 166,447, from which number will be selected those who will pass on to college or professional school.

There are 292 industrial institutions or classes, with an enrollment of 16,292.   These last figures are impressive but are smaller than they should be. It should be added, however, that they do not in-

[1] Dennis, *et al.*, " World Atlas of Christian Missions," p. 84.

clude the ordinary schools that provide industrial courses as a part of their regular curriculum.

Of elementary and village schools there are 30,185, instructing 1,290,357 pupils. This number of pupils is practically the same as the school enrollment for the state of Pennsylvania. These schools lay the foundations for all the higher educational work, and in some countries they furnish nearly all the missionary education.

The remaining institutions may be tabulated as follows :

```
Kindergartens . . . . . . . . . . 115 . . 5,597 pupils
Orphanages . . . . . . . . . . . 271 . . 20,383   "
Institutions for blind and deaf . . 25 . .   844   "
Medical schools . . . . . . . . . 111 . .   830   "
Nurses' training schools . . . . . 98 . .    663   "
```

This makes a grand total of 33,419 schools and 1,522,802 pupils. By way of comparison, it may be stated that in the New England States and New Jersey, according to the census of 1910, the number attending school was 1,652,506.

The distribution of these schools is significant as indicating where the emphasis has been put on education and where the higher education has been furthest developed. The mission fields that contain the largest number of colleges and universities are as follows :

```
India . . . . . . . . . . . 37, with 4,982 students
China . . . . . . . . . . . 18,   "    919    "
Turkey . . . . . . . . . . 11,   "  1,419    "
Japan (including Korea) . . . . 8,   "    517    "
Other countries . . . . . . . . 12,   "    791    "
```

India has 43% of the colleges and 58% of the college students.

Of the theological and similar classes, the distribution is wider, and every mission field, with but few exceptions, has at least a few such classes. Here again we find India in the lead, and the countries which contain the largest numbers are as follows:

India . . . . 141, with 3,755 pupils
China . . . . 129, " 2,544 "
Africa (with Madagascar) . . . 116, " 2,747 "
Japan . . . . 42, " 1,479 "

It will be noted that Africa has more pupils in such classes than any other field save India.

The distribution of boarding and high schools is similar to that of these professional schools.

India is the great home of mission industrial work, containing, as it does, 148 out of 292 schools, or 50%, with 8,999 pupils, while Africa has 70 of the remainder, with 3,485 pupils.

A somewhat similar situation is revealed in the matter of elementary education, although, like the theological and normal school, the day school is found in every mission field. Japan proper drops out here, because the government has practically the monopoly of elementary education, except for night schools or special classes. India has 11,503 of the 30,185 schools, or 34%, containing 361,726 of the 1,290,357 pupils, or 28%. Africa comes next with 8,271 schools, or 27%, with 447,196 pupils, or 35%.

In the matters of support and influence these mission schools differ from country to country. The Indian government gives grants-in-aid to all schools that conform to the prescribed standards, and these grants, added to the fees of the pupils, are almost, if not quite, sufficient to support the schools, except for the salaries of the missionaries. Most mission schools in India are thus aided or supported. A similar system prevails in parts of South Africa and in a few other British colonies. On the other hand, no government grants are available in Turkey, China, or Japan; and full recognition has not yet been accorded to mission schools in the two great nations of Eastern Asia. In fact, Japan expressly refuses to accord full recognition to any school that gives religious instruction within the school buildings, even outside of school hours. In some parts of Africa, for example in Uganda and Rhodesia, the mission schools have a practical monopoly of the field. The same has been true of Turkey, for the mission schools have been so far superior to other schools that they have dominated the situation.

In India, the mission schools are now meeting the competition of an increasing number of non-Christian and government schools, but they still set the standard in the matter of character building and moral tone, and many of them are without peers in efficiency.

In China, the Christian school for a long time had a monopoly. Recently, however, the govern-

ment and wealthy individuals have been starting
new schools and the enrollment in these already
greatly exceeds that in mission schools. In one
province, where Christian education is well organized and the government education has existed for
but five years, the enrollment in the government
schools is one hundred times that in mission schools.
Peking alone has two hundred schools with seventeen thousand pupils, while the total enrollment in
the mission schools of the whole nation is less than
eighty thousand. As yet the mission schools are
superior to all but a few of the best government
schools in pedagogical standards if not in equipment, but this lead will be lost unless they are
further developed.

In Japan, the Christian schools exerted a great
influence upon the generation now in active life
because of the high quality of their teaching and
the superior results obtained. Now, however, they
are relatively weaker than they were. The absence of a Christian university and the government
regulations make it impossible for the Christian
school to attract or retain the most ambitious
pupils. Christian education was never more needed
in Japan than at the present time, but it will be
necessary either to move forward or to move out.
A system of inferior Christian schools means that
Christianity itself is brought under reproach.

It would be difficult to exaggerate the influence of
these Christian schools, and especially of the higher
education furnished by the Christians of the West to

Turkey, Japan, and India. Robert College in Constantinople, the Syrian Protestant College at Beirut, and the other less famous Christian colleges in Asia Minor, have had a large share in making the new Turkey a possibility. It is a well-known fact that Robert College trained the leaders who made the Bulgarians' dream of freedom a reality. The leaders of the convention which framed the Bulgarian constitution were with few exceptions graduates of Robert College. Resolutions of thanks were even passed expressing appreciation of what Robert College had done for Bulgaria. This was in 1879. During many years, the majority of the college students were from Bulgaria. None of the leaders of the Young Turk party were trained in Christian schools, but, as has been mentioned, some of the leaders have not hesitated to declare that they would never have dared to undertake at that time the regeneration of Turkey, had they not known that there were scattered throughout the empire hundreds of young men who had been so trained in these Christian institutions as to understand the meaning and responsibility of constitutional liberty. The graduates of the college at Beirut and of its younger sister at Assiut, Egypt, are found in responsible positions, political, educational, and commercial, all through the Levant, and they exemplify those high ideals of character and service which they learned in college.

Those in a position to know declare that no force has had a greater Christianizing influence in Japan than the education conducted by the missionary. The literature of Japan has within a generation become Christian in its ideals and atmosphere. The Christian schools have produced a well-known novelist, Tokutomi Kenjiro, a poet, Shimasaki Toson, and writers on history and education. Twenty or more of the leading journals of the empire, including some of the most influential, have editors who were trained in Christian schools. Magazine literature in Japan was started by graduates of these schools. From them have come also the holders of important posts under the government as well as the leaders of the Japanese Christian community. No one who has read the remarkable tribute to the influence of Christianity in Japan that was written by a non-Christian Japanese and published in *The Century Magazine* for September, 1911,[1] needs to be reminded of the great impression made upon Japan by that pioneer of Christian education, Joseph Neesima, and of the influence exerted by his own work and that of his successors. The Doshisha University, founded by Neesima, reported a few years since two thousand baptisms among its six thousand students. Four other schools estimated their baptisms as about

[1] "Niishima and his fellow-workers, notably Prof. J. D. Davis, upon whom Mr. Niishima was wont to lean as upon the very staff of life, gave Japan a new national ideal. No achievements of man can be greater, more ambitious than this. In this the missionaries succeeded. Here, then, is the great fruit of Christian missions in Japan."—*Adachi Kinnosuke, "Century Magazine," September*, 1911, *p.* 747.

twelve hundred. Five years ago statistics showed that of the actual graduates of the middle or higher Christian schools, nearly one-half were dead, unknown, or still studying, that Christian work had claimed three per cent. of the total number, teaching twelve per cent., official life five per cent., and business, including farming, etc., the remainder, twenty-eight per cent.

Turning to India, one naturally thinks of a noted college which has often been severely criticized because of its alleged lack of a positive Christian influence.   Yet a leading missionary of that district, connected with another mission and passionately devoted to evangelistic work, declared to me that he believed this same college, the Madras Christian College, was to-day one of the mightiest forces for the Christianization of South India.   Much progressive legislation has been put through abolishing or mitigating social evils, and in these efforts, which aim at approaching more nearly to Christian ideals in social life, the leaders have been the graduates of this college, men who had never become avowed Christians but who had nevertheless imbibed the principles of Jesus and had applied them to the problems of their life.   The best of the colleges in India are equal or even superior to the best government institutions from the educational point of view, and in moral influence they are far superior. Because of this fact, the sons of an Indian gentleman, who was officially connected with a government institution, were a few years ago attending a

Christian college in North India. The father so highly valued the ethical influence of this Christian school that he preferred to run the risk of having his boys become interested in Christianity rather than send them to a non-religious government school. The Christian colleges in such great centres as Calcutta, Bombay, Madras, Lahore, and Allahabad,—to mention only a few,—are institutions in which every non-Christian student learns something of the Bible and of the teachings of Christianity. What is of equal importance, he studies each subject from a Christian view-point, and learns how the Christian regards the world, and the problems of thought and life. Like the government school, its teaching is destructive of old superstitions, but, unlike the non-Christian school, it does not stop there, but builds constructively upon a Christian basis, thus leaving the student with an intelligent, sane, and sound view of life.

The influence of the lower education has been equally marked. It is a matter of observation that by education and the impulse upward that comes from Christianity, the Christian communities at once begin to move up in the scale of intelligence and self-respect, and their ideals and manner of life improve. Nothing has made a deeper impression upon India than the utter revolution which Christianity has wrought in the lives of the outcastes who have been regarded by Hindus as hardly human and as incapable of being raised to anything approaching equality with the caste people. Not far from Cape Comorin, there is a professor in a Christian college, who, in spite of his humble origin, is an educational leader in his section and who is so highly respected by the Brahmans that a few years ago, when I was in India, one of these men put his wife in charge of this Christian gentleman for a short railway journey. The first Indian bishop under the Church of England comes from a family of similar origin. Teachers from the lowest castes are daily teaching classes that include pupils of all castes from Brahmans down.

The effect of all this upon the thought of Indian leaders has been profound. An educated gentleman is reported as having said publicly at Allahabad, "I am a Brahman of the Brahmans and belong, as you all know, to the most orthodox school; and I am an Indian and love my country, and I must confess that the way in which Christianity has raised the pariahs of Madras is beyond all praise and puts me to shame as a Hindu." A leading nationalist is thus quoted: "After all, when it comes to practice, Christianity alone is effecting what we nationalists are crying out for, namely, the elevation of the masses." [1] Some Hindus have even advised the depressed classes to embrace Christianity as the only means of escaping from the disabilities inherent in orthodox Hinduism.

The government of India does not prefer to employ Christian teachers, but the schools for girls have a large proportion of Christian women on

[1] Edin. Conf. Rep., Vol. III, p. 258.

their teaching staff, simply for the reason that the Christian community has women capable of teaching while the non-Christian community has not.

The influence of the Christian school in India has been a real contribution to social progress. It has raised the status of large numbers of individuals, who have found in Christianity the only avenue for realizing their inborn capacities. At the same time, it has demonstrated to the Hindus the possibility of raising the submerged classes and has shamed them into emulating Christian efforts.

Similar accounts may be given of the results in Africa. In British South Africa there has been a considerable agitation by colonists who claimed that mission-trained natives were filling jails and were a menace to society. At least, they were spoiled for the employer. A few years since two careful investigations were made. It was discovered that in Johannesburg every native employee who was occupying a position of trust or was earning an unusually large salary had been educated in a mission school. In 1906, Rev. A. E. Le Roy of Amanzimtote Seminary, in Natal, carefully investigated the records of the young men who had been connected with this school, even though they might have remained but a few weeks. Of the more than eight hundred pupils whose record could be traced, but eleven had ever been convicted of crime. Ten per cent. of the total number had turned out badly, twenty per cent. were good workmen merely, but not Christians, and seventy per cent. were reliable men, a credit to school and to church. It must be remembered that in these numbers were included those who had not attended the school long enough to receive a lasting impression. In particular, Mr. Le Roy investigated each former pupil employed at that time in Durban and Johannesburg. Of the forty-seven in Durban, their employers gave unqualified approval to forty-four and not one complained that the boys were disrespectful, which is the stock charge. In Johannesburg, which is five hundred miles away from their homes, the boys had a similar record. Of forty-four boys, thirty-eight merited unqualified approval ; three were satisfactory though they showed symptoms of laziness, and two were such though they occasionally indulged too freely in native beer ; only one had been discharged and that for drunkenness. In not a single case was education charged with "spoiling" a good workman.[1]

The educated Africans are more than good workmen ; many of them become useful preachers, teachers, and leaders of their race. One in Natal has even secured government recognition for his school. Even those who do not go into the so-called Christian professions oftentimes become earnest Christian workers. For instance, a few young men attended a Christian night school while working in a mine at Johannesburg. When they returned to their homes, they gathered their people around them, opened schools, organized churches,

[1] Le Roy, Rev. A. E., " The Educated Native."

and started the people of the vicinity upon the upward path intellectually, religiously, and socially. This is typical.

The missionary has also faced manfully the problem of industrial inefficiency, and by means of industrial training he has endeavoured to make possible a higher standard of living in the Christian community. In the early days, many pioneer missionaries believed that industrial development should go on side by side with the preaching of the Gospel. The missions to the North American Indians were largely industrial, and the first missionaries went to Hawaii with the idea of following that model. However, the present industrial work is of more recent origin. The most uniformly successful industrial undertakings conducted by missionaries have been those designed to make orphans and others, rendered destitute by famine or massacre, self-supporting. In Turkey and India, the thousands of people whom the missionaries have rescued from starvation have thus helped to support themselves, and at the same time have been trained for independent and productive lives.

Somewhat similar in its origin is the best known industrial mission work, namely, that of the Basel Mission in South India. In the early days of this mission, which was opened at Mangalore in 1834, the early converts were mostly from castes whose occupations were either incompatible with a Christian profession or dangerous for the converts and the Church. It was a question of keeping them from acknowledging their faith in Christ, permitting them to starve, or caring for them. The mission naturally chose the last, and was thus driven into devising means of making these Christians self-supporting. This was done by starting mission industries in which the Christians were set to work. The Basel Mission is one of the strong missions in southwest India and carries on all branches of missionary work. Its industrial centres are three: Mangalore, Cannanore and Calicut, with branch factories in seven other places. Here they conduct a large press. They also manufacture tiles for floors and roofs, make underclothing, towels, and the like, weave cloth, and make some of it up into garments. Master-weaver Haller, of Mangalore, invented the colour khaki and khaki cloth was first made in this mission. Coir-weaving, mat-making, knitting and embroidery are combined with some of the other factories. Since 1874 there has been an engineering workshop at Mangalore.[1]

Formerly, there was also a carpentering and furniture shop, but this has now been taken over by an Indian Christian. Commercially these industries have been very successful; the goods are of the highest quality and are sold all over India and abroad, and the profits are used for the furtherance of missionary work. The workmen are able to support themselves in comfort and to work under Christian conditions. There are dangers in such

[1] *Int. Rev. of Missions*, January, 1913, p. 165 *et seq.*

work, chiefly lest the mingling of business and evangelism shall hamper the spiritual influence of the mission, and lest the tendency shall be to induce individuals to profess Christianity for the sake of securing a lucrative position. Even those who for these reasons believe that only necessity will justify the starting of mission industries have to admit, however, that this Basel work has made a real contribution to economic progress and to the dignifying of labour as worthy of a Christian.

Three other main lines of industrial work are being carried on in India with the approval and assistance of the government. The first of these is the maintenance of technical schools of different grades. Some of these teach the boys to use native tools in a more efficient manner, others train foremen for machine shops and factories, while the highest technical college in India is said to be the Allahabad Christian College, which is under the Presbyterian Board. These schools are making a real contribution to industrial progress in two ways. They train men for leadership in the industrial development of India, and they furnish for such positions those who are loyal to Christ and will apply the principles of the Gospel to the new industrial problems of the country.

The second of these lines of industrial work is the development of institutions which are less utilitarian in their purpose. These include the manual training high schools, which teach the usual

branches and in addition the principles of wood-
and metal-working. Among these should be included classes where boys learn to do artistic work
in the precious metals or in weaving rugs.

The third line of work concerns the great industrial problem of India, the raising of the industrial
efficiency of the villager. The magnitude of this
problem is realized when one recalls that ninety
per cent. of the population of India live in towns of
less than five thousand, and eighty per cent. in
villages of less than one thousand. How can these
millions be assisted ? One American missionary
introduced into India the sisal plant, and invented
an inexpensive but effective machine for making
from the fibre of this plant, or of the native aloe,
the rope which every Indian uses. Much attention
has been devoted also to the improvement of weaving machinery. Thousands of Indians have earned
their living by making cotton cloth on hand looms.
The competition of the cotton mills of England has
driven many of these to the wall and missionaries
have been coming to their rescue. In particular,
one American missionary has succeeded in invent-
ing a hand loom which is simple, cheap, and at the
same time so efficient that for the present at least
the weaver who uses it can make a good living,
much better than had ever been possible with the
cruder machine. The development of agriculture
has also attracted the attention both of government
and of a few missionaries, and it is hoped that thus
something will be done to improve the condition of

the village-Christian and make it possible for him to support his family and the Church.

In all this work in India, especially in the south, one great obstacle has been encountered, namely, the opposition of caste, which prescribes the occupation of a man and proscribes any man who takes up any line of work into which he was not born. Besides this there has been the difficulty of the expensiveness of industrial or technical education which keeps the pedagogical aim in the foreground.

In Africa, the need of this industrial work is even greater and its difficulties less serious. It is strange that among people who tend to regard manual labour as beneath the dignity of one with a smattering of education, who leave the bulk of productive work to women, and whose standard of living is of the very lowest, the missionaries have not seen that all education should have an industrial basis. While a few of the leaders may not need to support themselves by their hands, every graduate of a Christian school, it would seem, should be given, with higher ideals, the means of realizing them.

The fact is, however, that much of the mission education here has neglected industrial training so that there is more than twice as much in India as in all Africa. Of course in population also India exceeds Africa. Now, however, the government officials and the educators are awaking to the necessity, and before many years the few centres for industrial work will no longer be peculiar. Among the chief centres for such work may be mentioned

Lovedale, the industrial high school at Adams Mission Station, Natal, known as Amanzimtote Seminary, the work in Uganda, now carried on independently by a stock company whose members are friends of the mission, and, above all, the Livingstonia Mission, in which all the education has an industrial basis.

In China and Japan, practically nothing has been done by the missionaries along industrial lines. The government is active in this department, and most missionaries feel that they are excused from undertaking this work. At the same time, it is coming to be seen that in all education there should be the manual element, both to dignify labour, to develop the pupil intellectually, and to make him feel that mere book learning is not sufficient preparation for efficient service.

Another incubus upon the development of peoples in mission lands arose from their ignorance of sanitation, hygiene, medicine, and surgery. The great epidemics, which swept away vast populations and left behind a trail of desolation and physical weakness, worked against economic efficiency. Likewise, the more ordinary physical ills reduced the vitality of the working force and lessened the number of workers. The missionary at an early day began the task of ministering to the bodies of the people in his field, and while the dominant motive was and still is the prevention and relief of suffering, the result has been that and more.

Modern medicine was introduced into Asia and Africa by the medical missionary. The beginnings were small and insignificant, but the outcome is most impressive. The total number of medical missionaries in the world is not large, numbering only 1,015, or one in twenty of the total missionary force. Of this number China has 365, India, 278, and all of Africa, including Madagascar, 113. In India, the women outnumber the men 163 to 115, but in all the world they furnish just about one-third of the medical workers. This is not a very large force to minister to the physical wants of almost a billion people. Yet the work which they are doing is impressive in itself and still more so in its outreach. Under their supervision are nearly six hundred hospitals and more than one thousand dispensaries. It is difficult to secure accurate medical statistics, especially as regards the distinction between the number of individual patients and the number of treatments. Hence the figures must be regarded as only approximate. According to the tabulated reports, the number of in-patients received into the hospitals during a recent year was more than 164,000 ; the out-patients visited were 145,000 ; the number of dispensary treatments was nearly 4,250,000 a year ; the number of individual patients more than 4,300,000 ; and the total number of treatments, 7,500,000.[1]

The quality of work done by these devoted physicians is extraordinary. Some of the great

[1] Dennis *et al.*, " World Atlas of Christian Missions," p. 83 *et seq.*

surgeons of the world are medical missionaries, who could command a princely income at home, but choose to live on a missionary's salary of not more than three or four dollars a day and devote themselves to the relief of suffering. In fighting the dread tropical diseases and in surgery they excel. Sometimes, in the midst of surroundings which the home practitioner would pronounce impossible, and usually, it must be confessed, without adequate equipment, these surgeons perform operations day after day. Merely from the view-point of medical and surgical science, visiting physicians have pronounced these missionary physicians an honour to the profession. Under these circumstances, they perform the most difficult operations, and succeed, too. In fact, they must succeed, for a few failures might shut the door for years against the foreign practitioner of strange medicine.

If the entrance of the Gospel has had the effect of raising people socially, as it has, then the means by which access for the Gospel was obtained should be credited with some of these results. Such has often been the function of medical missions. Dr. Peter Parker is declared to have opened China to Christian influence at the point of the lancet, and he was but one of these pioneers. Among Moslems especially, the success of the physician in curing supposedly incurable diseases commends him and his spiritual message.

Another social service of the medical missionary has been the breaking down of the power of the

medicine-man, who is always one of the greatest
obstacles in the path of progress. Whatever destroys his influence contributes vitally to the progress of the Kingdom.

Again, the medical missionary has done much in
the way of preventive medicine, through sanitary
and hygienic measures, to check epidemics. It was
a medical missionary, Dr. D. B. Bradley, who introduced vaccination into Siam and personally
vaccinated thousands. What he did there others
have done in other parts of the mission field, and
have thus checked the scourge of smallpox. It
was the medical missionaries who were among the
leaders in the task of halting the progress of the
pneumonic plague, which threatened China in the
winter of 1910–1911.

The sanitary conditions in the East are indescrib-
able and are often almost incredible to one who has
not seen them with his own eyes. No wonder that
cholera and plague are ever-present scourges in
India and cannot be eradicated until the people are
taught to understand the cause of their spread and
become willing to take the proper measures to stamp
them out. The Christian community has thus been
made intelligent and the results are really startling.

In the year 1896 there was a bad outbreak of
plague in Bombay. The Christians did not withdraw themselves but ministered to those in need.
Yet even so, the number attacked was very small.
The plague continued for a long period, and we
have the mortality tables for one week in June, 1898.

The comparative mortality of the different races and castes was in part as follows:[1]

Low caste Hindus	52.95 per thousand
Moslems	45.93 " "
Jains	45.35 " "
Europeans	27.63 " "
Caste Hindus	26.37 " "
Parsees	24.10 " "
Eurasians	24.01 " "
Brahmans	9.58 " "
Native Christians	8.75 " "

The low percentage for the Brahmans is accounted for by the facts that they are the most cleanly about their person and their homes, and that they kept themselves away from contagion.

This is not an isolated case. Cleanliness is a natural accompaniment of a vital Christianity. A Turkish official in Cilicia in a time of plague exclaimed,—" How is it, O ye Protestants ; has God spread His tent over you that ye are so spared ?" The Chinese are not given to overmuch cleanliness, partly due perhaps to the scarcity of water away from the rivers and canals. When plague prevailed in Hong Kong, heathen Chinese asked, " How is it that you Christians do not take the plague ? We have had processions and firecrackers, and made presents to our gods, but all in vain ; we are dying by hundreds."[2]

[1] *Vid.* Dennis, " Christian Missions and Social Progress," Vol. II, p. 464, foot-note.

[2] *Ibid.*, p. 465 *et seq.*

The medical missionaries have thus directly done much to relieve suffering and promote health. They are doing perhaps more in accustoming the people of these countries to a belief in the efficacy of medical science and in training native physicians and nurses. Attention has already been called to the number of classes which are conducted by missionaries for the training of doctors and nurses. Many of these give only an elementary training but even this is of some service. The poor over-worked medical missionary has neither time nor strength to do more than he is doing. The general education of his assistants is insufficient to serve as the basis for the highest grade of medical course, proper facilities are lacking in the way of books and laboratories, and in China it has not been permissible to dissect the human body.

In spite of these difficulties, much is being accomplished in this line. For instance, in Foochow and vicinity there are many Chinese practitioners who are proud to proclaim upon their signs that they have studied under one of the beloved medical missionaries of that city, Dr. Kinnear. In fact, it is difficult in these days, in most mission fields, to get far beyond the reach either of a medical missionary or of some native doctor trained in Western medicine and often by the missionary. This is true in Syria and Asia Minor, where one finds the graduates of the medical college at Beirut scattered over a large territory. China is the country in which authorities claim there is more unnecessary physical suffering than anywhere else on the globe. In that country, there are few trained physicians apart from missions, and this is the land in which Western Christians are doing the most to develop medical training of the highest order. The Union Medical School in Peking is the largest now in operation, but similar schools have been developed or are planned for other great centres, like Canton, Foochow, Shanghai, Hankow, and Chentu.

All these lines of activity tend to relieve the distress caused by poverty, for they aim at removing such poverty as is caused by ignorance, industrial inefficiency, and disease. At the same time, the missionary is not deaf to the appeals of present suffering, and through orphanages and in other less institutional ways is trying to relieve the suffering which presses upon him on every side. The latest statistics [1] indicate the existence of nearly 275 orphanages, containing over 20,000 inmates, more than one-half of whom are girls. Of these institutions, two-thirds are in India and the others are widely scattered. But one other country has more than twenty and that is Japan, with twenty-one. Here the Japanese Christians have taken the lead in caring for destitute children.

One has a very imperfect idea of what Christianity has meant to Asia and Africa in the removal of ignorance and its allied intellectual and

[1] Dennis et al., "World Atlas of Christian Missions," p. 85.

economic evils if one stops at this point. The peoples themselves have girded themselves for this task and are rendering the work of the missionary not absolutely but relatively less essential.

Japan has within a generation created a comprehensive educational system, which extends from the elementary day school, which every boy and girl must attend for six years, up through the high school and college to the university, with its schools of medicine, law, engineering, science, literature, and agriculture. To these should be added special technical schools of less than university grade and normal schools for the training of teachers. Children enter the elementary school when six years old, and the boys and girls receive the same education. Those who fail to enter the next higher school, the middle school or Chū Gakkō, may attend a higher elementary school for two or three years. Here they are prepared to pass the selective examination which is ordinarily required for entrance into the middle school. This examination is made necessary by the fact that the middle schools cannot accommodate all who desire to continue their studies. The middle school course is for boys and covers six additional years and includes the usual subjects for such a grade of school, to which is added English. In fact, three languages, Japanese, Chinese, which bears to Japan a much more intimate relation than Latin bears to England or the United States, and English, take nearly one-half of the entire time of the student.

The number of middle schools in the year 1909–1910 was 305, with 118,133 pupils. From here the successful boy passes into the Kōtō Gakkō, or high school, which is really a fitting-school for the university, and includes perhaps two years of what would be regarded in the United States as college work. Here, too, much of the time has to be devoted to language, each pupil studying two Western languages besides his own Japanese and the Chinese classics. The eight high schools contained in the year 1909–1910 6,029 pupils, the percentage of applicants who could be admitted being only 23.52. The percentage of successful applicants for the departments of law and literature was 36.38, for science, 25.24, and for medicine, only 11.02. As the goal of the ambitious student stand the imperial universities. Those at Tokyo and Kyoto are thoroughly organized. Two others are now being developed, namely, The Imperial North-Eastern University, which includes the Sapporo Agricultural College and the Science College at Sendai, and the Imperial Kyushu University, with colleges of medicine and engineering. These universities are groups of professional schools, and contained by the last report 7,559 students.[1]

Parallel to these schools for boys and young men are the schools for girls. The higher school for girls takes those who have passed through the six years of the elementary school and carries them on from three to five years longer, according to cir-

[1] "Japan Year Book, 1912," p. 175 et seq.

cumstances. The curriculum includes Japanese, English, history, geography, mathematics, natural history, drawing, housekeeping, sewing, music, and gymnastics. The number of such schools in 1909–1910 was 178, with 51,781 pupils.[1] There is no government provision for further education for girls, except normal schools, but private munificence has started in Tokyo the Woman's University which will doubtless ultimately be worthy of the name.

The Japanese Government controls the normal training of the empire. Each locality is required to maintain normal schools with a four years' course for young men, and a three years' course for young women. According to the statistics for 1909–1910, there were seventy-eight of these schools with 23,422 students, of whom one-quarter were women. The higher normal schools, four in number, enrolled 1,528, with a slightly higher proportion of women. The entire course extends for five years or more, with opportunity for advanced work and fellowships abroad.[2]

The Japanese have not only created their educational system, but they are seeing that it is used. The percentage of children under obligation to attend school who are actually in attendance is 98.1,[3] or 14.5 per cent. of the population.

The chief weaknesses of the Japanese education are its technical character, with little attention paid

[1] " Japan Year Book, 1912," p. 175 *et seq.*
[2] *Ibid.*
[3] *Ibid.*, p. 178.

to mere culture; its overcrowded curriculum, which can hardly develop great originality in the pupil; and its failure to give sufficient moral training, though moral instruction is prescribed.

The policy of the British Government in India has been to subsidize schools under private management rather than to multiply government schools. Such private schools, of course, must conform to the regulations of the Department of Education. At the head of the education of India have stood the five universities, Calcutta, Madras, Bombay, Allahabad, Punjab (Lahore), which are examining bodies with affiliated colleges. Other universities, both teaching and examining, are to be created. Normal, technical, medical, and art schools are found, and the movement to-day is in the direction of greater activity by the government in the field of elementary education, looking to the day when it shall be free and compulsory. The efforts of the Christians have stimulated the non-Christians to improve existing schools and to establish new ones of different grades up to colleges. Moslems and Hindus are alike engaged in this work of providing educational facilities for their respective constituents. The educational statistics for 1911[1] showed 172,292 schools, of which 15,038 were for females, and 6,354,772 scholars, of whom 873,553 were females. It is estimated that in British India only 28.1 per cent. of the boys of school age are in school, and 4.6 per cent. of the girls. All of this

[1] "Statesmen's Year Book, 1913," p. 131.

shows that much remains to be done before India will have sufficient educational facilities. It is also true that the native leaders of India are aware of the need and are urging great forward steps.

China has followed Japan in its plans for educational development. By an Imperial decree of January 13, 1903, the Manchu Government provided for the creation of a comprehensive system of schools, which was to include the following:[1]

1. Kindergartens for children from three to seven, which were to be located near orphanages or the homes of virtuous widows.

2. Lower primary schools of the first grade. Large sub-prefectures were to open at least three such schools, smaller ones two, and large towns one. Furthermore, each village of one hundred families was to have its school for the children living within half a *li*, about one-sixth of a mile. This standard was to be reached by degrees. Thus, within five years each group of four hundred families was to open such a school. In addition to official schools opened by local authorities, there were to be public schools maintained by the public funds of a city, market-town, country-town, or hamlet, and for this purpose they might use the revenues of certain landed property primarily given for works of benevolence or charity, for theatricals, and for superstitious festivities. So-called public schools could be maintained by subscriptions from private gentlemen or persons of good moral standing.

[1] "China Mission Year Book, 1911," p. 80 *et seq.*

Schools opened by private gentlemen in their homes for their own children or for the neighbourhood, or schools opened by teachers in their own homes might be called private primary schools. These schools were to be open to children of seven years. The course of study was to be for five years, thirteen hours a week, with attendance optional for the present, but free. The curriculum was to include morals, Chinese classics and language, arithmetic, history, geography, physical science, and gymnastics.

3. Higher primary schools. There was to be at least one in each sub-prefecture and they might be opened in market towns and in the suburbs of towns and cities. Provision was made for official, public, and private schools of this grade. The course was to be thirty-six hours a week and extend over four years. The curriculum was to include the studies of the lower primary with the addition of drawing. Instruction in these schools was not to be gratuitous.

4. Middle schools. These schools were to be a combination of a finishing school for those who would go no further, and a preparatory school for those who would go on to a higher education. Each prefecture was to have one, and the sub-prefectures might open them if they so chose. Schools were official if opened by Mandarins, public if opened by the gentry and associated persons, or private if the cost was defrayed by a private gentleman. The course in these schools was to be for five years,

thirty-six hours a week, and include instruction in morals, Chinese classics, Chinese language and literature, history, geography, mathematics, natural history, physics and chemistry, administration and political economy, drawing, and gymnastics. There was also to be instruction in foreign languages, Japanese or English compulsory, French, German, or Russian optional.

Public and private schools of these three grades could be opened or closed only with the approval of the local authorities and were to be subject to the same regulations as the official schools.

5. High schools. There was to be one high school in each province with a three years' course of six hours a day. As these high schools were to prepare for the university, they were to be divided into three divisions, corresponding to the three groups of faculties in the university. The first division would fit for the faculties of classics, law, arts, and commerce; the second for science, engineering, and agronomy; and the third for medicine. Ethics, law, Chinese literature, foreign languages, and gymnastics were to be included in the curriculum of each division. Students in the first division were to study, in addition, history, geography, elocution, law, political economy, English, and French or German. In the second section, the additional studies were to be mathematics, physics, chemistry, geology, mineralogy and drawing, with the same foreign languages. In the third division, these supplementary studies were to include Latin,

mathematics, physics, chemistry, zoölogy, botany, German, and French or English.

6. The university. This was to be located at Peking, with eight faculties and forty-six courses or specialties. Three courses were to extend four years, the remainder for three years, with from two to four hours a day in the class room. If a province wished to establish a university, it might do so on condition that at least three faculties be included.

7. The college for higher studies. This was to be an annex to the university, and provide for post-graduate work. The courses were to extend over five years without charge to the students, and with the privilege of travel.

In addition to this series of educational institutions, there was provision for lower and higher normal schools. Each sub-prefecture was to maintain one of the former. It was to offer a five years' course of thirty-six hours a week, and be open to persons from eighteen to twenty-five years of age, who were graduates of at least the lower primary grade and who possessed a good reputation, a strong physique, and a good knowledge of Chinese literature. Students who accepted free tuition were to teach for at least six years. The higher normal schools were to be located in each provincial capital, with a three years' course of thirty-six hours a week, and with the same provision in regard to the acceptance of free tuition. The students were to hold the diploma of a lower normal or middle school or prove that they had the equivalent.

For girls there were to be two grades of primary school. The first was to offer a four years' course for girls between the ages of seven and ten, of from twenty-four to twenty-eight hours a week, and the second a course of the same length for girls eleven to fourteen, of from twenty-eight to thirty-two hours a week. In addition to these there were to be girls' normal schools.

The provisions of this decree were never fully carried out. Some schools were opened only to find that there were no pupils fitted to pursue the prescribed course, and the teachers had to set to work to prepare them for it. Still, much progress had been made. A report submitted at the close of 1910 for the two years preceding showed that there were in Peking 252 schools with 15,774 students, and in the provinces 42,444 schools with 1,284,965 students.[1] This was an increase in two years of more than twenty per cent. The report showed that the public and private schools had passed the official schools in number. The strongest educational work is found in certain centres, especially in Chi-li, the imperial province.

The latest educational scheme of the Republican department of education includes the following schools : primary schools with a course of four years ; higher primary schools, with three additional years ; middle schools, four years ; university, with from five to seven years. Technical schools of three grades are also called for : a three years' course

[1] "China Mission Year Book, 1911," p. 79.

parallel to the higher primary schools, a higher course parallel to the first three years of the middle school; and the highest professional schools, parallel to the university, with one preparatory year and a regular course of from three to four additional years. Normal training of two grades is also provided. The lower is parallel to the middle school, and includes one year of preparatory study and four years of regular work. The higher normal training is parallel to the university and consists of a four years' course, one year being preparatory. For scholars who are not going on to the higher schools, supplementary courses of two years each are to be provided for those who have gone through the primary and higher primary schools.[1]

In the countries of the nearer East the movements are in the same direction, and if the present rate of progress is maintained, within a comparatively short time educational facilities should be at the disposal of every child.

In the field of industrial training, the progress has been less marked. The British Government is committed to this line of work in India, and public-spirited Indian gentlemen of wealth have aided in its development. In China, the government and local officials have taken up the matter with vigour, and in large centres one finds industrial schools where boys are being taught trades along modified Western lines. Shrewdly enough, the Chinese are careful not to go too fast. They recognize that for

[1] " China Year Book, 1913," p. 388.

a long time to come there will be room for hand-work, and so the boys who are being taught to weave cloth do not use power looms, which have not yet invaded China to any considerable extent, but use a hand-loom invented by the Japanese, which is more efficient than the ordinary Chinese loom.   In Japan, the government is developing the economic life of the country, is encouraging new industries, and is increasing the productivity of the individual labourer and of the country as a whole.

The standard of living is rapidly rising in Japan, China, India, and wherever Western influence has gone, even though it is far below that of the United States or of England.

The provision of proper medical facilities has attracted much attention in Japan.   The medical missionary helped to introduce modern medical science to the Japanese people, but now there is little call for such work.   To-day there are but eleven medical missionaries in Japan, including Formosa but excluding Chosen (Korea).   At least three of these are in Formosa and another is one of the pioneer physicians, who is permitted by his board to remain in the country, but whose place will not be filled when he drops out.   Years ago, there was a medical department connected with the Doshisha, but now part of the buildings have been taken over by the city and are used for a nurses' training home, while the medical practice formerly carried on by the missionary physicians is in the hands of a Japanese doctor.

Missionaries who maintain dispensaries in connection with work along the lines of social settlements find no difficulty in securing the assistance of Japanese physicians, who give their services gratuitously, after the American fashion, and who are fully as efficient as any medical missionaries could possibly be.   The medical schools, with their hospitals attached, are as well equipped as those of the West and have Japanese and European professors.   Hospitals are found all through the empire.   The missionaries themselves often employ Japanese physicians, and dentists as well, and there is really little place left for the work of the medical missionary as such, this work having passed from foreign into Japanese hands.   Now that Japan has annexed Korea, she is doing the same thing there, and is introducing hospitals for Japanese and Koreans alike.   In fact, in Seoul, we were told, the Japanese had to pay more for treatment in the hospital than did the Koreans.   The Japanese are likewise improving the sanitary conditions of the empire, and while they are hampered by lack of funds, the habits of the people, and the construction of their cities, yet they are rapidly securing a good water supply and proper drainage for their cities, and they are making the ravages of diseases next to impossible.   Their ability in such matters was conspicuous in the war with Russia, when their success in coping with such problems was in marked contrast with the failure of the United States at this point during the Spanish war.

Naturally China is far behind Japan in this regard. Yet the Manchu Government recognized the need. They started medical schools, chiefly for the army, planned for a medical faculty in their proposed university, and patronized the Union Medical School in Peking, under the direction of the London Mission. Then, too, the number of Western-trained Chinese physicians is increasing, both in connection with mission hospitals and independently. Some of these have only a smattering of medical knowledge, while a few are at the very top of their profession. I met one of these last in Soochow. He had given up a lucrative practice in order to live on the small salary paid by a mission hospital, because he thought he could do more good in that position. He got all the latest medical books and instruments from Europe and America, was an expert with the microscope, and was feeling very happy at the time of our visit because he had recently isolated a germ which is very rare and which few physicians of the West have ever seen. Another physician in another part of the country with somewhat less training goes out over every Sunday, preaches and teaches and also gives medical attention, and turns into the treasury of the hospital every cent of the comparatively large sums he receives from patients.

Siam has developed medical schools, but here the standards are too low. The Siamese physicians are not trusted by missionaries and are unable to cope with any serious situation.

In India, the British Government has been alive to the need and has made what provision it could for medical attention. Through the government, through private generosity, and through funds set apart for that purpose, physicians are located in different sections, and hospitals and dispensaries are also provided. A few of these physicians are foreigners, but most of them are Indians, a large proportion being Eurasians. These men do not always bear a good reputation either for medical skill or for character. Bribery is not unknown in the enforcement of sanitary regulations against plague and cholera, as I know from personal experience. Some of these doctors, however, are at the top of their profession, and while they do not command the confidence of the people like the medical missionary, yet they are doing a good work in relieving suffering and preventing the spread of disease. The British Government has a very fine sanitary code, but it is difficult of enforcement because of the prejudices of the people and the impossibility of entering homes to discover and remove sick persons, or to enforce sanitary measures. With the spread of education, this difficulty will disappear, until finally the situation in India will be similar to that in Japan. Wherever the British Government goes, it seeks to care for the health of the people and this is one of the blessings which flow from the British colonial policy.

Closely allied to this work of medical relief is that of providing relief in times of public calamity. Here, again, Japan leads. Since 1899, every prefecture has been required to create a fund for relief purposes, and the state adds to this an amount proportionate to that set aside by the locality. This entire fund amounted in 1908–1909 to nearly $19,-500,000, the yearly income standing at over $1,000,-000. The disbursements naturally vary. In 1905–1906 the amount was $327,000, but in 1908–1909 it was less than $22,000. Besides this, the general government expended in that same year, 1908, over $95,000 for the relief of paupers not cared for by their relatives or the local communities, and the state and communities together expended $25,000 for foundlings.[1] The forerunner of the Red Cross Society was started in 1877, and in 1886 Japan joined the Geneva Convention. At the end of 1909, the number of members connected with the society was 1,525,822, while the total assets came to a grand total of $7,940,000.[2] The people of Japan have also taken up the various lines of philanthropic work for the care of the dependent classes. The Japan Year Book for 1912 listed ninety orphanages, blind asylums, leper hospitals, maternity hospitals, and the like.[3]

Such, in brief, is an outline of what the missionaries and the people in mission lands are doing for

[1] "Japan Year Book, 1912," p. 233.
[2] *Ibid.*, p. 235.   [3] *Ibid.*, p. 245 f.

the removal of ignorance, inefficiency, and poverty.
If these were the only results of missionary work,
it would not have been in vain, and yet this is but
the beginning. At the same time, it is proper for
the Church to recognize the need there is for still
greater activity in this field. The spread of education and of the philanthropic spirit is most encouraging, but there are serious weaknesses in this
movement which only Christianity can remove.
The government education is, at its best, neutral
in matters of religion, and it tends to become directly and positively anti-Christian and anti-religious. The result is that the leaders of these new
movements have not the moral stamina they need,
they are not absolutely incorruptible, and they
lack Christian ideals. Unless these elements can be
furnished, these movements will be sterile of permanent results and may even become a curse. This
means that it is for the Christian forces at home
and abroad to develop Christian education to such a
degree and along such lines as shall create more
and more of a Christian atmosphere in these great
nations, and send out Christian men to be leaders
in the development of the intellectual and material resources of the great nations of Asia and of
the peoples of Africa.

The Christian schools are a force that has been
used for the conversion of individuals. They are
also a force for the Christianization of these countries. There is a tendency in some quarters to believe that the function of the Christian school is

exclusively to train men and women as pastors, preachers, teachers, catechists, and Bible women, and to regard any one who enters into secular education, into business life, or into government service as almost guilty of a breach of trust. It is true that the force of Christian workers is pitifully small. It is sadly true, also, that oftentimes graduates of these schools, who do not remain in the employ of the mission, or in distinctive Christian work, are lost to the Church and cease to exert a positive Christian influence. This is due in part to the temptations to which they are subjected, which will naturally become less powerful with the increase in the number of Christians in these callings, and with the development of a Christian atmosphere. May it not also be due in part to the fact that the missionary and the Church regard these men as having been false to their trust, and hence the men themselves lose the support and encouragement which would come from the sympathy and active coöperation of the Christian leaders?

It is time for the Church and for the Christian forces to see that there is a call for Christian men to become leaders in every department of the social life of the rapidly changing East, and that unless this call is heeded, the Church will have lost an opportunity that may never return. Such a failure to rise to the situation occurred in Japan twenty years ago, and it may never be possible for the Church there to occupy the position in the work of education which it might now be holding had the

missionaries had the foresight and the ability to
seize the opportunity at that time.   In these days,
the mission boards and the missionaries are awake
to the possibilities in China, and it is to be hoped
that before the crystallization that will follow the
inauguration of the new régime takes place, the missionaries will be able to secure such a recognition
for Christianity in relation to the development of
education that the new school system of China shall
not necessarily be positively anti-Christian.   This is
a time for statesmanship of the highest order, as
well as for the most earnest prayer that the Church
may be able to enter the open doors all through the
Orient, and thus aid in putting a permanently
Christian impress upon the new nations now developing under the eyes of the missionary and under
the impulse which originally came from Christianity.

III

PROGRESS IN THE IDEALS OF FAMILY LIFE AND THE POSITION OF WOMAN

NEXT to the problems of securing intellectual and industrial ability, in fundamental importance, may be ranked the problems that centre in the ideals of family life and the position of woman. The former concern primarily the individual; the latter affect the primary social unit, genetically considered, namely, the family. The family is the institution by which the race is propagated, and in which every human being, with the exception of a few abnormal cases, receives his earliest training, intellectual and religious. Here he learns the lessons of obedience and of adjustment to a social environment. In the home lies a centre of influence upon social development which can hardly be overestimated. Some of the serious social problems in our cities arise from the changes in the character of the home life which have come about within the last generation, and even within the last decade. The boy problem of the present day has arisen from a change in living arrangements by which the home has ceased to be what it formerly was, the centre of all the activities of the children, and the place where they learned to take an active part in the economic life of the household.

In the home life of the countries of the Orient, one may find the key that unlocks many of the problems of social development there. No more fundamental changes in the social organization of these nations can be found than those which touch the home. All that affects the position and status of woman has an important bearing upon this genetic social unit, the family.

As a preliminary to the discussion of the position of woman in typical mission lands and what has been done for her elevation, attention should be called to a fact that has often been overlooked. While woman has been despised and neglected, yet it is equally true in the East, as in the West, that the hand that rocks the cradle rules the world. Women have always exerted a mighty influence over men, and the ignorant women of the East are the last bulwark of superstition. If they can be induced to unite with the men in the advocacy of reform, the result is assured. Neither men nor women alone are able to bring about the necessary changes. Strangely enough, the social customs and abuses that primarily affect woman find their strongest supporters in the women who are their chief victims. Many a man in India would gladly reform his household and social relations, were it not for the influence of his unreformed mother, wife, and sisters-in-law. Woman holds the key to the situation in the Orient to-day. The men have come under progressive influences but they are held back by the conservatism of the women.

Thus, a prominent Indian gentleman in Madras told me that he could not go to England or America to study conditions with reference to the problems of his own country, because his mother, a lady of the old school, had threatened to kill herself the moment she heard he had set foot on a steamer. He believed she would do it rather than endure the disgrace of her son's having committed the heinous sin of crossing the ocean. This is typical. Hence, one can appreciate the profound significance and importance of the movements that are affecting the status of woman and the family.

A study of the position of woman among non-Christian peoples is not pleasant, and it affords little ground for pride in the inherent nobility of man's nature. Rather, it reveals the depths to which men may sink and the great debt which the world owes to Western Christianity and its ideal of woman. No detailed study of this subject is possible at this point. All that can be attempted is a sketch of the situation as it presents itself in certain typical mission fields.

It is not surprising to learn that among the less civilized tribes of Africa woman had no high position. She was regarded and, beyond the reach of Christian influence, is still regarded as a mere chattel; polygamy was practiced by all who could afford to buy many wives; and social standing depended upon their number. On the west coast every Bule man desired twenty or thirty wives, and some chiefs had from sixty to eighty. With many wives, the husband was relieved from the necessity of doing any work. In parts of the Congo Valley, the chief with many wives would hire them out to others. African wives were compelled to act temporarily in that capacity for guests. The purchase price of women in some parts of Africa was five large blue glass beads, while ten were demanded in exchange for a cow. During a famine in central Africa, the natives of Ushashi were selling their wives and daughters for two large potatoes. Under these circumstances, the women were the servants of their lords. The story is told of an African who ordered his wife to carry him on her shoulders over the deep and perilous ford of a river. A white man remonstrated with him after he was safely across, but the worthy native asked in astonishment: " Then whose wife should carry me over, if my own does not ? "

Similar facts are reported from the Pacific Islands. Dr. Paton remonstrated with a native of the New Hebrides for beating his wife savagely. He replied : " We must beat them or they would never obey us. When they quarrel and become bad to manage, we have to kill one, and feast on her. Then all the other wives of the whole tribe are quiet and obedient for a long time to come."

Among the great peoples of Asia, India presents the darkest picture, which in certain aspects more nearly approaches that of Africa. In discussing the position of woman in India, one is confronted by the difficulty that India is really a continent, not a homogeneous country, and that what is true of one section often does not hold in another. Even so, the population is so great that these different nationalities, castes, or language areas, contain so many people that, even if what is true of one section does not hold elsewhere, it yet affects a large number of individuals.

In the early Vedic times, the position of women was apparently one of power coupled with honour. They had fully as much influence as had the women of Greece or of Rome. They were equal to their husbands in the home; they were their necessary partners in the performance of religious duties; and even in politics and administration they had influence. Child marriages were not known and girls could choose their own husbands. Yet even so, women as such were held in little esteem, and it was only as wives that they were respected.

What a contrast this offers to the present situation! A bland Hindu confessed that upon two doctrines all sects were agreed: "We all believe in the sanctity of the cow and in the depravity of woman." The Tamil proverbs indicate the general esteem in which woman is held. Take two:

"What is the chief gate to hell? Woman."

"What is cruel? The heart of a viper.
What is more cruel? The heart of a woman.
What is the most cruel of all? The heart
of a soulless, penniless widow."[1]

[1] Jones, *op. cit.*, p. 152.

Under Hinduism woman suffers from serious disabilities. One injunction reads: "In childhood must a female be dependent on her father, in youth on her husband, her lord being dead, on her sons. A woman must never seek independence." The commentators thought this did not provide for every conceivable case; hence they added: "If she have no sons, she must be dependent on and subject to the near kinsmen of her husband; if he have left no kinsmen, on those of her father; or, if she have no paternal kinsmen, on the sovereign." [1]

No woman is permitted to be taught the Vedas or other sacred books. This comprised all the education there was in the old days, and the illiteracy of woman has been decreased but slightly. In 1911 only a trifle more than one per cent. of the women of India could read and write, and, if one subtracts the Christian and Parsee women, the percentage for the women of Hinduism would be still farther reduced.

Any high degree of education would be made difficult if not impossible by the early age at which girls are married. In the province of Mysore, which is regarded as a progressive state, the census of 1891 revealed the fact that one out of every five married women had been married under the age of nine. A census taken some thirty years ago in the state of Baroda, which had then a population of a little less than 2,000,000, showed that 558 females and 132 males had been married

[1] Wilkins, " Modern Hinduism," p. 327.

before they had completed their first year. By the census of 1891, among 222,000,000 out of the 287,-000,000 of India, there were:[1]

Ages	Married Boys	Married Girls
Below 4 years	89,051	223,560
5–9	nearly 602,000	more than 1,850,000
Below 14	2,725,124	6,871,999

Of course, in the most extreme cases, the marriage ceremony practically amounts to mere betrothal, and the girl does not go to her husband until later; but the day is not long delayed when she must go to her husband and become the household drudge for the older women of the family. It is not necessary to enter into the reasons for this custom further than to remark that one of the reasons adduced is that an early marriage is necessary as a protection to the girls, since they mature at an earlier age than with us.

Out of this marriage custom flow many evil consequences, both to the women of India and to Indian society. It propagates the unfit, as no one is relieved from the responsibility of having children. It makes impossible a high degree of education on the part of the young men, because, long before a full education can be completed, they must withdraw from school and assume the responsibility for the support of a family. This early entrance into the marriage relationship also prematurely exhausts the boys and young men, and saps their vitality, so that they lack energy and push.

[1] Chintamani, C. Y., "Indian Social Reform," p. 173.

The physical consequences to the girls are also serious. Many girls become mothers by the time they are twelve. Few are permitted to reach full development before they are compelled to bear children. Those in a position to know declare that, as a consequence of this pernicious custom, one-fourth of the women of India die prematurely, one-fourth become hopelessly invalided, and the majority of the remainder suffer in health. It is almost sure death for a girl of thirteen or fourteen to be married to a man of thirty-five, and yet hundreds of educated men of that age follow the custom and take girl-wives. Feeble-mindedness, hopeless idiocy, rickets, and scrofula result from this custom. Social reformers in India have declared publicly that, in consequence of the early marriages, the race has preserved the softer elements of character but has lost patriotism, love of enterprise, energy, aspiration, devotion to duty, and the like. A native physician at a congress in 1897 attributed to this custom the fact that the Hindus had fallen easy victims to every invading tyrant. No baby-born race, declared another,—and the Indian people are baby-born,—or one brought up by illiterate mothers, can develop virile qualities.

The fact that the wives are illiterate makes it impossible for their husbands to regard them as rational companions, and the sexual relationship is without the elevating moral influence it should have. "Very few people," declared a noted Pundit, "can justly apprehend the nature and depth of the social degradation caused by the contemplation of women, not as a rational and moral companion, but as an object of selfish pleasure." [1]

Among the Hindu population, there is, with two exceptions, little polygamy, though concubinage is tolerated. One of these exceptions is in the case of a man whose wife does not bear him a son within seven years. It is permissible for such a man to take another wife and this is almost certain to be done. The Kulin Brahmans, found mostly in Bengal, are the other exception. These are men who for a consideration will marry any number of girls. An investigation, made a little more than twenty years ago in 426 villages, showed 618 Kulin bigamists and 520 polygamists. One had 107 wives and others had 67, 52, and 50 each. Twenty-one had 25 or more wives, and 442 had from three to ten wives apiece. [2]

Still another count in the indictment of India's treatment of her women concerns widows. By the census of 1891, among 262,300,000 people in India there were 13,878 widows not over four years old and 64,040 between five and nine inclusive. The total through the age of fourteen was 252,450; from fifteen to forty-nine, 11,157,140; and fifty or over, 11,224,933. [3]

[1] Murdoch, J., "Papers on Indian Social Reform : The Women of India," p. 25.

[2] Dennis, J. S., "Christian Missions and Social Progress," Vol. I, p. 122 note.

[3] *Ibid.*, Vol. I, p. 124.

In the matter of the remarriage of widows, some of whom are married in infancy and have never lived with their husbands, there are differences of custom. Thus, in the North-West Provinces, out of a population of 40,000,000 Hindus, seventy-six per cent. permit and encourage the remarriage of widows. Of the more than 22,000,000 widows reported by the census, it is estimated that about two and a half millions are among the Brahmans and the Rajputs, and these strictly enforce the prohibition of remarriage.[1]

As to the general attitude towards widows, this also varies somewhat; yet a Hindu writer declares that the impression made upon his childish mind was that a widow " belonged not to the ranks of the two recognized sexes, that possibly she might be a being of a third sex, or else a member of a totally different species of the animal world."[2] Everywhere she is regarded as a person of ill omen. Until the practice was stopped by the British Government, she was urged, often compelled, to permit herself to be burned alive upon the funeral pyre of her husband. Some people believe that this was less cruel than her present lot, which is that of a household drudge, the slave of all the family, often the common property of the men, denied all pleasures, and without any escape, save through death or entrance upon an evil life. There are regions and castes in which the treatment is less cruel, es-

[1] Murdoch, J., op. cit., p. 116.
[2] Fuller, Mrs. M. B., "Wrongs of Indian Womanhood," p. 168.

pecially if she is the mother of children and above all of sons. A child widow or a childless young widow is the one upon whom the abuse chiefly falls, and this is because she has nothing to set over against the fact that she is regarded as the murderer of her husband. No marriage is arranged unless the astrologer declares that the horoscopes indicate long life for the parties. Hence, if the husband dies young, the Hindu concludes that it is due to some sin committed by the wife in a previous existence. Hence, she is virtually his murderer.

In addition to all these evils in the position of woman, we must mention still another, namely, their seclusion, which probably dates from the time of the Mohammedan conquest of India. This affects only a portion of the women of India. In the south and west, only the better classes are affected by it, and these only to a limited extent. In the north and north-west and in the Moslem native states, it is fully enforced among the higher classes, and the custom tends to filter down through society. It is a mark of social distinction if a man can afford to keep his wife and daughters behind the purdah. In a place like Hyderabad, the women and their slave attendants are practically prisoners. A husband killed his wife because a man by mere accident had seen her back through an open door, though she was unaware of it. The effect of this system is to injure the woman's health, make her constantly conscious of her sex, prevent her from getting into touch with the world, and keep her horizon as narrow as possible.

This is a mere sketch of some of the features of the treatment of women in India, but it is enough to indicate the need of change and the lines along which it should be made.

China is the only country in the world with a female population exceeding that of India. The situation here is interesting. In general, woman in China is in bad odour. The radical which signifies " woman," when doubled, means " to wrangle "; tripled, it means " to intrigue," also " seduction," " fornication," and " adultery." Of the one hundred and thirty-five more common characters which are written with this radical, fourteen have a good meaning and eighty-six may be said to be indifferent in meaning; but there are thirty-five that have a bad signification, and these include some of the most disreputable words.[1]

Woman is proverbially the incarnation of jealousy, and hence it strikes the Chinese as most irreverent to speak of God as a jealous God. An ancient verse of Chinese poetry has been rendered into English thus :

" The serpent's mouth in the green bamboo,
The yellow hornet's caudal dart ;
Little injury these can do ;
More venomous far is a woman's heart." [2]

[1] Smith, A. H., "Chinese Characteristics," p. 246.
[2] *Ibid.*, p. 245.

There is a general feeling that woman cannot express filial piety, and hence, when a case occurs of a woman's sacrificing herself for her parents, great honour is paid her.

The general attitude towards women is indicated by the sorrow which is felt when a girl is born into a family. She is regarded as a burden, not as a source of joy. The main object in marrying her off is to get rid of having to support her. The sale of girls and of women has been frequent, especially in times of famine. During such periods, the sale was carried on as openly as that of mules or donkeys. During the famine of 1878, the export of women and girls from the three northern provinces was so great that in some places it was difficult to hire a cart for any purpose, as they were all being used to transport the human goods to the homes of the purchasers. Another method of securing a similar result was to lease a wife. An early inquirer at Ningpo had leased his wife for ten years. When he realized the wrong, he tried to redeem her, but the party in possession refused to release her. Before the expiration of the lease, the second husband died and the family or clan sublet her to a third party for the remainder of the term of ten years. Among officials a common and polite present used to be a favourite concubine. Among the common people, who could not afford an additional wife, a wife was often loaned.

. The poorer people devised a method of escaping the financial burden of a daughter's support. This

was known as the "rearing-marriage." By it the
girl was made over to the family into which she
was to marry, was reared by them, and married
at their convenience. This was regarded as a confession of poverty. It was superior to the Indian
custom of child-marriage, but such girls might
have a hard lot. Mothers-in-law resented having
to feed and clothe such children, often treated them
cruelly, and sometimes murdered them.

Christianity teaches that a man shall leave his
father and mother and cleave to his wife. Chinese
ethics teach that the man must cling to his father
and mother and compel his wife to do the same.
Before her marriage, she is a servant of her parents.
The word in Chinese that is used like the English
word "daughter" means "slave girl." After marriage there is a change in masters. Her husband,
whom she is to serve for time and for eternity, regards her as little more than a chattel. The power
of a husband and the parents-in-law over the women
of the household is almost unlimited. Yet even
here human nature will assert itself, and the hen-
pecked husband is ridiculed in Chinese literature as
in that of America. One of the classic stories is
that of ten husbands who felt themselves aggrieved
by the attitude of their wives, and who decided to
organize themselves into a society for the purpose
of asserting their prerogatives. They had met for
this purpose, when the wives, who had got wind
of the plan, marched into the room, with the result
that all but one of the men fled. With a con-

temptuous sniff, they marched out; whereupon the nine timid husbands decided to elect the tenth, who had stood his ground, as their president. They went in to announce the election, only to find him dead from fright!

While China does not force the marriage of mere children, yet the marriage customs lead to great abuses. The matches are all arranged by the professional match-maker, and one who is unscrupulous may work great injustice. One missionary knew of two young men who found their wives to be idiots, while a young girl of a high family found herself married to a badly formed imbecile covered with loathsome sores.

The Chinese family is supposed to be monogamous but the emperor set the example of polygamy. By law he was entitled to wives of three ranks. First was the empress, who was alone in her dignity. In rare cases two princesses shared the imperial throne. The secondary wives were unlimited in number, and one of them usually succeeded the empress in case of the latter's death. The third rank was filled to suit the taste and desire of the emperor. Rarely did one of these attain the throne. When the Emperor Kuang Hsu was married in 1889, two secondary wives were chosen for him in addition to the empress. Those who have been able to afford such a family have followed the example of the emperor, but as a rule only one wife is married with the full ceremony. The second wife owes obedience to the first, unless she has children while the first has none. In that case, they are on an equal footing. While the introduction of an additional wife or concubine is sometimes resented, yet not infrequently the ladies of the household are pleased to have it done, because it lends additional dignity to the household. Somewhat similar is the custom by which a Chinese merchant, who must spend much of his time in another city, away from home, may support there a second home with wife and children.

Theoretically, divorce is easy in China. There are seven reasons for which it may be granted : disobedience to the parents-in-law, childlessness, improper conduct, jealousy, loathsome or contagious disease, stealing, and talking too much.' Practically, divorce is not easy. The population of China presses very closely upon the margin of subsistence. The social system makes no provision for an unmarried daughter, as the land is divided among the sons of the household. Hence, there is no way by which a divorced daughter, who returns to the parental home, can be supported, and the family will use every influence to prevent the breaking up of the marriage tie, unless there is a valid reason or they have a chance of marrying her to another.

In China, the lot of widows is not so bad as it is in India, and yet suicide is encouraged. A woman is supposed to belong to her betrothed and to her husband, and, if he dies, the truly honourable thing for her to do is either to kill herself or to remain a

[1] Dennis, *op. cit.*, Vol. I, p. 117.

widow throughout life. A widow may become a concubine and suffer less disgrace than if she becomes a lawful wife. It has been customary to report the suicide of widows to the government, which has then publicly announced such cases in the official *Peking Gazette*. One finds in China many a monument erected in honour of widows who have shown their conjugal loyalty by following their husbands into the spirit world.

The women of China have suffered from another disability, namely, foot-binding. In some parts of the country, practically all the women have had small feet. Elsewhere, the coolie women, but no others, have been exempt. The effect of this custom has been to cause a terrible amount of needless suffering, to cut women off from the possibility of outdoor life, to reduce their vitality, to remove them from a position where they could exert a helpful influence in a broad way upon society, and in general to cramp them physically, intellectually, and socially.

Family life in China has not been ideal. The Chinese make fond parents and the boys are under no real discipline. Only the ingrained feeling of filial piety, which is enforced upon each individual by all his education and by the institutions and customs of society, prevents this lax family discipline from resulting in greater evil.

In pleasant contrast to India and China, Japan is a country in which woman has occupied a relatively high place.   Of the one hundred and twenty-three Japanese sovereigns, nine have been women. The chief deity in their mythology is a woman.   In the seventeenth century, Japanese women made brave martyrs.   Their feet have never been bound. Among the middle and lower classes they are free to move about and visit their friends.   Yet woman has been regarded as inferior, the plaything of man, rather than as his companion and equal.   A Japanese gentleman is reported to have said to the American wife of a Japanese: "Woman is a fool. But if she will obey her husband, people won't laugh at her.   Japanese women are much better than European women, though.   The Western women rule everything; they think they are great gods.   Their husbands are very unwise and cowardly to let them behave in such proud style.   The European wife, instead of waiting on her husband, makes him get everything for her."   And the whole was uttered in a way that implied " disgusting and preposterous."

The educated wife of a prominent Japanese official made a trip to America and Europe a few years ago.   An American lady asked her what impressed her most during her first days in this country.   She replied, " The way women are treated here.   Now I understand what ———— meant when he used to tell me, 'When we are with Europeans, you go first; when we are with Japanese, I go first'"! Until very recently the pronoun used by all Japanese women in speaking of themselves was *shō*, the primary meaning of which is "concubine," and in Japanese novels Western women are represented as speaking of themselves in the same way. The late emperor of Japan did much for the progressive development of the empire, and when the new constitution was promulgated in 1889, his wife rode by his side. Yet it should be added that his heir, the present ruler, was not the son of his empress, and when he celebrated his silver wedding anniversary, an addition was made to the royal household. A military officer once expressed the hope that the prince would set a better example.

The seven causes for divorce mentioned under China hold in Japan also, and the seventh reason, that of talking too much, is the most common ground, or so it was alleged some years ago. The result of this laxity in the divorce laws was seen in 1891, when there were 345 divorces for every thousand marriages.[1] This proportion was nearly fifteen times that in France for the same year, where it was only twenty-four per thousand. During the last twenty years the proportion has diminished to a marked degree. The new edition of the "Encyclopædia Britannica" gives it as 160 per 1,000. Even now, in Japan, a civil or religious ceremony is not required for marriage. All that is necessary is for a couple to begin to live together. If pregnancy ensues and the parties are satisfied with one another, before the child is born, the marriage is registered. Otherwise, they may separate, the girl is sent back

[1] Dennis, J. S., op. cit., Vol. I, p. 117.

to her parents, and such a case does not enter into the statistics of divorce because there was never a marriage. About half the marriages, it is alleged, are begun in this informal way. Until recently, also, woman has been kept in ignorance. Thus, Count Okuma declared a few years ago, " Heretofore the education of women has been very much discouraged." This is now entirely changed, and six years of education are now prescribed for every girl equally with the boys.

Such are some of the facts regarding the position which woman occupied in non-Christian lands before it was modified by Christian and other Western influence. One of the first things the missionaries undertook was Christian education, and as soon as possible this was offered to girls as well as to boys. In the beginning, parents had to be hired to permit their children, and especially their daughters, to attend school, and one worthy gentleman of Calcutta exclaimed, " They will be educating our cows next, now that they are trying to teach our girls." From small beginnings the work of Christian education for women has spread until schools are found in all mission fields. They range all the way from kindergartens and primary day schools up to colleges and professional schools. This is not to claim that all the schools which are called colleges are doing true college work, and it is to be doubted whether any such institution on the mission field offers four years of what American educators would regard as college work. Nevertheless, these schools are working up towards it as rapidly as funds permit and as their constituents are prepared for such education.

The latest missionary statistics do not accurately differentiate the students between the sexes and do not specify the schools which admit girls or women. All that can be asserted is that at the present time, in all mission fields, there are at least the following numbers of girls and women under instruction:

In college and university classes	427
In theological and normal schools and classes	3,256
In boarding and high schools	41,313
In industrial training schools and classes	5,414
In elementary and village schools	259,639
In kindergartens	1,751
In medical classes	136
In nurses' classes	515
Total	312,451[1]

From these schools are being graduated year by year the women who become teachers in the Christian schools, Bible women, wives of native Christian workers, and, in short, those who are destined to be leaders in the emancipation of their sex.

No one who has seen these schools in operation can fail to be impressed by their value. Not that they are above criticism, any more than are similar schools in England or the United States. In those countries or among those classes where cleanliness of person and modesty of costume are not common,

---

[1] Dennis, *et al.*, *op. cit.*, p. 83.

neatness and decency are so thoroughly inculcated that they become a part of the girls in after life. The contrast between an African woman, whose costume consists chiefly of grease and dirt, and the Christian schoolgirl can hardly be imagined; it must be seen to be understood. I well remember our journey across Batakland in Sumatra. On the east of the Toba Sea the Bataks, especially the women, looked more animal than human. Here no Christian schools had been established. Then, as we journeyed west, we began to note a change until, when we had reached Silindong, which is thoroughly evangelized, the whole appearance was that of intelligent men and women.

This latter effect of education is universal. The uneducated non-Christian woman has few interests outside of the home. Her intellectual life is almost negligible. Her Christian-trained sister, on the other hand, while no less devoted to her home, takes an intelligent interest in life and is in consequence a more efficient wife and mother. The vacant expression has given place to one of alert intelligence. Their æsthetic sense is developed, and above all they are aroused morally, and made to realize that they are not things but self-respecting individuals, who are as precious in God's sight as their fathers, brothers, or husbands. All schools, even the primary schools, have something of this effect, and the higher schools and colleges, like the girls' colleges in Smyrna, Cairo, Lucknow, Peking, Kobe, and Tokyo,—not to mention others,—are training girls who can be leaders of their sex in the effort to realize their inherent God-given possibilities.

Not in all countries are the girls permitted to attend the ordinary school, and in India, for instance, even those who are permitted to enter must soon leave in order to found new homes. To meet the needs of such women, there are a few schools which admit girls without compelling them to violate the time-honoured customs of society. The principal means, however, of helping such social prisoners is through the labours of the unmarried evangelistic women missionaries and Bible women, who visit them in their homes and teach them regarding Christ and His message for womanhood.

Beside this work of Christian education must be placed the example of the Christian home. While the relations between the members of a Christian household at times excite the disgust of prejudiced gentlemen of the old school, who claim that the Indian home, for example, is the most nearly perfect home in the world, yet the power of the Christian home is marked everywhere. There are arguments that may be adduced for a celibate missionary force, and they are not to be dismissed without consideration. Indeed, there may be circumstances under which the single missionary is more efficient than a married man. This is true particularly in pioneer work and amid unhealthy surroundings. But when all due allowance has been made, it yet remains that the Christian home is one of the most powerful Christianizing influences in mission lands. In its peace, in the beauty of the relationships between husband and wife, and between parent and child, and in the whole atmosphere, there are elements of purity and of uplift that no country ever knows apart from the influence of Christianity. A missionary in Tokyo declared some years since that many who did not know English had come to understand and use the phrase "Christian home" as an expression for an ideal household.

A few years ago a cultivated Christian woman went to China as a bride. After a short period, and before she had begun to do any real missionary work, her health failed and for years she hardly left her home. Yet at her death, it transpired that she had exerted a mighty influence over the whole region. Her patience in suffering, the peace and beauty of the home life, even the attractiveness of the home itself, had so impressed the servants and all who had occasion to enter the home, that they had spread the story far and wide. People had even peeped through the shutters into the house after dark, although only the servants were aware of it, in order to see something of this Christian home. The shut-in invalid had through the home been making the appeal of a Christlike life known to persons who might never hear a sermon.

In addition to these two lines of approach, the missionary has often taken the lead in the agitation against the worst abuses of which woman is the victim and has succeeded in many instances in mitigating, if not in abolishing, some of the sad features of her social treatment.

The effect of Western influence, missionary and other, upon the position of woman, has been marked, in some places revolutionary.

A few instances from Africa and the Pacific Islands will indicate the direction and the degree of the progress. In Uganda it was formerly a source of shame for a man not to have a large number of women to cultivate his land. Now it is a cause for shame to have more than one wife, and this is the direct result of Christian influence. In Khama's country, likewise, Christianity has stopped polygamy. Khama's wife is a queenly woman with all the grace of a princess, while her face reflects her beautiful Christian character. Her home, which she built with her own hands, is in native style, but is attractively decorated and is scrupulously neat. In the South Seas, where women were formerly downtrodden, they have become able to hold their own. The wives of the two most remarkable native missionaries sent to New Guinea were able to conduct the Sunday and week-day services, preach acceptably, and carry on the schools whenever their husbands were prostrated with fever. At the same time, they were good housewives.

The difference between the home of a heathen Zulu and a Christian Zulu is like that between light and darkness. The number of the Zulu's wives is indicated by the number of huts within the kraal. Inside the hut there is neither light nor air, save what can get in through the low door, or the vent hole for the smoke, which blackens everything. All clothing is discarded inside and the ground serves for chairs. Dogs and small domestic animals have free access to everything and there is nothing to be damaged among the simple storage and cooking utensils. The Christian home, on the other hand, is open to light and air. Compared with the hut, it is cleanliness itself. A few books, perhaps a sewing-machine and portable organ, not to mention the ordinary furnishings of a Christian home, are in evidence.

Another field which the Christian home has entered is Sumatra. No longer do Christians live as they used to in common houses. In the village of Purba Saribu, which had hardly been touched by the Gospel, we saw the old home life in full swing. From eight to twelve families lived in a single house, rectangular in shape, without partitions, each family being assigned to a certain section of the floor on either side of the open passageway, which extended from end to end. The four corners were the honourable places, in a certain fixed order. There was no chance for privacy save that furnished by the semi-darkness. The Christians, on the other hand, live in comfortable dwellings, one family to a house.

The effect is the same whether in Sumatra, Zululand, Bechuanaland, or Uganda. The Christian home is unique and attests the power of Christianity.

The position of woman likewise changes. A traveller passing along the paths in parts of Africa is able not only to tell from the appearance whether a village is Christian or heathen, but often also to gauge accurately the religion of the passers-by. If one sees a family walking along the trail or road with the man carrying the bundles, one can safely conclude that he is a Christian, especially if his wife is with him and is treated as his equal. The non-Christian would naturally stalk on ahead and leave his wife, that is, his servant, to manage the baggage and supervise the children as best she could. Such an incident is typical of the new status which Christianity accords to woman.

These are instances of the change in regions where Christianity has had an effect quantitatively greater than it has had in a country like India, where the vast majority are still beyond the direct and positive influence of the Gospel. Qualitatively, however, the change in India is equally great, perhaps even greater, and it has spread far beyond circles which are even remotely identified with Christianity.

Take, for example, the matter of the creation of a public sentiment that demands a change. Such statements as these from influential native sources are indications of what Christian influences are doing :

"Nor can a people who treat their women as if they were intended for no higher duties than the personal service of their husbands, and who heartlessly consign their unfortunate widows to a lot of perpetual privation, show much chivalry, generosity, sympathy with the weak, self-sacrifice, dignity of family life."[1]

The Hindu is one of the most influential journals in South India. It is in no sense a Christian organ, and yet as long ago as September, 1888, it was publishing such statements as this:

"There is one evil which is a standing hindrance to reforms of every kind, and if that is remedied the natural aptitudes of the nation will receive an unchecked stimulus towards development in all directions. We mean the present degraded condition of our women. . . . It will be no patriotism but foolish and ruinous vanity to assert that women in India are now in that condition which enables them in other countries to exert vast influence on the character and life of the nation as well as of the individual. The hard and unreasonable marriage laws, their seclusion and their ignorance have made them entirely unfit for the exercise of that elevating and chastening privilege which is theirs by nature. The character of the nation is formed by its youths, and the character of the youths is formed at home by their mothers. . . . If our country too should produce its patriots, warriors and statesmen, our mothers should receive a different training and should be given a different lot from what are deemed to be appropriate to them at present. The kitchen would cease to be their

[1] Chintamani, *op. cit.*, p. 347.

world, the priests should cease to be their moral preceptors; cruel marriage laws should cease to rob them of their youth, and their minds should be opened by a high and liberal education." [1]

These reformers recognize the impossibility of raising a nation by improving the condition of only one-half of the population. A member of the Imperial Legislative Council of Madras declared:

" One serious drawback . . . is that in these . . . matters the effort has been, almost solely, on the part of *males;* and it is a feeling which I cannot get rid of, that, so long as *this* is the case, so long shall we be working as with a lever without the fulcrum. A good percentage or a strong contingent of self-reliant, self-respecting and—let me add—self-assertive womanhood is what I look upon as that fulcrum; and it is my conviction that, with them for co-workers and—if I may say so—for active and belligerent malcontents, the rate and amount of success ought to astound the sceptic and sanguine alike." [2]

With such a change in public sentiment, it naturally follows that there has been progress in the removal of disabilities. Woman in the old days was kept in utter ignorance. To-day the leaders are seeing the importance, yes, the necessity, of giving her an education. Statistics for 1911, already quoted, gave the number of schools for females as 15,038 and the number of female scholars

[1] Murdoch, *op. cit.*, p. 1 *et seq.*
[2] Chintamani, *op. cit.*, p. 29.

as 873,533.[1] These figures indicate to what extent India is beginning to move in the direction of education for all her women. Even the Moslems in India are awaking to this necessity, and they are securing schools for their daughters.

To be sure, the motive may not always be the highest. Thus, in a city of north India there was an Indian gentleman of the highest social standing whom I met in 1908. He had been a leader in an agitation which resulted in the city's opening a high grade school for girls. A most excellent step this was, but after the school was running and was being patronized by the best families, the gentleman gave away the secret. He had held advanced ideas concerning the education of girls and had been scored by his less progressive friends for sending his daughters to school. He resolved to get his revenge. He knew that if the municipality should open a school, all these men would patronize it. Hence, as a member of the municipal government, he put the measure through, largely in order that he might have the satisfaction of sitting in his home and watching the daughters of his detractors pass by on their way to school. Thus do various motives coöperate in bringing in the new day.

Another evil which has been attacked by reformers, missionary and Indian, has been that of the marriage age and the age of consent. In this matter the native Christian community has been a standing protest against too early marriages, for

[1] "Statesman's Year Book, 1913," p. 131.

they have not married their daughters so early as the non-Christians. All progress in the education of woman tends to postpone the date of marriage. A Hindu reformer stated some years since that in the peninsula of India the age at which the Brahmans married their daughters thirty years before had been from seven to eight; within that period it had been pushed up to from ten to twelve; and some had even delayed the marriage beyond the age of twelve and done it without incurring any reproach. In 1889, the Bombay Social Conference recommended that the penal code be amended so as to protect all girls, whether married or unmarried, until they reached the age of twelve, a violation to be punishable as a felony. This became the law two years later. The Maharajah of Mysore, the second in importance among the native states, had a law enacted in 1893 that a girl below eight or a boy below fourteen was to be regarded as an infant, and any person who caused, aided, or abetted the marriage of such an infant was to be imprisoned for not more than six months or fined not more than Rs. 500, or both. The same penalty was prescribed for a man above eighteen who should marry an infant girl. A man over fifty who married a girl under fourteen was to be liable to two years' imprisonment. From that day to this, the agitation has been kept up, and progress has been made in the direction of raising the marriage age to a decent point.

How slow it has been may be surmised from the

reception given two bills introduced in 1898 into the legislative council of the Madras Presidency. One made a man liable to criminal prosecution for violating an age of ten for girls; the other prescribed imprisonment or fine as a penalty for violating an age limit of eight. These were strenuously opposed because they were thought to be too far in advance of public sentiment.

The Parsees have secured special legislation, making fourteen the legal age for them. The Brahma-Samaj, in 1872, secured a law establishing the ages of eighteen and fourteen as the marriage age, and requiring the written consent of the parents for the marriage of any person under twenty-one.

This whole agitation was started in 1856 by Dr. Chevers, who showed the inadequacy of the protection afforded child wives. Matters came to a crisis in 1890, when a little girl of twelve died in horrible agony because of the treatment given her by her husband, who was imprisoned for a year.

The abolition of *sati* was due to the efforts initiated by William Carey. As early as 1799, he entered an energetic protest against its farther toleration by the government. Had there not been a change in governors, *sati* would have been abolished in 1808. The first regulations restricting the practice were passed in 1812 and 1817, but it was not until 1829 that Lord Bentinck issued an order which declared *sati* to be culpable homicide, and threatened severe penalties on all who encouraged it or in any way assisted at the ceremony.

Carey absented himself from church one Sunday morning in order the sooner to translate Lord Bentinck's order and have it issued, lest any delay might sacrifice a widow's life. This act of 1829 applied only to British India. As late as 1880 isolated cases of *sati* were heard of. No sooner was the abolition regulation of 1829 promulgated than in Bengal a monster petition, representing some of the best families and containing 18,000 names, was presented for its withdrawal. In all this agitation Carey and the missionaries had the active assistance of natives, especially of the pioneer Hindu religious reformer, a Brahman, Raja Ram Mohan Roy.

The next object of attack was the prohibition of widow remarriage. Under the lead of a native reformer, this agitation was maintained until, in 1856, the Widow Marriage Act was passed, which legalized the status of Hindu widows who had contracted a second marriage and declared their children legitimate. At the same time, the law did not protect them in their civil rights. They still forfeited all property inherited from the husband and were not afforded sufficient protection for their own private property. The first public widow marriage ceremony in Bengal was performed in Calcutta in 1865. Four years later came the first such marriage in Bombay. Since that day progress has been made, but even now the cases are rare enough to excite much attention.

Thus, along these various lines, there has been

marked improvement in public sentiment and in the legal status of women in India.

The women of China are coming to the front. The impression made by the Christian home has been profound. The Christians are not permitted to marry their daughters to men of bad character, to dispose of them as second wives or concubines, or to force them upon men to whom for moral reasons the girls feel an antipathy. A Christian who abuses his wife, divorces her for more than one cause, or takes a second wife, incurs church discipline. Non-Christians have been impressed with the desirability of securing Christian girls for wives. The influence of the Christian family in purifying and elevating social life has been acknowledged, for instance, by non-Christians in Hong Kong. A missionary in Shantung testified, long before the present movements began, that it was common to hear outsiders comment admiringly upon the improvement in the Christian women. As a result, native ideas regarding the rights and capabilities of women steadily changed. Some years ago, a man in Hankow came to a missionary and brought him his idol, the god of riches, with the explanation: " We never have any peace in our house. I am told if I give up idols and believe on Jesus my home will become a little heaven on earth. Here is my idol."

Christian women have come to the front as leaders. There are several fine Christian women physicians, the first of whom was graduated in New York at the head of her class in 1885. The example of the Christians in securing education for their daughters has influenced leading women in China. One sister of Prince Su some years ago opened the first school for girls in Mongolia, while the other sister started the first purely Chinese school for girls in Peking, which soon had nearly one hundred pupils from the highest families. She undertook the work in spite of opposition and ridicule, and declared to the missionary ladies that but for them this school would never have been.

The first woman's daily paper in the world was started by a Chinese woman of means in Peking, and was published until funds failed. Women's clubs have been opened. One of these, in Ningpo, has had a flourishing existence and has discussed such weighty and knotty problems as that of foreign loans for railway development. In Peking, under the lead of lady missionaries, lectures were given for the benefit of the women of the aristocracy, and this did much to open them to Christian influence as well as prepare them for the part they were destined to play in the New China.

In the revolution which overthrew the Manchus, and which was so largely the work of the young men who had studied in Japan or in the United States or Europe, the young women were actively interested. The students in the Girls' College at Ponasang, Foochow, were on fire with zeal. Several of them joined the "Dare-to-Die Society," and started for the north to die for their country. When they were urged to return home, they declared: "We are Christians. Jesus died to save His people, and we will die for China." In these last few years, there has appeared in China, and to a less extent in other Oriental countries, the New Woman, who is even more *outré* in China than in America. Women have come to a new consciousness of their power. They have been given greater liberty and have tasted the sweets of it, and a few have desired to follow in the footsteps of their Western sisters and live an independent life.

Unfortunately, they have not grown into this liberty gradually and so they tend to confuse it with license. Friends in China have given me instances that fell under their own observation of the boldness of these new women, which would be marked and would excite unfavourable comment even in one of our cities. Judge of the impression produced by such actions in the midst of a most conservative civilization, in which for generations women have been kept in the background as inferiors. Such tendencies are apt to bring into reproach the whole cause of progress along Western lines, and the work of education to which such results are attributed. Needless to add, these extreme cases are not Christian women.

The change in Japan with regard to the position of woman has been very marked. We have already noted that Miss Japan is being educated alongside of her brother. Women are beginning to assert their rights as women. In 1902, they began to protest against the use of the humiliating word *shō*, concubine. Partly because foreigners are beginning to read and interpret Japanese books, the word was purposely omitted from the statute entitled " Family Law." The difficulty is that this word is rooted in Japanese customs so firmly that, as writers declare, " really there is no other way for a woman to talk of herself." Even the abuse of men, which is indulged in by a certain type of the New Woman, has spread to Japan. Last year a woman's magazine was started by discontented women, the contents of which are of this nature. This is but one sign of the revolt of the women of Japan, which will have serious consequences unless Christian standards can be enforced.[1]

[1] " It is a statement heard again and again that the influence of the new life has been detrimental for women morally and spiritually. People who remember the old régime are unanimous in deploring the lowering effects of the present conditions on both men and women, the change being shown perhaps in women more conspicuously of late than in men. The criticisms made are that women have grown less refined, less faithful to duty, that they are selfish, luxurious, vain and fond of display. The simple Spartan life of the past has vanished, and nothing of true worth has taken its place. But the careful thinker will add, no doubt, that the present apparent retrograde condition is probably temporary. Women who in the past were kept from contact with the world are now meeting all its allurements; whereas little power was in their hands, and they were fully protected from temptation, they are now obliged through circumstances to act for themselves. The old-time conservative training and teaching do not touch the new conditions of life. . . . Impulses are now being set free which were held in check in the

During the war between Japan and China, the value of the Christian home was impressed upon the nation. For nearly three years the soldiers were separated from their wives and families. Many wives, it was reported, brought disgrace upon their families, and even used the savings sent them for abominable purposes. During this period, the Christian wives of the Christian soldiers kept their homes pure, performed their duties towards their husbands' parents, and attended to the education of their children. Regarding not a single one was there any report of misconduct. Concubinage used to be respectable. Now it is coming to hide itself. Formerly husband and wife were never seen together. Now they may be observed walking and

past by external forces, while there is yet lacking judgment and knowledge of true values, and restraint from within, to guide the awakened mind. . . .

"Theoretically, the ordinary woman not under Christian teachings is now taught, in schools and by masters and parents, ethical standards not greatly changed from past ones. She is more or less all her life to be under the guidance of others, she is not to be given the freedom of thought or action which Western women take for granted, her life is to be in the home and for the family ; but in reality the life she often has to lead, through new conditions or from financial necessity, calls for more recognition of her worth and individuality. The old teachings alone are not sufficient for the future Japanese woman; there must be more acknowledgment of her place and true value.

* * * * * * *

"What part has Christianity among these conditions? The answer is almost too apparent to need statement. The restraints formed under the feudal days, together with many of the teachings of the past, are going rapidly by with the changing times.

talking together and even riding in the same jin-ricksha, so it is declared.

In all this movement, the sane leadership has been largely in the hands of the Christian women of these lands, who have revealed to the world both the beauty and the power of an educated and con-secrated womanhood.· Take India as an example. The Christian community has produced a group of women who have shown the possibilities of develop-ment inherent in Indian womanhood. The *In-dian Christian Messenger*, a few years ago, printed the following paragraph :

" Who was the first Indian lady that graduated in Arts ? Miss Chundra M. Bose, a Christian. Who was the first Indian lady that graduated in medicine ?

They will mostly pass away with the older generation, of whom few remain. The old religions have little ethical influence and only a feeble hold at best on modern men and women. Chris-tianity will not replace them but rather fill a void. Japan is singularly ready for all the ethical ideals of Christianity in all points, with the exception perhaps of those concerning patriotism and filial duty. Christianity especially fills the needs of women at this time of awakening. The glamour of Western life and the freedom of the women of the West attract them. They seek it without a knowledge of those deeper things that make freedom a blessing. Buddhism gave to woman humility, but at the price of self-effacement and degradation, not by the teaching of lofty ideals for her. It took away her individuality, even her soul. . . . Christianity places woman on a level with man ; her individuality and worth in herself is recognized and full scope is given to her powers. At the same time by teaching self-sacrifice and service founded on the higher, broader ideal of love for others, it replaces the narrow old standard of self-sacrifice for the

Miss Mary Mitter (now Mrs. Nundy), a Christian. Who was the first Indian lady that graduated in law? Miss Cornelia Sorabji, a Christian. Who was the first Indian lady that encompassed the wide, wide world, both old and new, in search of knowledge and means for the amelioration of the condition of millions of Indian widows? Pundita Ramabai, a Christian. Who are as yet the only Indian ladies whose writings have earned the approbation of European critics? Miss Toru Dutt and Mrs. S. Satthianadhan, Christian ladies. Who have rendered signal help towards making an accomplished fact that eminently Christian movement for which millions of Indian females bless the honoured name of Lady Dufferin? The Indian Christian girls. Confining ourselves to our own North-West Provinces and Oudh, we may well continue: Who was the lady that first graduated as M. A.? Miss S. Chuckerbutty, a Christian. Who was the lady that attained a position hitherto unsurpassed by any lady candidate amongst M. A. candidates of the Allahabad University? Miss Lilavati Rapheal Singh, a Christian. Who was the first lady in Bengal that graduated in two subjects

good of one's family. While not laying such stress on efforts for family, clan or country, it inculcates, with a higher motive and on broader lines, the efforts to be made for humanity in general. Through its ethical and philanthropic side, Christianity makes the strongest appeal to our women, an appeal which meets a wonderful response in the hearts of sensitive natures, made singularly receptive by the discipline of the past."—*Miss Ume Tsuda, " Int. Rev. of Missions," April, 1913, p. 295 et seq.*

with the degree of M. A. ?   Mrs. Nirmala Shome, a Christian." [1]

A word or two may well be added about a few of the Indian Christian women, to make clearer the significance of their work.   The first Mrs. Satthianadhan was the daughter of an early Brahman convert to Christianity.   When the Madras Medical School opened its doors to women, she left her home in the Bombay Presidency to take up this work as the pioneer Indian woman in the study of medicine. In spite of the difficulty of facing the prejudices of Indian society, she entered the school and was enthusiastically welcomed by the men students.   On account of her health, she had to stop her course before graduation.   She married and produced well-known writings in which she gave brilliant descriptions of the life of Indian women.   She was also prominent in philanthropic work.

The hymn, " In the secret of His presence how my soul delights to hide," is the production of an Indian Christian, Miss Goreh.

The Sorabji family is one of the most famous of the Christian families in India.   The father was one of the few Christian Parsees.   A useful minister of the Gospel, he is best known as the father of his brilliant daughters.   One of these married an Englishman and used to delight Queen Victoria by her rendering of Persian songs.   Another was the only woman of the Orient in the Parliament of Religions.   Another became a distinguished surgeon ;

[1] Dennis, J. S., *op. cit.*, Vol. II, p. 188.

a fourth became an artist who exhibited at Paris and London; while the most famous of all, Miss Cornelia, is a prominent legal light. At the age of twenty-one, she had graduated from college and was lecturing to a class of men at the Gujarat College, Ahmedabad, on English literature and language, and later was Acting Professor of English. Her success in teaching men marked an epoch in the history of women in India. She graduated in law at Oxford and was admitted as a barrister.

The greatest modern Indian woman is Pundita Ramabai, whose noble work for the widows of India and now, also, for thousands of orphans, is too well known to require description. At one time neutral in her work as regards Christianity, she is now aggressively Christian and is respected by all classes.

A Christian community that can produce such women as these is to be reckoned with in the days to come.

The large majority of the Japanese women in their prime who are prominent in Christian work were educated in Christian schools. Even some women, not themselves Christians, who are prominent in public work, were thus trained. The mission schools were the pioneers in the education of the girls of Japan, but they no longer take the lead. This is not due to any decrease in their efficiency, but to the remarkable improvements in the government schools. The result is that the next generation of leading women will not come from Christian schools in any such proportions.

What the effect of this diminution in the number of Christian-trained women will be no one can forecast. The leading woman educator of Japan, Miss Tsuda, quoted above, who has the highest grade Japanese school for girls in the country, a school with government recognition, is herself an earnest Christian.

Any one who has visited the Orient and seen the difference between the Christian and the non-Christian homes, who has contrasted the expression upon the faces of the women whom Christ has made free with that upon the faces of those who are still without Him, will need no further argument to prove the success of the work of Christian missions. Had there been no other effect, the undertaking would have paid for itself. As it is, the women, who hold the key to the Orient, are being reached, and if the Church at home will do its part, more than half the women of the world will before many generations cease to be a drag upon social progress and will become a force speeding on the emancipation of their sisters and the uplift of the great nations on the continents of Africa and Asia.

IV

PROGRESS IN ETHICAL IDEALS

A FAIR-MINDED man approaches the subject of ethical progress in mission lands with hesitation, because he realizes how great is the danger of misrepresentation. It is so easy for the outsider to misunderstand what he sees. It is so easy for the best observer to look at but one side of the picture. The general method in the past has too often been to describe the darker phases of life in non-Christian lands, their cruel customs, or their lack of such virtues as honesty and purity, and then to contrast with these the ideals of Christian nations. This is unfair for two reasons: it overlooks the brighter and better side of non-Christian life; and at the same time it forgets that in our own civilization the Christian ideals are but imperfectly realized. On the other hand, one who is prejudiced against missionary work dwells upon all the attractiveness, to him, of the Orient, the beautiful thoughts that here and there find expression in their sacred writings, and the charm of life in the East. He contrasts with these the crudity and cruelty of Western life, and then concludes that the West has nothing to teach the East.

Similarly, the Oriental traveller or student comes

to this country, sees the industrial and moral conditions in our cities, the openness of vice, the corrupting influence of some of our amusements, and he returns convinced that their own customs and institutions need only minor modifications.

What shall one say as between these two diametrically opposed conclusions? Neither is just. It is not fair to compare the best of one country or civilization with the worst of another country or civilization. For instance, I had a friend in India whose acquaintance with Americans had been confined to missionaries and to such travellers as Dr. Charles Cuthbert Hall and President Henry Churchill King, while the Englishmen he had known had been army officers and civilians. Needless to say, the erroneous conclusion he drew was that Americans are far superior in every respect to the British. The best of the East should be compared with the best of the West, the worst of the Orient with the worst of the Occident, or, better still, the general level of the standards in the two parts of the world should be set over against one another.

At the same time, it should be borne in mind that, while the vice in our cities should make Christians ashamed of their failure to eradicate this evil, yet it exists in spite of our Christian public sentiment, which is constantly striving to suppress it. On the other hand, this same evil in India is sanctified by religion, and its worst phases are connected with the religious life and worship of certain sections of the people. The Western nations are constantly struggling to suppress thievery, but graft has been taken for granted in China. Stealing is a recognized profession in India, and it is only under the spur of Christian and Western influence that any very earnest attempt has been made to eradicate it. Hence, while scrupulous fairness must be shown towards these peoples, and while it must be admitted with shame that Christianity has not yet succeeded in raising the ethical ideals of Europe and America to a truly Christian level, yet it is still true, as this chapter and the last should show, that the nations which have gone the farthest in adopting the principles of Jesus are, ethically speaking, immeasurably ahead of those that have not followed Him.

The ethical precepts and ideals of a nation like China are high. The same may be said of the best portions of the literature of a country like India, although much of the literature of India would never be tolerated in an English translation. The real difference in ethical level is seen in the social and individual standards as embodied in actual life. One glaring instance is the position accorded to woman, as set forth in the last chapter.

The root of the difficulty is the fact that under the non-Christian religions,—and even, it must be confessed, under a dead and formal Christianity,—there is a divorce between religion and ethics. This does not mean that these religions do not enforce a certain moral code. They do. For example, the belief, prevalent in China, that the spirit of a murdered man returns to plague the murderer, deters many a man from making way with one whom he dislikes. In such matters as sex relations, certain rules may be enforced with great rigour, even though the standard, as Westerners regard it, may be very low. At the same time, these religions are relatively powerless to transform lives, and in many cases there is an absolute divorce between ethics and religion, the most religious persons being the most corrupt. Even under Roman Catholic Christianity, where it has lost its vitality, as it so largely has in the countries of South America, this is true, and the priests have at times been a stench in the nostrils of all decent people. The open violation by many Buddhist priests in Japan of their vow of chastity, even their frequenting of houses of prostitution, has been notorious. A famous Buddhist priest whom I met personally in Burma was not ashamed to confess himself guilty of such deeds.

Similar offenses occur in India. Some of the holy men are sincerely desirous of attaining the higher life, and live pure, though selfish, lives. But others are unspeakably corrupt and have reached the point where it is believed that they are guilty of no sin when they violate every rule of purity or decency. What else could be expected in a country where the amours of the gods are portrayed in sculpture, painting, and story, and are familiar to the very children in the street? Prostitution is the handmaid of religion in India.

To be sure, one finds in both India and Japan the doctrine of salvation by faith, but it is radically different from the Christian belief bearing the same name. Not only is faith regarded as a meritorious work, but, according to some schools, it makes no difference what content the faith has. Believe in any god or in any formula, and that faith will save you, no matter what your life may be. Some of the Japanese have been driven to take refuge in faith as the means of salvation by their belief that their sins are ineradicable, and in the hope that they may thus attain future happiness without having to rid themselves of their sinful practices.

It would be unfair to say that Islam teaches no ethical standards, but it is not unfair to claim that it not only tolerates but caters to ethical standards for which no enlightened religion can stand.

The distinctive glory of Christianity is that it contains a dynamic which can transform the man who loves sin into the man who loathes sin, and still more into the man who has broken with sin and is living a new life. It also proclaims and maintains that any religion is unworthy of the name, unless it manifests itself in a changed life, which is constantly rising ethically.

It is sometimes claimed by the critics of missions that the acceptance of Christianity means an ethical deterioration and that the only natives one can trust are the raw heathen. This criticism is especially frequent in Africa. There are reasons, which might be given, that would explain why this criticism may at times seem to have some justification. They do not, however, disprove the claim that the members of the Christian community, as a rule, have higher ethical standards than the same class of people among the non-Christians, and that usually this standard is the highest that can be found anywhere in the country. This is in spite of the fact that these Christians have often come from the lower ranks of society, whose standards may be lower than those of the higher classes.

There is everywhere evidence of the ethical progress that has been made under the influence of Christianity, a progress that is now extending far beyond the Christian community and is producing a real ethical revival in the countries of Asia.

Intemperance has been a serious vice among the peoples of Africa and the South Seas. Most of the primitive races have their own intoxicating liquors for use at social gatherings, but the effect of these, bad as it is, does not compare for a moment with the demoralization produced among such races by the strongest distilled liquors. These were practically forced by Western traders upon these people.

Against this vice the native Christian rulers and the Christian communities have taken a decided stand. Khama, the great chief of Bechuanaland, South Africa, used all his influence to exclude imported liquors from his territory. In an address delivered in London, he declared: "It were better for me that I should lose my country than that it should be flooded with drink. . . . I dread the white man's drink more than all the *assegais* of the Matabele, which kill men's bodies, and it is quickly over; but drink puts devils into men and destroys both bodies and souls forever. . . . I pray your Honour never to ask me to open even a little door to drink."[1] The result is that, except at the railway stations, no such liquors can be obtained. He attempted with equal earnestness to stop the making and drinking of the native beer. His reasons were that it debauched the people, led them to waste their time, and kept the children out of school. The intervention of British officials, which was probably due to some misunderstanding, forced him to stop these efforts or run the risk of the withdrawal from under his dominion of all the beer-loving people. The very Sunday I spent at his capital, Serowe, he initiated a new attempt to curb this evil, with what success I have never learned.

In New Zealand a young Maori chief was a leader in urging that "no intoxicating liquor be sold or given to any man of the native race, and that no license be renewed or fresh license be granted within a mile of Maori-land." Thirty chiefs and sixty representative men supported this petition. In the Zulu Mission in South Africa every church-member is expected to take the pledge of total abstinence. The Christians around Lake Nyasa agreed together, "we will neither make beer nor drink it." In twelve villages in Formosa, where

[1] *Vid.* Dennis, J. S., *op. cit.*, Vol. II, p. 107.

churches had been planted, the change was so great that the heathen Chinese declared, "The aborigines are now men and women." In Assam and Burma nearly every Christian is a total abstainer. In a country like Japan, also, Christians have been leaders in fighting intemperance, although now the work is by no means confined to them. There are about seventy-five temperance societies in Japan, including Korea, and nearly twenty more among Japanese elsewhere. The active membership is about eight thousand. The Japanese branch of the World's Women's Christian Temperance Union has some three thousand members in more than seventy branches.[1]

Again, take such a matter as human sacrifice. For the purpose of averting calamity or securing good harvests, victory in war, or success in any new undertaking, it has been customary among some peoples to offer human sacrifices. Closely connected with the animistic beliefs so prevalent among all primitive peoples is the custom of killing human beings to serve as attendants to deceased persons of dignity and station. This degenerated until, among some savage tribes, human sacrifices became a part of their ceremonial etiquette.

The Vedas and other sources reveal the fact that in the early days of India such sacrifices were common. The particular kind of human being required was specified in the case of no less than one

[1] "Japan Year Book, 1912," p. 232.

146 Sociological Progress in Mission Lands

hundred and seventy-nine different gods. In Assam, not long since, children were offered as a sacrifice for the forgiveness of sins. The Shans in upper Burma believe that human sacrifices bring good harvests and that certain spirits can be appeased in no other way. The guardian spirit of one of their ferries required such a sacrifice annually, and a Chinaman was preferred. Very conveniently, the spirit used to capsize the boat at the proper moment and thus secure his victim. Before 1837, in a single city in east central India, one hundred and fifty human sacrifices were annually offered. In 1892 the head man of a village came to the missionary, requesting him to intercede with the government for permission to offer a living child in sacrifice for the purpose of removing disease from their homes and bringing rain.

During thirty years, a king in the Society Islands sacrificed as many as two thousand such victims. Most public occasions, even the launching of a new canoe, required such offerings.

Africa is the scene of some of the worst of such atrocities. The resting place of the body of a chief was often a bed of living women. Forty victims were killed within two days after the death of one king. When King M'tesa of Uganda rebuilt his father's tomb, the throats of two thousand victims were cut at the grave. A chief in the Congo region, whose hand was diseased, killed thirty of his subjects because he thought they were eating it. The brother of another king lay unburied for two months because they could not capture and kill enough people to satisfy their superstitions. One hundred had been killed, and another hundred were required. One beast in Africa killed four hundred virgins and mixed their blood with the mortar in order to get the right shade for the painted stucco of his palace. A whole quarter of his city was assigned to his executioners.

Against such barbarous customs the Christian forces have waged relentless warfare. The British troops destroyed the shambles of the last named king and took him prisoner. The British Government has entirely suppressed such sacrifices in India, unless there is an occasional secret offering in spite of the vigilance of the police. The native leaders of Uganda are dominated by Christian principles, and under their influence human sacrifices are a thing of the past in that country. In Old Calabar, the missionaries fought the custom with all their might and finally won the day. In 1850 two chiefs had died and several wives and slaves had been killed. Then a missionary appealed to the king, and he and his chiefs were induced to consent to the passage of a law abolishing all executions except for crime. The people were rallied to the support of this law and organized themselves into a "Society for the Suppression of Human Sacrifices in Old Calabar." The law was passed and its enforcement gradually improved until human sacrifices became unknown.

The great French missionary Coillard induced

the notorious King Lewanika in Zambesia to abolish the rite of human sacrifice. In the Yoruba Mission of the Church Missionary Society the progress was gradual. First, the public parading of the victims was discontinued. Then public opinion came to regard it as wanton cruelty to sacrifice men and women, since no beneficial results were secured. This drove the practice under cover, until it finally ceased, unless in rare instances. Thus, wherever Christian influence is dominant, human sacrifices have disappeared.

Cannibalism is another evil that has prevailed widely among primitive peoples. The chief basis of this custom was the animistic belief that by eating the bodies of slain enemies the victors acquired the strength and courage of the victims. Dr. Warneck instances cases where triumphant warriors, as a matter of principle, devoured human bodies, even though they so disliked the taste that it caused nausea. Again, the lack of animal flesh for food may have helped to establish this custom, which, in not a few cases, degenerated until it became a matter of mere beastly enjoyment.

In Fiji the people ate human flesh from the love of it, to express vengeance, and to excite terror. Human flesh was regarded as an essential part of any feast for the entertainment of visiting chiefs. One chief used to return from his tributary islands with the bodies of infants hanging from the yard-arms of his boat. Another registered the number of bodies he had eaten by setting up a stone on end for each body. A missionary counted eight hundred and seventy-two such stones.

It is to the credit of North and South Africa that there has been little cannibalism in those parts. Not so in the Congo region. One fortified city there with four gates had the approach to each paved with human skulls, most of them the relics of cannibalism. In one pavement there were more than two thousand skulls. In this country, that of the Batelas, every person who became old was killed and eaten by his children. A missionary in Old Calabar reported one region where slaves were sold for food in a regular cannibal market.

Cannibalism has rapidly disappeared before Christian influence. Raratonga, one of the Hervey Islands, was transformed by two native teachers within the two years 1823–1825. Fiji has been Christianized. Lifu, one of the Loyalty Islands, was converted by a native evangelist from Raratonga. He was condemned to be eaten by his hearers, but within ten years cannibalism had been stamped out. The Maoris of New Zealand have been transformed and, within the range of Christian influence, no cannibal Maori can be found, if there are any survivors anywhere. Yet these people in the old days not only feasted on slain enemies but specially fattened slaves for such feasts. In Africa the progress has been in the same direction. For example, Bishop Crowther reported a tribal war in which one hundred and fifty prisoners were taken. The heathen chiefs received one hundred and thirty-nine, and these were all eaten. The remainder were assigned to Christian chiefs, and their lives were spared.

Infanticide is another heathen custom that has taken its toll of human life. This is true of Africa. In one town in East Africa the missionaries knew of at least forty children who had been killed at or shortly after birth within a single year, 1895. In extenuation of some of these murders in Africa may be cited the belief that, unless a child about whom there is some untoward circumstance is killed, the father will die. Some people regard the cutting of a lower tooth first as such an evil omen, while other tribes regard the cutting of an upper tooth as rightly punishable with death. On the West Coast the mother of twins is disgraced for life. In other regions their birth is a cause of great rejoicing.

In Old Calabar the king of Creek Town was induced in 1851 by missionary influence to pass a law pronouncing the murder of twins or their mother a capital crime. It was added, however, that since such mothers and children could not be permitted to live in the town, a place outside should be found for them. By 1878 these women were given full liberty of visiting the town and trading there without molestation. In the same region, twins were born to a Christian couple in 1894, and, thanks to the influence of Christianity, were regarded as a source of great delight. Infanticide used to be prev-

alent in Madagascar; the Christian communities
have blotted it out from their midst. In the Fiji
Islands infanticide was added to cannibalism.
Mothers themselves often strangled their children,
especially the girls, and the early missionaries testified that no less than two-thirds of the children
were killed. Now these islands are one of the most
law-abiding communities in the world. On the
island of Mbau the stone, now hollowed out and
used as a baptismal font, was formerly the place of
slaughter for those who were to be eaten. Except
in the Samoan Islands, infanticide was practiced
throughout the small Pacific islands. Now, among
all the Christians in these islands, the old custom is
abhorred, and even where Christianity has only a
partial hold, it has been much reduced.

Cannibalism and human sacrifices are marks
chiefly of savage society, but female infanticide has
been common in many countries where in other respects there existed a high degree of civilization.
The facts set forth in the third chapter go far to
explain some of the reasons for this custom.
Mothers who had come to loathe their own lot were
unwilling that their daughters should suffer the
same disabilities, while the great expense of bringing up and marrying a daughter led fathers to desire to escape this financial burden. A pagan
woman in China expressed it thus: "A daughter is
a troublesome and expensive thing anyway. Not
only has she to be fed, but there is all the trouble
of binding her feet, and of getting her betrothed,

and of making up her wedding garments ; and even after she is married off she must have presents made to her when she has children.   Really, it is no wonder that so many baby girls are slain at their birth!"[1]   On the other hand, the necessity of having a son to perform the sacrifices and rites after the death of the father, confined the killing of infants to those of one sex.   These statements apply to such countries as China and India.

Whatever the reasons, the facts are indisputable. One of the early missionaries in Foochow learned from the statements of natives that fifty and more years ago about sixty or seventy per cent. of the female infants in that region were drowned at birth, or destroyed in some other way.   Special inquiries for the province of Fukien gave an average of forty per cent. for the girls that were murdered. For the vicinity of Amoy, it varied from ten to eighty per cent.   Even if we make a large allowance for exaggeration, the result is sufficiently appalling.   A Christian woman in the adjoining province of Cheh-kiang confessed that before she became a Christian she had had five daughters, all of whom she had drowned, because she could not afford to bring them up.   It is suggestive that in this region foot-binding is carried to an extreme, beyond that in most of the other provinces.   This may account in part for the unusually high percentage.   Parents who did not kill their children might leave them in an exposed place, or they

[1] Dennis, J. S., *op. cit.*, Vol. I, p. 129,

might be cast into the baby tower. Such towers still exist, though they are supposedly used only for the disposition of the bodies of dead babies. I have myself visited one in the vicinity of Foochow, and a friend saw it when it was so full that little bundles were lying around outside.

Christians have taken the lead in checking infanticide in China. The old pond in the centre of the city of Amoy, into which babies were thrown, gradually ceased to receive these deposits, and the pond long ago dried up. Some thirty-five years ago the protests of missionaries in Foochow led to the issuing of a proclamation that "the drowning of female infants is forever forbidden." Later edicts threatened severe punishment for those guilty of such murders. The result was a great diminution in this practice. At a later date, the imperial government issued edicts forbidding such murders, and opened foundling hospitals for girl babies. It must be said, however, that until recently some of these institutions were anything but well managed. Little attention was paid to cleanliness and sanitation. The children were at least horribly neglected and even worse charges have been brought against these hospitals. Others were fairly well conducted and the girls were trained for marriage. Now, however, a new day has dawned and, under Christian leadership, improvements are being made. There was six years ago an admirable institution in Tientsin in charge of a Christian Chinese woman doctor. Meantime, this lack of care by the Chinese gave the missionaries an opportunity to supply the deficiency.

Still more important, perhaps, has been a change in public sentiment. The example of the Christians, among whom the practice of infanticide, of course, entirely disappeared, affected the outsiders. Some twenty years ago, a missionary in Hankow was surprised to find several baby girls in Chinese homes, and was told, "We see that the Christians are keeping their girls, and we think perhaps we might be able to do the same." Everywhere the influence of Christian missions has tended to heighten the regard paid to women, to make more sacred the life of girls, and thus to lessen the evil of infanticide.

In some parts of India, chiefly in the north, infanticide used to be most shockingly common. The Rajputs and other tribes were sinners above all others. In 1843, in one clan, the Chauhans, there was not a single female child. In 1836, a Rajput chief estimated that the annual slaughter of infant girls in the two provinces of Malwa and Rajputana amounted to not less than 20,000, and this in spite of an order of the British Government, issued in 1802, declaring infanticide murder, punishable with death. An army officer, writing in 1818, stated that, among the children of eight thousand Rajputs, probably not more than thirty were girls. Ten years after the government had begun to suppress the custom in Gujarat, only sixty-three girls were known to have been saved. One Deputy Inspector of Police was asked if he had any children. He replied, "Yes, I had the misfortune to have two daughters, but I have dispatched both of them. May God now bless me with a son!" In one district, some years since, several hundred children were returned as having been carried off by wolves. Strangely enough, all of these were girls![1] In many sections, there has been no conscience in the matter; the custom has been a matter of course. When Kathiawar, the peninsula west of Bombay, came under British rule, the Jains expressly stipulated that no cattle should be killed for the use of British troops, but they had been practicing female infanticide for ages. The result of all this is seen in the proportion of the sexes. Thus, several years ago, in upper Burma, where woman is highly honoured, there were 102.79 girls to every 100 boys, practically the same as in Europe. Contrast with this the Indian averages: for Quetta, in British Baluchistan, 69.78; Sindh, 83.17; Rajputana, 87.48; all India, 92.00.[2]

In addition to this cold-blooded infanticide, there used to be another, a sacrificial infanticide, to appease the deities. Thousands of children were cast into the Ganges to be devoured by crocodiles and sharks, while another method was discovered by William Carey, in 1794. A mother, who was too poor to go on a pilgrimage to a sacred river spot,

[1] Fuller, Mrs. M. B., *op. cit.*, p. 155 *et seq.*
[2] Dennis, J. S., *op. cit.*, Vol. I, p. 133.

left her child in a basket, hanging from a tree, to be devoured by white ants.

Against all such practices the Christian forces, backed by the British Government, has waged determined warfare. The Christians themselves regard the custom with horror. The efforts of the government are hampered by the secrecy and inviolability of the Indian zenana, which make very difficult the detection and punishment of the murderers of children at home, and also by the fact that the father has from time immemorial possessed the power of life and death over his children. Mere neglect and exposure will accomplish the purpose, and an overt, positive act is almost necessary for action. As early as 1802, infanticide was declared murder, and the penal code of 1860 made it a crime. Meantime, government had succeeded in preventing the exposure of children at such festival spots as the mouth of the Ganges, where so many children and older people, too, had perished. This was done soon after Carey's gruesome discovery of the baby's bones in the basket.[1]

Even these measures were not sufficient, and the Female Infanticide Act of 1870 required the registration of all births. It went still further, and laid down the principle that the number of girls born must bear a certain proportion to that of the boys ! Thus, a tribe in which there were eighty boys under twelve and only eight girls would be at once suspected and put under strict surveillance. This

[1] *Vid.* Smith, G., "Life of William Carey," p. 281 *et seq.*

is no imaginary instance.   In this effort to prohibit
female infanticide, the British Government has had
the support of the feudatory states, which have
made similar prohibitions.   In spite of these efforts, in 1897, a census of the Thakur villages in
the North-West Provinces showed that eighty-five
per cent. of the children were boys.   Within a recent period of fifteen years, 12,542 cases of infanticide were officially reported, and in 1895 it was declared in the *Indian Social Reformer* that the custom seemed largely on the increase in the Madras
Presidency.   All of which goes to show that a custom that has prevailed for centuries is not often
eradicated within a generation.

Suicide is another evil of non-Christian society
which Christianity has opposed.   This practice is
associated with the old ethical standards of the
samurai class in feudal Japan, among whom loyalty was regarded as the preëminent virtue, in comparison with which life itself was of relatively little account.   Out of loyalty to a leader, as a method
of testifying to loyalty to one's beliefs, or even as a
means of escaping the disgrace of failure, it was
customary to commit suicide.   The samurai, as all
know, used their short sword for committing *hara-
kiri*.   This is one of the most painful of deaths,
but they were trained to commit it without moving
a muscle of the face.   In these days suicide is committed by others than the descendants of the samurai.   Women commit it more frequently than

men. Students especially are given to ending life thus when they fail in their examinations ; and certain beautiful spots in Japan, which are favourites with such visitors, have to be guarded to prevent their being used for such a purpose. The recent suicide of General Count Nogi and his wife is proof that the old standards of the samurai have not passed into oblivion, as is testified to, also, by the acclaim with which this deed was hailed by many.

Suicide is not unknown in India, where a native journal declared that eighty per cent. of the suicides are married women. Suicide has also been common in China. Here the object has been not merely to escape from the pains of this life, but to secure revenge. The Chinese believe that one who thus leaves this world may return as a spirit to haunt the life of the oppresser or betrayer. Many of the suicides have been women. Some of them have been driven to this by the betrayal of their virtue. Others have done it in order to escape cruel treatment or to avoid the necessity of being married. Favourite methods have been by the use of opium, by drowning, or by eating matches. As it is believed that any mutilation of the person received during this life must be retained in any future existence, these methods are favoured because they leave no mark. Christian missionaries rescue many suicides in China every year. The pessimism of heathenism, especially where Buddhist and Hindu views regarding transmigration have had influence, accounts for much of this, added to which is the cruelty with which women are often treated. Then, too, there is the low estimate put upon life.

Suicide is too common in the so-called Christian West for us to be too censorious upon this point. At the same time, the whole influence of Christianity is against it, whether in America or in Japan. Christianity teaches the sacredness of human life and the responsibility of each individual before his Creator, which cannot be avoided by self-destruction. Christianity teaches that there is a future life. It inculcates a spirit of faith and joy. It opposes the spirit of revenge. It does not reject loyalty, but it teaches that this should be loyalty to the highest ideals and should be exhibited by a life of service. The result is that Christians on the mission field rarely if ever commit suicide unless insane. Moreover, the Christian view of suicide is coming to prevail among non-Christians. Thus, Japan is seeking to prevent suicide and the second, sober thought of the nation disapproved of the act of General Count Nogi, even though it was strictly in accord with the old standards, which would have been accepted by all as proper two generations ago.

Self-torture is another evil to be mentioned here. This is very common in connection with religious rites, especially in India and China. In India, there are bodies of ascetics who always remain standing; others who keep their hands uplifted above their heads until they cannot be taken down; others who hang head down from the bough of a tree; and others who are at all seasons surrounded by five fires, or who remain immersed in water, or under a jet of water from sunset to sunrise, etc. In connection with festivals in honour of the god Shiva, hook-swinging used to be in great vogue, the hooks being thrust through the muscles over the shoulder blades. Walking upon live charcoal, rolling upon "cushions" of thorns, lying upon beds of spikes, piercing the tongue and sides with heavy javelins, are other methods of self-torture.

In China, the mutilation may be from religious motives, as in these examples from India; or it may be due to filial piety or even to the hope of gain. Dutiful sons and daughters cut off pieces of flesh to make soup for aged or sick parents. One famous case, which received the approbation of the government, was that of a Miss Wang. When she was thirteen and her betrothal was hinted at, she retired to her room, drew blood from her arm, and with it wrote a sentence declaring that she would remain single and care for her parents. Her father and second brother were killed in battle in 1852. As she could not leave her mother's side to follow her father's body to the grave, she gashed her arm and let the stream of blood mingle with the lacquer on the coffin. Ten years later she cut a piece of flesh from her left thigh to be administered to her mother during a serious illness. The mother recovered. In less than a year the mother was sick again, and she repeated the operation with the right thigh. Later, when her mother was slightly ill, she applied burning incense sticks to her arms and put the burned flesh with the medicine. Such conduct was regarded as most commendable and very unusual on the part of a mere woman.

This whole practice of self-torture is contrary to the teachings of Christianity. No Christians ever indulge in it. As Christian influence spreads, it is seen that this is not the avenue of approach to God or a means of securing either peace or pardon. Religion must be on an entirely different basis from this. Thus, Christianity cuts out the very basis on which religious self-torture rests. Some asceticism and torture have been for the sake of gain. Here the Christian doctrine, that every man should seek to support himself and those for whom he is responsible, and do it in a manner worthy of a child of God, takes away the basis for such asceticism. The whole Christian idea of the worth of the body as a temple of the Spirit makes its mutilation not only useless but sinful. Wherever Christian influence has gone, and through preaching or through education has dispelled the old superstitions, the practice of self-torture ceases. Even the agnosticism, which is invading these mission lands, tends in the same direction. Asceticism and self-torture are losing their hold in the East.

Cruel ordeals have been characteristic of savagery and even of more advanced civilizations. Certain primitive tribes of India used boiling oil. If any of the Kois died a natural death, it was thought to

be due to the machinations of an enemy. The
most likely person was settled upon, the corpse
was carried into his presence, and the accused was
made to thrust his hand into boiling water or oil.
Siam and neighbouring countries used such tests,
some of them in an exceptionally cruel form.
Poison was used in Madagascar. A well-known
missionary of the early days declared that at that
time three thousand perished thus every year. It
was computed that one-tenth of the people were
subjected to it at some time during their life, and
that of these one-half perished.

On the continent of Africa, the ordeal has been
common and has persisted to the present day. Old
Calabar used as the poison a powdered bean. A
different poisonous drink was used in Nyasaland,
and cases of its use were reported as late as 1893
by the Livingstonia missionaries. In one tribe
several hundreds of persons have been compelled
to take the poison at one time, of whom from
thirty to forty died. In such cases, the rule was
that the wives and children of those who died
passed to the accuser. This may account for the
willingness of the people to accuse others of witchcraft. This practice has played an important rôle
in Africa. Upon witchcraft and ordeals rested the
whole legal system of many African tribes.

The basis of all such ordeals lies partly in ignorance of the laws of evidence. Still more it rests
upon the belief that all calamities are due to the
action of spirits or of men, who have caused them

out of revenge. Then, too, there is a belief that if a person is innocent no harm can result. Superstition and ignorance thus lie at the root of such customs. Both of these bases disappear under the influence of education and the Christian view of the world. Wherever the missionary has gone, he has striven to put down such needless cruelty.

The missionaries of the Old Calabar Mission in Africa had a long and hard struggle to suppress the custom. It lasted for nearly thirty years, but finally resulted in victory. In 1878, the British consul and the men of the country drew up and signed articles of agreement by which any one who administered the poisonous esere-bean was to be executed as a murderer, whether the victim succumbed or not, and any one willfully partaking of the poison was to be fined and banished as guilty of attempted murder. It was the testimony of the consul that such an agreement could never have been secured but for the persistent efforts of the missionaries to suppress the custom.

On the Gold Coast, natives have been known to declare themselves Christians in order to escape the perils of witchcraft and poison ordeals, because it was generally understood that Christians would not tolerate any such customs. An American missionary in the Congo Valley secured an agreement from all the neighbouring chiefs, pledging themselves to prevent any further administration of the poison. In Nyasaland, the result of missionary effort was the gradual disappearance of the custom, under a growing public opinion against it. Pastor Coillard with brave audacity preached before the cruel Lewanika against his use of the poison ordeal and in this way and by private interviews began the abolition of the entire system there. In Madagascar, where the poison cup was in constant use, the fatal draught is never mixed, and this was true before the French took the island. In India this savagery has been suppressed by government.

Slavery is an evil which has been all but universal. In Africa and in Asia slavery has generally prevailed. Slavery has always prevailed in Mohammedan countries. It has existed in China, Korea, Siam, Assam, some of the native states of India, etc. Japan appears to be an important exception, for here slavery, in the proper sense of the word, has not existed, although there used to be many serfs and a class of outcastes, as will appear later. It has been universal in Africa and still persists beyond the range of European influence. It has not been banished from the Philippines even to-day. In some of these countries the slavery is of the milder domestic type. In others, the only slavery is that due to the selling of children or the taking of a person in payment of debt.

Wherever slavery exists on a large scale, there must of necessity be a trade in slaves. The slave-trade in Africa and the South Seas annually took its toll of human lives. A generation or more ago, it was estimated that the number of lives annually sacrificed through the African slave-trade was not less than half a million, and that the number actually transported, added to those who were exiled by the burning of villages, would bring the yearly toll of sufferers up to two million. Some twenty years ago, nearly every important town in Hausaland had its slave market. In one of these the average daily offering was five hundred slaves. A missionary estimated that one-third of the population of that region in the western Sudan were slaves. From the Sultanate of Zanzibar, in 1895, some eleven thousand were being shipped annually to Arabia, while the maintenance of the number of slaves within the Sultanate, who comprised two-thirds of the population of 400,000, required an additional importation of six thousand a year.

Against these twin evils the Christian forces have waged a generally successful warfare. For three centuries the subjects of Christian nations carried on the slave-trade until an aroused public sentiment, originating in and sustained by Christian principle and feeling, could tolerate it no more. The traffic in slaves was abolished throughout the British Empire in 1807, after a struggle which had lasted for twenty years. The United States acted simultaneously with Great Britain and these two nations were quickly followed by others. The refusal of the United States, however, until 1862, to grant the Right of Search, made it difficult actually to abolish the trade. The American importation was estimated in 1837 at as high as 200,000 annually. From about this time, a new crusade began, in which the British played the leading rôle, and which resulted in the suppression of the slave-trade. Ships of war were stationed along the African coast to prevent native boats from carrying slaves from the continent, especially to Arabia. Missionaries co-operated by caring for the rescued slaves.

In all this period, one heroic figure stands out prominently, that of a Christian missionary, David Livingstone. From soon after his first journey, in 1852, until his death in 1873, his life was devoted to the exposure of the horrors of the African slave-trade and to arousing the powers to the need of its suppression. His biographer Blaikie thus summarizes his influence: "From the worn-out figure kneeling at the bedside in the hut in Ilala an electric spark seemed to fly, quickening hearts on every side. The statesman felt it; it put new vigour into the despatches he wrote and the measures he devised with regard to the slave-trade. The merchant felt it, and began to plan in earnest how to traverse the continent with roads and railways, and open it to commerce from shore to centre. The explorer felt it, and started with high purpose on new scenes of unknown danger. The missionary felt it,—felt it a reproof of past languor and unbelief, and found himself lifted up to a higher level of faith and devotion. No parliament of philanthropy was held; but the verdict was as unanimous and as hearty as if the Christian world had met and passed the resolution—'Livingstone's work shall not die: *Africa shall live!* ' " [1]

The great authority on British Central Africa is Sir Harry H. Johnston. His testimony to the influence of Livingstone is unequivocal. He writes : " Dr. Livingstone, however, appeared on the scene, and his appeals to the British public gradually drew our attention to the slave-trade in Eastern Central Africa, until, as the direct result of Livingstone's work, slavery and the slave-trade are now at an end within the British Central Africa Protectorate, and are fast disappearing in the regions beyond under the South Africa Company; and the abolition of slavery in Zanzibar will shortly be decreed as a final triumph to Livingstone's appeal." [2] The status of slavery was abolished in Zanzibar in 1897, shortly after Sir Harry H. Johnston had published this statement.

The Universities' Mission to Central Africa has had for one of its chief objects " the ultimate extinction of the slave-trade." Bishop Mackenzie induced chiefs to agree not to permit the slave-trade or to buy or sell slaves. In Lewanika's country, traffic in slaves was stopped under the influence of Coillard. The internal slave-trade has also been abolished within the sphere of European influence, except for isolated instances under Portuguese or Belgian rule. It was the Christian queen of Madagascar who, in 1877, declared that any slave im-

[1] Blaikie, " Personal Life of David Livingstone," p. 480.
[2] Johnston, " British Central Africa," p. 157.

ported into the island should be set free, and thus stamped out the slave-trade there, the suppression of which had been provided for in a treaty with Great Britain half a century before.

Equally important have been the efforts to suppress the institution of slavery itself. One of the most notable victories of missionaries at this point did not occur in the East, but in the West. This was the fight that was waged in the West Indies, centering in Jamaica. It was maintained in spite of the most determined opposition. The slave owners went so far as to foment a slave insurrection and then charged it against the missionaries. The fight, however, was won in 1834 and resulted in the total abolition of slavery. Some of the freed slaves wished to return as missionaries to West Africa, to the very region from which they had been kidnapped. They declared their willingness to do this at the risk of reënslavement. " We have been made slaves for men," they said, " we can be made slaves for Christ."

Christian influence abolished slavery from the Christian community in Old Calabar. The law recognized but two classes of persons, slaveholders and slaves; free servants had no legal status. Under Christian teaching, public sentiment changed until, in 1854, a declaration was drawn up, which all Christian slaveholders were compelled to sign when they united with the church. According to this, they solemnly promised to regard their slaves as servants, not as property; pay them

just wages; encourage them to obtain education
for themselves and their children, and to attend
religious worship; sell no slave unless he was
liable to suffer death and could not be otherwise banished; endeavour to secure the abolition
of slavery; set the slaves free as soon as it should
be legally possible; and treat them in accordance
with the Golden Rule.[1] In 1893, forty native
chiefs in Uganda, who had become Protestant
Christians, freed all their slaves. The status of
slavery was abolished in the territory of the Royal
Niger Company in 1897. The first step towards
this notable achievement on the West Coast was
taken by the missionaries, by whose aid the government officials made their first approaches into the
territory affected.

It is not only in the suppression of such cruel
customs as the foregoing that there has been ethical
progress among Christians and under the influence
of Christianity. Similar results may be cited in
such matters as truthfulness and honesty. The
situation here is one which the people of the West
can hardly appreciate. We regard truthfulness as
the very corner-stone of all virtue, beside which
most of the other virtues are of minor importance.
Courtesy, politeness, and the like are all right
enough in themselves, but a lack of these may
easily be condoned. Not so in the Orient. Here
the order is reversed, and truthfulness tends to be

[1] Dennis, J. S., *op. cit.*, Vol. II, p. 325.

regarded either as no virtue at all, or at best as a rather minor one. Even native Christians in India have been known to declare to a missionary to whom they were devoted that they would lie in order to please or help him. I have been credibly informed of a case in China, where Christians confessed sins of which they were not conscious out of loyalty to a dearly beloved missionary. When such statements as this are true, one can imagine that truthfulness is not to be expected to mark the non-Christian community. An authority on China, like Douglas, declared that " a universal dishonesty of mind poisons the sap of the nation and produces all the cancers and evils which have made China a byword for deceit and corruption." An educated native Christian in India declared to a missionary, " You who have been born in Christian families and have been trained from infancy to speak the truth and to hate lying, can have no idea of the difficulty we Bengalis have in overcoming the natural tendency in us to lying and deceit. You are taught that it is dishonourable and evil to lie ; we are taught that the dishonour is not in lying, but in being discovered."

In spite of these handicaps, the Christian community has made marked progress in the direction of greater reliability. A few illustrations must suffice at this point. When the Japanese invaded Formosa, they used as guides, wherever possible, the native Christians ; for these, they knew, could be trusted. On reaching a village, they inquired whether there were any native Christians, and then they compelled these to assist them. On the other hand, the " Black Flags " killed the Christians, because of the certainty that they would not play false. Again, a Buddhist orange merchant in Japan praised his oranges and added, " I don't lie ; I am a Christian." This statement was itself a lie, but the incident illustrates the reputation of the Christians. Similar testimony comes from China and India. A non-Christian Chinese in Shensi was asked whether he saw any good points about the Christians. He replied, " Yes, there are three things I am bound to admire. (1) There is no need to watch our crops around their villages. (2) They neither sow, sell, nor swallow opium. (3) They cause little trouble in paying their taxes." A law case in a district in India, where the fruits of Christian work had proved discouraging, is also to the point. A group of men were called as witnesses in a trial which involved their landlord, who was in a position to injure them. It was supposed that their testimony would, therefore, be favourable to him ; but no, their statements were against him. They had heard the Bible, had learned that a lie was wrong, and hence refused to utter the lie that would have helped them financially. In another place, a company of shopkeepers formed a combination of a strange sort. Their agreement was not to keep up prices, or to increase their profits, but to carry on their trade without lying.

The introducton, in and through the Christian
community, of these higher standards of conduct is
not the only sign of ethical progress. Christianity
is also producing a new type of personality, that of
the incorruptible, public-spirited Christian, who is
seeking not his own salvation but the welfare of
others. In Buddhism, Hinduism, and Confucianism
there is little public spirit. All is selfish. The
officials in the Old China were in office for what
they could make out of it. The roads were neglected because any one repairing them would benefit others more than himself. Temples and such
buildings were erected, but as works of merit and
in order to advance the spiritual interests of the
builders or to increase their reputation. Only in
Japan does there seem to have been any great feeling
of patriotism and of willingness to serve and to die
for one's country. Buddhism and Hinduism embody
many high ideals and aim at union with the divine.
But salvation is a personal matter, and does not include the service of others. Mozumdar was a great
theistic reformer of Hinduism, and was regarded by
many as almost, if not quite, a Christian. He
showed his deep appreciation of the Saviour in his
remarkable book, "The Oriental Christ." Yet
even this man could not get away from the ideals
of his old religion, and towards the end of his life
he retired to the solitudes of the Himalayas. He
left in explanation of this course a pathetic statement, which is worth quoting:

"Age and sickness get the better of me in these

surroundings.   I cannot work as I would—contemplation is distracted, concentration disturbed, though I struggle ever so much.   These solitudes are hospitable ; these breadths, heights and depths are always suggestive.   I acquire more spirit with less struggle, hence I retire.

"My thirst for the higher life is growing so unquenchable that I need the time and the grace to reëxamine and purify and reform every part of my existence.   The Spirit of God promises me that grace if I am alone.   So let me alone.

"The rich are so vain and selfish, the poor are so insolent and mean, that having respect for both I prefer to go away from them.

"The learned think so highly of themselves, the ignorant are so full of hatred and uncharitableness, that having good-will for both I prefer to hide myself from all.

"The religious are so exclusive, the skeptical are so self-sufficient, that it is better to be away from both.

"What are the dead?   Have they not too retired?   I wish my acquaintance with the dead should grow, that my communion with them should be spontaneous, perpetual, unceasing.   I will invoke them and wait for them in my hermitage.

"What is life?   Is it not a fleeting shadow, the graveyard of dead hopes, the battle-field of ghastly competitions, the playground of delusions, separations, cruel changes and disappointments?   I have had enough of these.   And now with the kindliest love for all, I must prepare and sanctify myself for the great Beyond where there is solution for so many problems and consolation for so many troubles." [1]

Contrast with this the type of personality created by Christianity in various mission fields. Consider a man like Chief Khama of Bechuanaland. From those days when, as a young man, he dared the anger of his father and his chief and risked death for disobedience rather than enter into a polygamous marriage, through all the days of his own rule, he has sought to enforce Christian standards among his people. There has recently passed away in Natal a simple Zulu preacher, who as a young man went out into a region of rank heathenism. The people did not want him and threatened to kill him, but he stuck to his post and to-day that whole region is Christianized; and all this was achieved without the aid of a missionary or of foreign money. Or take the leaders of the Christian Church in India, like Mr. Tilak, the Maratha Christian poet, or Bishop Azariah whose heritage is of the lowliest but who has been a power among Indian students and who is now the first Indian bishop of the Anglican Church in India. Go to China and what higher type of Christian can one find anywhere in the world than that simple pastor-evangelist, Rev. Ding Li Mei? Through his efforts hundreds, yes thousands, of the Christian youth of China have turned deliberately away from

[1] Jones, J. P., "India's Problem, Krishna or Christ," p. 350.

the hope of lucrative positions in order to prepare themselves for leadership in the Christian community. In Japan there are scores of Christian leaders who have revealed to the Japanese people the possibilities of a Christian character.

The report of Commission IV to the Edinburgh Conference, which treated of the missionary message, is suggestive at this point. No reader of this remarkable book can help being struck with the statement again and again that one of the most powerful forces attracting persons to Christianity is the life of the Christians. Because of the demonstration in the lives of individuals of the ability of Christianity to create a new type of manhood and womanhood, others are compelled to believe that Christianity has a power of which they have not dreamed. Such evidence cannot be gainsaid.

Take India, for instance. What is the greatest apologetic that Christianity can present? What it has done for the outcastes. Hinduism believes these submerged millions to be less than human. Such people used to be treated worse than the cow or even the monkey, who might be sacred. They were doomed to this existence because of sins committed in some previous existence, and there was absolutely no hope for them. And then the Christian missionary appeared, reached out to these despised ones, educated them, made them men and women, until the second generation, if not the first, has produced men of culture and influence. They teach schools in which Brahmans are pupils. A

Christian in South India, who came from the car-rion-eaters, the lowest of the low, is mayor of a city, and this Christian pastor is treated in his official capacity by the Brahmans as their equal. Such miracles were unheard of before, and men have seen that even these lowest, when touched by Christ, can be made ethically and intellectually equal or even superior to those whom Hinduism pronounced of finer stuff. Christianity is, indeed, creating a new type of personality, and such a religion commends itself to open-minded men.

The effect of this rising standard of morals and this new type of character is to produce ethical changes beyond the ranks of the Christians. This is seen in all the great countries of Asia, such as China, Japan, and India.

The twin evils of China have been opium and gambling among men, with foot-binding as a cruel and disabling custom affecting women. Years ago China was a nation of heavy drinkers, but sub-sequently threw that vice completely off. Now it is engaged in a life-and-death struggle to throw off the opium habit, with the purpose of making China strong. There is no need of dwelling upon the earlier struggles of China against this evil, but it is interesting to call attention to the connection which missionaries have had with the present attempt. In May, 1906, Dr. DuBose of Soochow, President of the Anti-Opium League, had an interview with the Governor-General of the River Provinces, who promised to forward to Peking a memorial signed by missionaries of all nationalities. This promise was at once taken up, and in August there arrived at Nanking a petition of sheets from 450 cities, with 1,333 signatures.

It is claimed that the result of this petition was the issuing of the edict of September 20, 1906, which urged the speedy suppression of the opium habit. In January, 1907, the Chinese Government ordered the viceroys to reduce poppy growing by one-half before the spring of 1908. By May, the opium dens in Foochow and Peking were closed, and the next month the edict was issued prohibiting opium smoking and planting. Other more stringent edicts followed ; and then came the international opium conference in 1909, with a second conference three years later. In March, 1909, Viceroy Tuan Fang reported that 3,000,000 people had given up the opium habit since the issuing of the decrees, that opium smokers had been reduced sixty-five per cent., and that the cultivation of the poppy and the revenue from opium had been decreased one-half. The government has sacrificed from 100,000,000 to 150,000,000 taels of revenue. Some opium smokers have died as the result of breaking off the habit. Substitutes are coming in, and the fight may not be won for a generation; but the progress has been marvellous and far beyond the expectations of the most sanguine.[1]

The new penal code of China prescribes severe

[1] "China Mission Year Book, 1910," pp. 11, 12, 398 et seq.

penalties for manufacturing, dealing in, storing for later sale, or importing opium; for making, selling, storing for later sale, or importing opium-smoking instruments; for smuggling or permitting the smuggling of opium or the smoking instruments; for opening opium dens; for planting the poppy for the manufacture of opium; for smoking opium or failing to enforce these regulations.[1] There is such solidarity in the Chinese people that when they make up their mind to do a thing, especially if it has an ethical bearing and is designed to benefit their country, they carry it through. The need of the reform may be judged from the statement that in certain of the remoter provinces as many as eighty per cent. of the men and fifty per cent. of the women were addicted to the use of the drug. It is the poor man's vice. A few cash are sufficient to enable a man to forget his miseries, his poor home, scanty clothing, and insufficient food.

Gambling has been the other evil in China, and has been indulged in by people in all ranks of society. The moral interest aroused in the crusade against opium has, in certain quarters, resulted in a movement to suppress gambling, or at least to separate the government from connection with it. For some years there has been growing in Canton a feeling that the government should not exploit this vice for the purpose of gain. In this city the licenses from gambling establishments have produced no inconsiderable part of the provincial

[1] "China Mission Year Book, 1911," p. 445 et seq.

revenue. The provincial assembly passed a resolution urging the viceroy to abolish the system. Because of the revenue difficulty which would result, he temporized. The gentry came to the support of the assembly and carried the matter to Peking, with the result that finally in March, 1911, the revenue from gambling was abolished, and strict regulations were issued against public gambling.[1]

In all this, the Christians have been setting an example to the other Chinese. Every Christian has been required to give up gambling. Some of the most prominent Christian workers have been converted gamblers. One Christian in Ningpo lapsed back into the habit, but when he came to himself, his repentance was so deep that, in Chinese fashion, he chopped off a finger so that it would remind him never to do it again. A missionary was once lamenting the little spiritual progress of the Christians in a certain village. Thereupon one of the prominent church members replied, "Sir, you don't know. Formerly, before we knew the truth, gambling was common; now it has been utterly abolished. Then we had feuds and lawsuits every month; now harmony prevails."

Foot-binding is, for China, a modern custom, dating from long after the time of Confucius, but it has entailed untold suffering upon the part of women and has condemned them to lives of comparative idleness. The early missionaries so vividly realized the difficulties in the way of removing this custom

[1] "China Mission Year Book, 1911," p. 47.

that they took no positive stand against it. About forty years ago, however, the attitude changed. Schools for girls began to require that all their pupils should unbind their feet as a condition of remaining in the school. The first allusion to such a rule that Dr. Dennis was able to discover dated from 1870. At about this time, in 1877, it came to be understood in at least two missions in Foochow that no church member was to bind the feet of his daughters. About this time Dr. Macgowan and other missionaries in Amoy organized the Anti-Foot-Binding Association, with a membership of over forty.

This was in 1874. The result of all these movements was that there gradually appeared a group of women with natural feet, who were neither slaves nor working people and entirely respectable. Twenty years later, the movement took on new life and enlisted the aggressive support, not only of the missionary ladies, but of the Chinese and civilians. A Natural-Foot Association was organized in 1894, at Shanghai, composed of these varied elements, and through publications and in other ways an active propaganda was carried on. To the leadership of this movement came Mrs. Archibald Little, who devoted years of time and much money to this reform. Still more recently, this movement has been taken up by the Chinese, and whereas formerly the Chinese ladies made their feet look as small as possible, it is declared that in some places women with small feet pretend to have natural feet.

A Chinese friend in Shansi remarked to me, when I called on him in 1908, that he believed that within ten years there would be no bound feet left in China. That is expecting too much, but the ethical revival in China, which is crushing out political corruption, the opium degradation, and the gambling mania, will help also this movement for relieving the women of China of one of their greatest disabilities, the cause of untold misery. Foot-binding has already been declared illegal.

The ethical revivals in Japan and India centre chiefly around questions relating to purity. The moral standards in Japan are far below what they should be. To be sure, one might conclude from the fact that prostitution is licensed, that the situation there is worse than it really is. Dr. Griffis estimated that in the early days of the New Japan but five per cent. of the population actually practiced concubinage, although this may have been twenty per cent. of the population financially able to afford such a luxury.[1] The licensed quarters are under strict control and are the first to be searched when a crime is committed. In many cases they are outside the city. Vice is never so open as in some cities of the West. Yet, when all possible allowance has been made for this, it yet remains true that illicit relations between the sexes are far too common. Facts could be adduced which would reveal the extent to which this vice invades the pub-

[1] Griffis, W. E., "Mikado's Empire," p. 557.

lic educational institutions. All this is due largely to the fact that the Japanese, even more than Western people, have maintained two standards of morals, one for men and another for women. Bakin, the great teacher of Japan through fiction, taught this. Jealousy is regarded as a womanly sin, and is represented as a female demon. Chastity in Japanese signifies womanly duties, and one cannot express the idea of male chastity without a circumlocution. A pure girl will, at the command of her father or for the sake of her parents, enter a brothel. An inmate may marry a relatively respectable man and have her past buried.

Christians have waged relentless war against this institution. In 1890, the native Christians of Kyoto petitioned the government for the abolition of licensed prostitution. Christian Japanese in California succeeded in stopping the traffic in Japanese girls in San Francisco. Some years ago, when much of the licensed quarter in Osaka was burned, the Christians, Japanese and missionary, succeeded in preventing its rebuilding in immediate proximity to the railway station. Similar action was taken in Tokyo after the recent conflagration there. In the city of Maebashi, the Christians have succeeded in preventing the licensing of prostitution in that city, even though many merchants desire it, at least during the time of a large county fair.

These protests by Christians against impurity have had a far-reaching influence. A paper by a Japanese, published as long ago as 1896, paid tribute to the impression made upon the Japanese mind by the Christians' insistence upon the doctrines of monogamy and personal purity. "I do not mean to say that the Japanese people have been, as a rule, polygamous, or that womanhood among them, especially in the better classes, had not a very high ideal of faithfulness and chastity. But monogamy as the only true principle of social order, and purity as obligatory upon men as upon women, was never properly understood. If to-day our best ethical opinion has practically endorsed these truths, we must give a large measure of credit to the foreign missionaries who have been living among us for nearly forty years." [1] A native paper about the same time declared that there was not a boy or girl in the empire who had not heard the one-man-one-woman doctrine, while their ideas of loyalty and obedience were higher than ever. And the paper declared that the cause of this advance was none other than the religion of Jesus.

A similar awakening has been witnessed in all the ethical thinking of the empire. The spirit of the literature in the Tokugawa period was Buddhistic in its ethics and its philosophy. That of the Meiji period, just closed, is declared to have been Christian. Christian standards are held up before the people. The nation is so proud of its past and so sensitive of all criticism that it is setting itself earnestly to the task of reforming its customs and institutions until no one can point the finger of

[1] Dennis, J. S., *op. cit.*, Vol. II, p. 142.

scorn at Japan. The difficulty arises from the fact that in not one of the religions of Japan is there a moral dynamic equal to the task, and the educated youth of Japan find no sufficient moral sanction in their agnostic or positively atheistic position. In nothing short of Christianity will they find a power that can accomplish such a task.

India has suffered from these same evils, only there they are even worse because they are buttressed by the religion of the people. This renders them almost immune from attack by a government which is pledged to neutrality in all matters of religion. Apart from the question of the moral standards of the individual, the chief evils are three in number: indecency in art and literature, indecency in worship and religious festivals, and religious prostitution.

It is a well-known fact that there is hardly a god in the Hindu pantheon who did not violate the laws of purity, some of them on a wholesale scale and in the most disgraceful manner. Temples are often ornamented with obscene representations of these gods. Especially in South India, there are temple cars on which the gods ride during festivals. These have been erected at public expense and have stood out in the open where the children in the neighbourhood have played around them. Usually these cars are ornamented with carvings of this character. When the British Government attacked the obscenity of the land some years ago, it was necessary to add this proviso: "This Section does not extend to any representation sculptured, engraved, painted, or otherwise represented on or in any temple or on any car used for the conveyance of idols, or kept or used for any religious purpose." This was added because the government was convinced, upon the testimony of British and native officials, that "native public opinion was (is) not yet sufficiently advanced to permit the destruction of such indecencies."[1] At the same time, it is a sign of progress that, in at least some villages and cities of South India, the temple cars are no longer out in the open, but are under cover, bricked up, so that they are invisible except when in actual use.

The more enlightened people are becoming ashamed of the obscene carvings and paintings. This was evident when, a few years since, a missionary in North India purchased for me some photographs of the decorations in one of the most sacred temples, but one that is not open to the public. The man had the photographs but he was evidently ashamed to have them seen by foreigners. The native literature contains books and passages so vile that they cannot be published in English, and the government has punished men for attempting it. For the same reason, the universities cannot use some of the literary classics.

Then, too, the public religious festivals used to contain features of the most disgusting indecency. They were so vile that no detailed description may

[1] Dennis, J. S., *op. cit.*, Vol. I, p. 90.

be printed in English. The same is true of the worship of certain sects. The festival Holi is celebrated all over India, and this is one of the most unholy of all. In the old days no decent woman would be seen upon the streets at such times, and acts were performed publicly which are too bad even to hint at. Now public sentiment has arisen against these excesses and they have been appreciably toned down. Hindu teachers devise games to keep their pupils from participating in these demoralizing festivities. In this they but follow the example of the Christian teachers.

Finally, in India the public woman has a recognized place in society. The dancing girl has been the only means by which an Indian gentleman could entertain his guests. Women of this character are a necessary factor in every marriage ceremony. The marriage necklace, which corresponds to our wedding ring, has to be tied by such a woman, for she can never become a widow, and hence her presence is a good omen. The leaders in social reform in India have come out openly against this, and the anti-nautch movement has had a large growth. It was not until a comparatively recent period that the British officials began to take a stand against having their hosts entertain them by means of the nautch dances. This was the more natural, because their real significance is not apparent except to the initiated. The Indian Social Conference, in 1895, unanimously passed a resolution which read: "The Conference records its

satisfaction that the anti-nautch movement has
found such general support in all parts of India,
and it recommends the various Social Reform Associations in the county to persevere in their adoption of this self-denying ordinance, and to supple-
ment it by pledging their members to adhere to
the cardinal principle of observing on all occasions,
as a religious duty, purity of thought, speech, and
action, so as to purge our society generally of the
evils of low and immoral surroundings." [1]   At this
same time, influential citizens of Madras petitioned
the British officials to discountenance such forms of
entertainment.   In 1896 Lord Elgin requested his
host in Madras to stop a dance which had been provided against the protests of the reform element.

Of a similar character to the nautch-girls, and in
some regions identical with them, are the temple
girls. These women are known under various
names in different parts of the country. They are
married in young girlhood to some god or to the
dagger of the god Khandoba. They sing and
dance before the god and perform on festival occasions. Their real life, however, is that of religious
prostitutes, and they are thus used by the priests
and other worshippers. The number of these is
not accurately known, but it goes up into the tens,
if not into the hundreds, of thousands. The British
Government has felt itself unable to remove this
disgrace, but the agitation against it is bearing
fruit, and within three years the government of the

[1] Dennis, J. S., op. cit., Vol. II, p. 145.

progressive native state of Mysore, in South India, has prohibited the performance of the ceremony of dedication to such a life in any temple within the control of the government. It is to be hoped that this is but the beginning of an earnest movement upon the part of native rulers to end this sacrifice of low-caste Hindu girls to lives of shame. Then, perhaps, the British Government will dare to take similar action. Already, at the last session of the Supreme Legislative Council, one of the Indian members introduced some drastic bills dealing with this whole question. Thus, a new day is dawning in India and it can be traced to the influence of the Christian thought of the West, which has revealed to the leaders of India the real character of their age-old customs.

The whole ethical atmosphere of Africa and Asia is being purified, and the time will come when the ethical standards of Christ will prevail.

V

PROGRESS IN SOCIAL RECONSTRUCTION

SOCIAL organization is the stereotyping of the adjustments of men to their environment; it is the embodiment of the experiences and ideals of a people. For this reason it is natural that the increase in intelligence and in industrial efficiency, and the raising of the ethical standards, which have been outlined, should already have resulted in changes in social organization.

While the social organization in the different lands of Africa and Asia varies widely, yet it is uniform in one respect, that until very recently, at least, the individual has counted for comparatively little. The unit has been the family, the tribe, the clan, the guild, the caste, or the feudal lord with his retainers. While in some instances the man of ability might rise, and while great influence attached to certain positions, social, political, or religious, yet the ordinary individual counted for very little. In the civil societies which have developed in the West, the government deals directly with the individual, who is responsible for his own deeds and who is more or less free to change his station in life in accordance with an agreement or contract mutually satisfactory to all concerned.

Not so in the East. Here the individual has been born into his station in life, and he has had his standing, not as an individual, but as a member of a group. He has not been accustomed to independent action or even to independent thinking. He has thought and acted as his ancestors had thought and acted for generations. He has been responsible primarily to the head of that social group to which he belonged, and that group might be held responsible for its members.

This description is not everywhere applicable in all its details, but, in general, it may be said that individuality and personal responsibility were little encouraged by any Oriental country, and that individuals were accustomed to act, not as units, but only with others. The nearest to an exception was China, where the essential democracy of its local communities and its civil service system made it possible for a man of ability to work his way up to the top; but even he could do this only with the permission and the assistance of his family, to whose authority he was subject. Westerners sometimes wonder why it is that progress is slow in certain quarters, and why it is so hard for the individual who is intellectually convinced of the truth of Christianity to break with the past and come out as an avowed Christian. The explanation lies largely in this characteristic of the social organization, under which he has been brought up. It has discouraged the development of individual independence and initiative and has thus made it difficult for the reformer to stand out against the members of his own social group.

The outstanding feature of the old social organization of India is caste; of Japan, feudalism; and of China, a combination of absolutism or theocracy with democracy, which had for its basis the family or clan.

For the mass of the people of India, caste is synonymous with their entire social organization and even with their religion in its social aspects. Hinduism and caste are almost interchangeable terms. To be sure, the caste spirit is not confined to India. The class spirit is akin to caste. Make the class an absolutely closed body without inter-marriage or interdining with other classes; make the membership a matter of heredity; buttress it with the sanctions of religion; and the result would practically be the caste system as it has been developed in India. Men everywhere like to form themselves into groups, among whom there is a consciousness of likeness, and to develop this likeness both positively, by cementing the union among the members, and negatively, by emphasizing the differences between them and others. In the older days, especially, there was a very strong professional feeling, and an instance of something very akin to caste survives, for example, in the refusal of an English club to admit a worthy gentleman to membership because his family had been "in trade." The attitude of superiority Americans tend to take towards the immigrant and the feeling that they are of a finer stuff than he are other evidences of a spirit which is common among mankind, and which has been worked out to its logical conclusion by the Hindu.

According to the Hindu tradition, all the members of their society fall into four castes:[1] the Brahman, or priestly class; the Kshatriyas, or warrior class; the Vaishyas, or agricultural class; and the Sudras, or servile class. The first is said to have come from the mouth of Brahma, the second from his arms, the third from his thighs, and the fourth from his feet. Other castes originated from intermarriage between these. Another theory, equally untenable, is that the system was devised by the Brahmans for the purpose of retaining their control over the rest of the people, in accordance with the rule, divide and conquer. This purpose may have been active at some times, but it is not sufficient to explain the origin of the system.

The present caste system is most complex. There are more than three thousand divisions, each of which is an independent community. The average membership is but 80,000. Such an organization is too complicated to have its origin and growth attributed to any one cause. In general, it may be said that caste is functional and racial in its essence and origin. When the Aryan tribes entered and conquered India, they needed different classes to

[1] *Vid.* Bhattacharya, J. N., "Hindu Castes and Sects"; Chintamani, C. Y., "Indian Social Reform."

perform different functions. They had to have priests and civil rulers, and an agricultural population to support the other two. They needed soldiers and scholars, and while the inducements to these pursuits are slight in an agricultural community, they were secured, it is suggested by an Indian student of caste, by assigning to those who thus served the people a position of high honour. Just as in other parts of the world social organization and even civilization have been greatly developed after the conquest and subjugation of other less vigorous peoples, so it was in India. There is little doubt that the Sudras, or servile class, are the descendants of aboriginal tribes, which were conquered and forced to serve the Aryan conquerors. Whatever its origin, its later development has had at least five sources:

1. Race. India is a congeries of races. No fewer than seven distinct types of races were distinguished by the census of 1901, and the number of languages in use is 147. The question of unifying such a heterogeneous population would tax a statesman of to-day. The Hindu solved it by regarding these miscellaneous peoples as castes, and assigning to each its place in society. This process has gone on until very recent times. In fact, it is still proceeding here and there. Aboriginal tribes, which have remained in isolated spots outside of the social organization, are being admitted to a definite position in Indian society as castes.

2. Locality. When sections of a caste have

migrated to another region, the bond between them and the main body has gradually weakened and they have become independent castes.

3. Trade. In one aspect, especially to-day, the caste is the Indian trade-union. As new occupations are taken up by the members of a caste, who have lost their former work or who wish to improve their condition, these men gradually come to feel that their interests are different from those of their former fellow caste-men, and, with the cessation of intermarriage and dining, the new trade becomes a new caste. This process is going on to-day.

4. The elevation or degradation of a section of a caste. Some sections of castes have, by sheer force, pushed themselves up in the social scale. Others have for some reason been degraded, so that the other members of the caste regard them as unworthy of treatment as equals.

5. Religion. As each caste has its own religious cultus, when a new religious movement arises, the tendency is for its members to become a separate caste. There are castes to-day whose origin can be traced to a break with the Brahmanic religion.

Far more important than the origin of caste are its rules, spirit, and social consequences.

The chief characteristic of caste is exclusiveness, which covers three realms, business, hospitality, and marriage. In the matter of business, the restrictions are the least binding. The law of Manu permitted persons, when necessary, to subsist by occupations belonging to the lower castes, and the members of the lower castes might practice any profession but that of priest.   Members of different castes may have business dealings with one another, and the tendency of education to-day is to break down the stringency that survives here.   At the same time, a caste of manual labourers takes the position of a strong trade-union with reference to the outsider who seeks to become a competitor, but with an important difference.   Whereas the " scab " labourer can usually avoid all trouble by joining the union, the Indian labourer cannot change his caste.   Into it he was born, and in it he must die, unless he becomes a Christian.

There is greater exclusiveness in the matter of hospitality and social intercourse.   In general, no member of one caste will eat in the home of a member of another caste, or partake of food cooked by a member of a lower caste.   So great is the demand for Brahmans as cooks by those who can afford such a luxury, that in some large towns the words " Brahman " and "cook" have become almost synonymous.   In certain prisons they also serve in this capacity.   Curiously enough, it has been decided that bottled waters or crackers put up in tin boxes may be taken by caste people without fear of pollution.   These restrictions and the seclusion of women seriously limit social intercourse between Indians and all foreigners.

The greatest exclusiveness of all is in the matter of marriage.   While it was not so in the earlier days, yet to-day the rule is rigidly enforced among all orthodox Hindus, that the girl must marry a boy of the same caste. Their rank must also be equal and their horoscopes harmonious.

The spirit of caste is the very opposite of democratic. At its centre is the exaltation of the Brahman to the position of a deity. The laws of Manu declared: "Whatever exists in the universe is all the property of the Brahman; for the Brahman is entitled to all by his superiority and eminence of birth."[1] No greater wrong is to be found than that of killing a Brahman. No Brahman ever bows his head to make the salutation due to a superior, except to another Brahman. A Sudra addresses a Brahman as "venerable god." The more orthodox Sudras will not cross the shadow of a Brahman, and some vow to eat nothing in the morning before they drink water in which the toe of a Brahman has been dipped. The use of water is one of the matters most minutely regulated by caste. Thus, a high caste man may use water fetched or touched by a clean Sudra. Ganges River water is not rendered unfit if brought by an unclean Sudra. Even this sacred water, however, must be thrown away, if it has been touched by a non-Hindu, Moslem, Christian, or outcaste.

Nine-tenths of the people of India are either Sudras or below them. Manu prescribed that servitude is innate in the Sudra, and, even if his master frees him, he is not released from servitude.

[1] Murdoch, J., op. cit., "Caste," p. 16.

The Brahman "may take possession of the goods of a Sudra with perfect peace of mind, for, since nothing at all belongs to this (Sudra) as his own, he is one whose property may be taken away by his master." [1] It was provided that the lowest peoples must live outside the village, be deprived of dishes, wear the garments of the dead, eat their food in broken dishes, and constantly wander about. If a Brahman talked with one of these outcastes, he had to be purified. The same penalty was exacted if he walked on a road with such a creature, touched one, drank water from a well sunk by one, or from a well which had been touched by the pot of one of these creatures. One who permitted an outcaste to live in his house, not knowing him to be such, had to burn his house. At the end of the eighteenth century, they could not cross a street where a Brahman lived, and they were either naked or clothed in hideous rags. On the Malabar Coast, they were not allowed huts, they could not walk along the highroad, or come within a hundred paces of another caste. If they were on a road and met a caste man, they had to utter a certain cry, and go a long way around to avoid him. Under the British rule, the situation has been improved, but even to-day there are out-castes who have no rights, who may not enter courts of law, whose only meat is carrion, and who may never, under the régime of caste, rise to a plane of living which can be called human.

[1] Murdoch, J., op. cit., "Caste," p. 17.

The penalties for violating the rules of caste are so severe that comparatively few are willing to run the risk. The chief of these are that friends, relatives, and fellow townsmen refuse all exchange of hospitality. The offender cannot obtain brides or grooms for his children. Even his married daughters cannot visit him without risk of being excluded from caste. His priest, barber, and washerman will not serve him, although barbers and washermen are less likely now to refuse their services. His fellow caste-men will not assist him at the funeral of a member of his household, and he may even be excluded from the public temples.

Perhaps the most serious aspects of the caste system are the social results. It has condemned the mass of people to ignorance and to a standard of living below what progressive people accord to favoured animals. It ministers to an overweaning pride on the one side, and to a sense of inborn inferiority and servility upon the other. It divides society into water-tight compartments and deprives the members of society at large from having common interests. It thus makes unity of thought and action next to impossible. It encourages utter indifference to suffering; for no caste person dares to help a stranger, for fear of pollution. It has enforced a closeness of intermarriage that has had serious consequences in physical deterioration, if not degeneracy. It has produced a civilization which is not progressive, which, in fact, stands like a rock in the pathway of progress. Most serious of all is the effect upon the individual, who is held in the most rigorous control, and is not allowed to disobey the traditions of his caste in matters of religion, ethics, or social order.

Social reformers generally regard caste, in its present form, as the greatest single obstacle to progress. The conviction is common that it must be either abolished or, at least, radically modified, before India can take her place as a unified, self-governing member of the family of nations. On the other hand, its critics ought to remember that in the early days caste probably served as a unifying force. A recent writer declares: "There is no doubt that it is the main cause of the fundamental stability and contentment by which Indian society has been braced up for centuries against the shocks of politics and the cataclysms of Nature. It provides every man with his place, his career, his occupation, his circle of friends. It makes him at the outset a member of a corporate body; it protects him through life from the canker of social jealousy and unfulfilled aspirations; it ensures him companionship and a sense of community with others in like case with himself. The caste organization is to the Hindu his club, his trade-union, his benefit society, his philanthropic society." [1]

Just as caste is the unique element in the social organization in India, so feudalism [2] was the char-

[1] Low, Sidney, "Vision of India," p. 263. *Vid.* "Encyc. Brit.," ed. 11, Vol. V, p. 465.

[2] *Vid.* "Encyc. Brit.," Vol. XV, p. 255 *et seq.*

acteristic of Japanese society before the advent of the new era. In the early historical period, beginning with the fifth century, there was a remarkable tendency to organize the nation into groups, based upon occupation or function. The heads of the great families had their titles, and the most renowned of these leaders administered the affairs of state, subject, however, to the will of the sovereign. The provinces were ruled by younger members of the imperial family, though they, too, were subject to the Throne. In the first legislative epoch, beginning in the middle of the seventh century, attempts were made to reform the social system, to check the abuses which had grown up with the system of forced labour, by commuting it for taxes, to stop the absorption of the land into great estates, and to parcel out the land into lots for each adult. Internecine warfare was also checked. These reforms were short-lived, however, and, by the adoption of the Chinese administrative system, the Emperor became the source, but not the wielder, of power.

This function was relegated to a bureaucracy and a military class. Soon after this, the foundations of the feudal system were laid, by the granting of large tracts of tax-free land to the noblemen, who had wrested it from the aborigines or had reclaimed it by the labour of serfs. At the same time, the tax laws were such that the peasants moved off from government lands and took up land on the estates of these nobles. The development of this dual form of government and the centuries of civil strife, which continued with brief intervals from the latter half of the twelfth century to the beginning of the seventeenth, firmly fastened feudalism upon Japan. During the Tokugawa era, which began in the last of the sixteenth century and extended until the beginning of the Meiji era, fifty odd years ago, the social organization of Japan included three groups: first, the Throne and the court nobles; second, the military class or samurai; third, the common people or *heimin*. The function of the Emperor or Mikado was to mediate between his heavenly ancestors and his subjects, while all the affairs of state were entrusted to the Shogun and the samurai. The Mikado became what has been characterized as "a sacrosanct abstraction." The court nobility, comprising one hundred and fifty-five families, were the descendants of former mikados. They ranked above all the feudal chiefs, filled the court offices, lived lives of proud poverty, and devoted themselves to literature and art.

Below these came the samurai, military families that had hereditary revenues and filled the administrative posts, which were mostly hereditary. About fifty-five out of a thousand of the population belonged to this class. These families were the retainers for the holders of the great estates, which formed feudal kingdoms with their own laws and usages, subject to review by the Shogun's government. The produce of the peasants supported the chief and his retainers, half of the assessed income going to them and the other half to the peasants. The revenue of the richest daimyo, or feudal chief, amounted to about $2,500,000 a year. In 1862, there were two hundred and fifty-five daimyos. The chiefs had their castles, occupying commanding positions, within which lived their military retainers. The samurai lived frugally upon the rations of rice given them from the granaries of their chiefs. They despised money and all devices for making it. The right of wearing the sword of a samurai was to them the highest conceivable honour, and they were willing at any time to lay down life for their lord or their country. Their word was inviolable. Courage was to them the primary virtue and stoicism came next. No insult to their honour could be condoned. Courtesy to one another and contempt towards the commoner were their rule. Martial exercises and book learning occupied their attention. Their greatest fault was faithlessness to women. The samurai women were equal to their husbands in courage.

Below these classes were the great mass of the people, about fifteen-sixteenths, known as the *heimin*, or commoners. These were divided into three classes, the husbandmen, the artisans, and the traders. The farmer was honoured and one who cultivated his own estate might carry one sword but never two. The artisans, with whom were ranked the artists, swordsmiths, armourers, etc., were respected. Many of them were permanently in the service of feudal chiefs at fixed salaries. Trades-men stood lowest of all. Below these, quite in the spirit of Hinduism, stood the *eta* (defiled folks) and the *hinin* (outcastes). The *eta* were probably de-scended from prisoners of war or the enslaved families of criminals. They tended tombs, disposed of the bodies of the dead, slaughtered animals, and tanned hides. They were not permitted to marry, eat, drink, or associate with those of higher classes; they lived in segregated hamlets, and were governed by their own head-men under three chiefs. Some of them, however, were able to amass much wealth. The *hinin* were mendicants, and removed and buried the corpses of executed criminals. When the pro-scription was removed, and the members of these classes were admitted as commoners in 1871, there were 287,111 *eta* and 695,689 *hinin*.

This organization of society was fairly efficient during the days when fighting was constantly go-ing on, but during the centuries of peace, which marked the Tokugawa era, it ceased to serve the needs of the public. The large hereditary fighting force maintained by public funds became an anomaly. The agricultural and commercial classes became more important but they acquired no new privileges or rights. The standard of living went up, luxury, the theatre, the dancing girl, and the brothel arose, wrestling became an important insti-tution, and plutocracy asserted itself against aris-tocracy. At the same time, the power of the Sho-gun and of the feudal chiefs passed into the hands

of retainers and subordinates, and the chiefs themselves became voluptuaries or *dilletanti*.

A mere recital of these facts shows that this social
organization was out of harmony with Western
ideals, that it was not conducive to unity of action
or public efficiency, and that it paid no regard to
the interests and rights of the majority of the
people. It could not survive after Japan came into
contact with Western thought and Western institutions. At the same time, one can see that in such
a society as this the individual had little place. In
every emergency the question was, How will my
experience of danger or death affect my family or
my nation? Life, chastity, property were all held
subject to the interests of the family. From this
source, coupled with the deification of the Emperor,
came the absolute loyalty to country and the desire
to die for its upbuilding, which has been and still
is characteristic of the Japanese people. Moreover,
these military ideals, which filtered down through
society, also resulted in a spirit of predatory patriotism that tends to seek the glory of Japan without reference to the interests of other peoples.
This is based upon the belief that Japan is to be
regarded as the leader of the world and her interests as paramount.

When one passes from Japan to China, one passes
into a radically different political and social atmosphere. Here, also, we find the idea of filial piety,
as in every country where Confucianism has had

influence. Here, too, the family is the unit; but
instead of a feudal organization of society, we find
a strange combination of democracy and absolutism.

The unit of government in China is the *Hsien*,[1]
which consists of one walled city, or part of one,
with the villages surrounding it, the boundaries extending until they reach the territory of the con-
tiguous *Hsien*. In the eighteen provinces there are
1,443 *Hsien*, which, together with twenty-seven in
Manchuria, make 1,470. Every Chinese is registered in his *Hsien*, and this registration he clings
to, no matter in what part of the world he
lives. Here is his ancestral home; here he passes
his old age; and to this spot his bones will be
sent for burial if he dies elsewhere. He is
always identified by his fellow countrymen by
his *Hsien*. The official head of this district may
be called the mayor. From his small salary he
has to provide for the maintenance of his subordinates and superiors. His associates often hold
their positions by hereditary right or custom.
This official has important judicial functions, is
the agent of the provincial and imperial admin-
istrations for collecting the land tax and the
grain tribute, is registrar of land and famine com-
missioner, and as such he is expected to keep the
granaries full. He is responsible, save along the
Yellow River, for the prevention of floods and the

[1] Morse, H. B., "The Trade and Administration of the Chinese
Empire," p. 46 *et seq.*

reparation of their damage. He has custody of official buildings, repairs the roads and bridges, sees that schools are maintained, preserves order, and is the guardian of the morals of his district. This is enough to tax the powers of the most paternalistic official, one would think. However, he comes into little contact with the people, eighty per cent. of whom, perhaps ninety per cent., experience no evidence of government pressure.

The people in China govern themselves according to their customs. These customs constitute the common law, and it is interpreted and executed by themselves. For this common-law administration the village is the unit. The fathers of the village, who really hold office with the approval, if not under the appointment, of the villagers, exercise this authority. The official head of the village is the land warden, who is nominated by the mayor from the village elders, but is dependent upon the good will of his constituents. He is constable and may have jurisdiction over more than one small village. The criminal law of China is national, but in civil matters the custom of each district is observed, and the constable, the mayor, and the higher officials have to fall in with this, or else they are bound to get into trouble, which may lead to rebellion and removal. Even the governors of the provinces are not absolute masters but must conform to local usages.

Above the *Hsien* is the *Fu* or prefecture. Of these there were 183 within the empire, each composed of from two to six *Hsien*. There are certain officials for groups of prefectures but for purposes of administration the province is next above the *Hsien*. These provinces have occupied a semi-autonomous position. They are like satrapies in some respects; in others they are like the constituent states of a federation; or still more like a territory of the American union, which has executive and judicial officers appointed by the central authority and removable at will, but with local autonomy for the levying of taxes and administration of law. To show how the authority filters down from the throne to the district magistrate, we may quote a part of a specimen proclamation: " The magistrate (*Hsien*) has had the honour to receive instructions from the prefect (*Fu*), who cites directions of the *Taotai* (group of *Fus*), moved by the Treasurer and the Judge (province), recipients of the commands of their excellencies the Viceroy and Governor, acting at the instance of the Foreign Board, who has been honoured with his Majesty's command." [1] The affairs of the province have been under a general board, consisting of the Viceroy, Governor, Treasurer, Judge, Salt Officer, and Grain Official. The last four were the executive board of the provincial government. These officials were appointed for a three-year term, and, with the exception of governors and viceroys, were reappointed but once. No official ever held a post in the province of his birth, and the officials in each province represented

[1] Morse, H. B., *op. cit.*, p. 67.

different political parties. These rules are now being modified.

At the head of the empire stood the Emperor, who was in theory an absolute monarch, but in practice was bound by the unwritten constitution, that is, by the customs that had been handed down and by the precedents of his predecessors as defined in their edicts. He was also bound by the opinions and decisions of his ministers. Next to him was the metropolitan administration, one of whose objects was the registering and checking of the provincial administration. Originally there were six boards, namely, the Boards of Civil Office, Revenue, Ceremonies, War, Punishments, and Works. Each board had two presidents and four vice-presidents, equally divided between Manchus and Chinese. Under foreign pressure, a Foreign Board was organized in 1861 and changed in 1901. The Boards of Commerce and Education were added in 1903. The Court of Investigation, the Office of Transmission (dealing with memorials to the Throne), the Court of Revision (supervision of administration of criminal law), and the old College of Literature should be mentioned.

A few things stand out prominently from this summary and from other facts not mentioned:

1. The provincial autonomy, emphasized in many cases by differences in dialect and even in language. This made unity of opinion and action difficult, if not impossible.

2. The insufficiency of the salaries. These had

to be supplemented by means of the graft which was all but universal.

3. The frequent rotation in office. This made any continuity of policy difficult, except as it was secured by following the local customs.

4. The lack of representation outside of the local community.

5. The general inefficiency, from the point of view of Western political theory.

6. The domination of the whole system by the foreign Manchu dynasty.

The paternalistic spirit pervaded this government, and this was due to the fact that, after all, the institution at the basis of China and most affecting the individual is the patriarchal family. Backed up by the ancestor worship, the family is the real unit of Chinese society. And it is a family of a type that has long since ceased to exist among the peoples of the West. With us, when a son marries, he usually sets up a new home. Not so in China. Not only do the parties have nothing to do with the selection of each other, but, with the marriage ceremony, the girl ceases to be a member of her own family, and becomes a member of her husband's. The typical Chinese family consists of the parents, their sons, who probably married young, their daughters-in-law, who have come as servants to their mother-in-law, and the grandchildren. The daughters have all married and gone to other homes. They have no rights in the old family, and are seen only occasionally. The property is held in common, though there may be a division before the death of the father. The father, and, after his death, the mother, may chastise, sell, or even kill a son. A wife has no wish that her husband is legally bound to respect. Further than this, the wider family, the clan, the members of which live together in villages and have a common ancestral temple, can keep the young man or woman in hand. While a young man is supposed to become of age at sixteen, he is practically under the control of his father, uncles, and older brothers, and when the average man comes to the headship of a family, his powers of initiative have largely atrophied. Custom and morals become identified, and both of them have the sanction of religion.

China has enforced corporate responsibility. Any official was held accountable for any offense within his jurisdiction, whether he was to blame for it or not, and whether he could have foreseen its occurrence or not. The same responsibility extended to families and villages. A case was known where a man, aided by his wife, flogged his mother. The pair were flayed alive; the grand-uncle, uncle, two elder brothers, and the head of the clan were executed; the neighbours on either side, the father of the woman, and the head representative of the literary degree the man held were flogged and banished; the prefect and the district ruler were temporarily degraded; and the child of the offenders was given another name.

While the Chinese have thus lost much of their

ability to take the initiative, they have developed coöperation to the full. In matters of religion, trade, amusement, and the like, they work together. Societies, secret or open, are organized for every conceivable purpose, for burying the dead, for holding feasts, for making public improvements, for any or for no purpose. The guild is the power in the business world. The system of markets has ramifications all over the province and brings each individual within reach of a market on a larger or a smaller scale. It is in their proved ability to coöperate, in their inherent respect for orderliness, and in their habit of governing themselves, in accordance with the customs which have for them all the sanctity of a moral law, that we have the promise of the success of the present republic.

This is a sketch of the social organization of the three great peoples of Asia before the advent of Western influence. Within a generation great and radical changes have taken place.

Caste has begun to weaken its hold in India. Two provisions of the British Government for the public welfare have had much to do with this ; namely, the building of railways and the introduction of a good water supply. The expense of railway travel in India is very low and the people travel in droves, from the Brahman to the coolie. The railway carriages are not built on the lines of caste, and this promiscuous intermingling of the different castes cannot fail to cause some relaxing of the stringency of caste regulations. Then, too, when persons are away from home and among strangers, as those who travel are, they naturally—at least in India—tend to overlook those minute regulations of caste which hamper freedom of movement. Mention has already been made of some of the restrictions that caste imposes upon the use of water. In the old days, the different castes would have separate wells, to which low caste people, and especially outcastes, could have no access. But the British Government does not permit such discrimination, and this, too, tends to break down the exclusiveness. Among the educated young men of India, these restrictions upon the use of food have lost their compelling force. They may conform among their families and friends, but when away from home, they do not hesitate to eat with others, contrary to the rules of caste. At a recent Social Congress, the delegates had a common meal together. The remarkable thing about it was, not that they thus broke the rules of caste, but that when they returned to their homes, not one of them was called to account by the heads of his caste.

In the old days, any high caste Hindu who crossed the ocean was *ipso facto* thrown out of caste and could be restored only by a long, expensive, and disgusting process of purification. To-day this requirement is either greatly reduced or entirely waived.

The party of reformers in India, who have come to realize the evil social consequences of caste, are seeking earnestly to remove some of the worst features. One line of effort is the attempt to break down the barriers between the sub-castes, in order to reunite the castes which were originally one. This would prevent the evil results of too close interbreeding and at the same time broaden the interests of the individuals. Inter-caste marriages are by no means unknown, especially among the members of the reforming Hindu sects. I met in northern India a gentleman who had been devoting his time for years to arranging such marriages.

The leaders in the movement for political progress also recognize in caste one of the obstacles to the attainment of their desires. They see in the condition of the outcastes a lasting blot upon Indian society. Some of them have openly advised the members of these depressed classes to become Christians, as the only avenue of escape. Others deplore the movement towards Christianity upon the part of these people, and are summoning their co-religionists to missionary efforts, in order to prevent the Christianization of these millions, which would mean, they believe, "in no small measure the wiping out of the hoary Hindu civilization."

Equally important with this social movement is the political agitation for a greater degree of self-government. The agitators range all the way from those who calmly, though vigorously, request a greater share in the government of India and the removal of some of the disabilities from which India has suffered, up to those who urge the expulsion of the British and are ready to use violence in order to emphasize their demand. The demands are equally varied. In this connection, it should be remembered that as yet a very small fraction of the population of India is in the slightest degree affected by this agitation.

The causes of the agitation are too many to be discussed fully here, but a few of the grievances should receive a bare mention:

1. Certain disabilities from which the Indians have suffered, such as their exclusion from some of the higher offices.

2. Until recently, the control by government rather than by the electorate of the majority in the legislative bodies.

3. Certain fiscal and tariff regulations which unduly sacrifice India to British interests.

4. The attitude of superiority assumed by many a Britisher towards the cultivated and educated Indian.

5. The acquaintance of the Indian student with the history and political philosophy of the Western nations, and his consequent desire to enjoy similar political rights and privileges.

6. The selfish wish to exploit the country, or at least to hold office. The educated Indian has believed himself above everything but a position under government, in administrative or educational work, and the graduates have far outnumbered the positions.

7. The fear that Hindu institutions are being

undermined, and the consequent attempt to expel the British, in order that full control may revert to the Brahmans and other leaders of Hinduism.

Whatever may be said of the justification or lack of justification of these reasons—and I am both an admirer and a critic of British rule in India—it should be stated that the Indians enjoy a far greater degree of self-government than was ever granted them under any former régime, and that the British Government is moving in the direction of satisfying the legitimate demands of the people and perhaps permitting India to become a self-governing member of the British Empire, with its own parliamentary institutions.

Even before the recent reforms, less than 6,500 Englishmen were employed in the task of ruling India, backed up by less than 80,000 British troops. While of the 1,370 higher positions in India, those paying a salary of $4,000 and more, 1,263 were held by Europeans, fifteen by Eurasians, and ninety-two by natives of India ; in the lower appointments, paying from $4,000 down to $300 a year, there were but 5,205 Europeans, 5,420 Eurasians, and 16,283 natives.[1]

As early as 1850,[2] provision was made for consultative committees in towns. In 1870, local committees were given control over the funds for local improvements. In 1882, municipal committees and local boards were provided for ; the members were to be elected ; and the non-official members were

[1] "Encyc. Brit.," Vol. XIV, p. 386.　　　　[2] Ibid.

to be in the majority. In 1910–1911 [1] there were 715 municipalities which cared for all local interests, subject to the approval of the provincial government. According to the system, the number of official appointed members and of elected members varies according to local conditions. A community that behaves itself is granted a larger proportion of elected members, and the choice by these members of a mayor. On the other hand, as a punishment for wrong-doing, the right to select the mayor may be taken away and the majority of the council be appointed. Thus, a premium is put upon good behaviour, and the people have an inducement to develop their capacity for sane self-government.

At the head of the government in India is the Governor-General, or Viceroy, together with the Executive Council appointed by the Crown. In 1909, a Hindu barrister was for the first time appointed to this body, the members of which had hitherto been exclusively British. The supreme legislative body is this same Council, but with additions. Previous to 1909, the additional members numbered sixteen, all of whom were nominated by the Viceroy to represent different sections of the population. Now, however, the legislative members have been increased to sixty-one and, what is of greater importance, a minority of the members, twenty-five in number, are elected, directly or indirectly, by the people of India. The nominated members still comprise the majority, thirty-

[1] "Statesman's Year Book, 1913," p. 122.

five, but of these not more than twenty-eight may be officials and they are not necessarily British. In the provincial legislative bodies the elected members are in the majority, ranging from thirteen or fourteen in Bengal to three in Burma, exclusive of the head of the province.[1] The purpose of preserving so large a number of nominated members is to make sure that the councils contain experts and the representatives of special interests and of minorities. Already, in the supreme legislative council, an Indian member has brought up the matter of free and compulsory elementary education, and it is certain that in the coming days the Indian people will constantly grow in ability and power to control their own affairs.

In India, the process of social reconstruction is hardly more than well begun. On the other hand, Japan is a nation which has entirely reconstituted itself. It has organized its government and society along lines which are designed to secure increased efficiency and also greater opportunity for the individual. The story[2] of the process by which Japan emerged from feudalism into constitutionalism is fascinating, especially as one sees the willingness with which the samurai, who had been the backbone of old Japan, gave up their old privileges and, out of loyalty to Emperor and country, adapted themselves to the new régime. At first, the leaders

[1] "Encyc. Brit.," Vol. XIV, p. 385.
[2] *Ibid.*, Vol. XV, p. 266 *et seq.*

of the revolution desired merely to unify the nation. But this could not be done, it came to be realized, unless the feudatories were deprived of their local autonomy and of their control of local finances. In 1871, the four most powerful feudal chiefs in the south, those of Satsuma, Chōshū, Tosa, and Hizen, surrendered their fiefs to the Emperor. While they may not have realized what it would cost them, only seventeen of the more than two hundred and fifty feudatories hesitated to follow this example. The motives behind this step may have been mixed, but undoubtedly the chief motive was that of loyalty to the Throne. Any one who had hesitated for selfish reasons would have seemed to forfeit his right to be called a samurai. Especially after this change, the position of the samurai became anomalous, and their pensions, amounting to about $10,-000,000 a year, became too great a burden upon the taxpayers. In 1873, they were asked to commute their pensions and lay aside their swords, the most cherished privilege they possessed. The terms were very unfavourable, but many of them promptly complied, and stepped out into life as ordinary citizens, to make their own way.

Three years later, this change was made compulsory. The samurai had been trained to despise money and the financial measure evoked no complaint. The extreme conservatives, however, thought that the abolition of the sword-wearing was too much to demand. Armed protests ensued, and finally, in 1877, a rebellion broke out in the south.   One of the most portentous changes in the reconstruction of Japan had been the depriving of the old military class of its monopoly of the army and the navy.   In this most bloody rebellion, in which the killed and wounded aggregated one-third of the whole force engaged, on the one side were the old soldiers, trained to fight for generations; on the other side was the new army, consisting of recruits drawn from every class of the nation.   The result proved the fighting quality of the people, and established the principle that the days of the samurai had passed forever.   They have come to their own, however, as leaders in the new Japan, and even in the Christian Church.

The government of Japan [1] is an interesting combination of centralization and local autonomy.   At the head stands the Emperor, with a cabinet subject to him rather than to the majority in the House of Representatives.   The Imperial Diet is composed of two houses, the House of Peers and the House of Representatives, each being vested with the same legislative powers.   The upper house is composed of hereditary princes and marquises, representatives chosen by the lower orders of nobility in the ratio of one member to every five peers of each class, life members nominated by the Emperor for distinguished services or for erudition, and representatives, one from each prefecture, elected by the highest taxpayers therein.   The last two classes may never exceed the former.   In 1910 the house

[1] " Ency. Brit.," Vol. XV, 202 et seq.

contained 207 titled members and 164 non-titled. The lower house is composed of 379 members, a fixed number being elected by the male electors of each district. The urban population elects 76, the rural 303, but the latter includes all the population of Japan outside of the three large cities of Tokyo, Kyoto, and Osaka.[1]

Japan proper is divided into three urban and forty-three rural prefectures. The latter are subdivided into counties, and these into towns and villages. In general, in each of these subdivisions there is a chief officer, the governor in the prefecture, the head-man in the sub-prefecture or county, the mayor in the municipality, and the chief magistrate or head-man in the town or village. These officials are all appointed by the central administration. Associated with each of these is an elected body, or assembly, which is chosen by the electors, who number a little more than 2,000,000. By a simple device of classifying the electors, those who pay taxes on one-third or one-half of the property in a district elect the same proportion of the assembly. From this franchise are excluded such persons as local salaried officials, judicial officials, and any contractor for public works or public supplies. The chief function of these local assemblies relates to local finance, subject in certain instances to the approval of officers in the central administration. In connection with all the larger administrative districts, there is also a council, of which the

[1] " Japan Year Book, 1912," p. 497 *et seq.*

chief official is the president, and which has certain executive powers, acts for the assembly in cases of emergency, when the latter is not in session, and decides matters referred to it by the assembly. The effect of this system has been to give the people a good training in self-government. In fact, they had been somewhat prepared for this even in the days of feudalism, when the common people were divided into groups of five families each, which were held jointly liable for any offense committed by one of their members.

The Japanese Government has also energetically taken up the task of developing a country which had not been given to industry into a great industrial and commercial nation. By subsidies and by public ownership, it has sought to extend the influence of the empire throughout the Orient and the Occident. It has had to meet problems of sanitation, housing, and the like, which had never been dreamed of in the older days. The aim has been to make Japan superior to all other nations in every line, and the people believe that already they have done this in many respects.

Within a little more than a generation, Japan has thus passed from feudalism into a social organization which Europe reached only after centuries of struggle, and it is facing the future with confident optimism. At the same time, the Japanese people have still preserved the old virtues which glorified their past, such as their intense patriotism and their feeling of solidarity in family and nation.

Individualism is developing but there is little prospect that it will ever be carried to the extreme which is found in the West.

In all this story of progress, Christianity has played an honourable part. Men like Drs. Hepburn, Verbeck, and S. R. Brown, and Captain Janes influenced the leaders of Japan through their teaching and their lives. Count Okuma declared in 1909, at the semi-centennial of Christian missions in Japan, "Though I am not a Christian, I have indirectly received an immense influence from Christianity. . . . The first missionary I ever met was Dr. Verbeck, whom I first saw in 1864. He was my English teacher, and . . . his Christian conduct was a constant example. . . . It was the life of Dr. Verbeck that influenced me more than his teaching."[1] The Japanese Christians likewise, from Yokoi, down through Neesima, to Watanabe, Ishii, and Nitobe, have played their part well. In public life and in the army and navy, they have shown that Christianity can increase the efficiency and the loyalty of the Japanese patriot. The leaders of the Christian church, likewise, have been and still are influencing the social as well as the public life of the nation. Preachers who attract, Sunday after Sunday, the students in the universities and public schools, and preach to them the doctrines of Christianity and their applications to the needs of Japanese life today, are a social force in the new Japan.

[1] "Christian Movement in Japan, 1910," p. 59.

Japan has naturally moved from feudalism into a constitutional monarchy, with an aristocratic and property basis. China has moved from a combination of absolutism and democracy into what was supposed to be a constitutional monarchy but which turns out to be a republic. The steps by which China came to the successful termination of her revolution were very rapid. It was not until 1905 that a commission was appointed to study the forms of government in other countries. This was followed, a year later, by the issuing of an imperial edict, September 1, 1906, which foreshadowed the inauguration of a parliamentary system for the empire. The next year, 1907, an advisory council was established as a first stepping-stone towards a representative government. On August 27, 1908, an edict announced that Parliament would be convoked nine years from that date, in 1917. Provincial assemblies met in October, 1909, and in May, 1910, the names of the National Assembly or Senate were announced, and this body met for the first time on October 2, 1910. At once this Assembly began to assert for itself prerogatives which were not within the purview of the Crown when it issued the plan of constitutional development. The agitation within and without the Assembly sought two ends, first, the immediate calling of the real parliament, and, secondly, the organization of a responsible cabinet to advise the Crown, and to carry out the wishes of the people, that is, of the Assembly.

The pressure became so great that the Prince Regent promised a cabinet within a year and a parliament at the end of three years, or four years before the time originally agreed upon. Even this did not satisfy the radical party, and, before the National Assembly gathered for its second session, in the autumn of 1911, the rebellion was in full swing, and it culminated in the issue of the edict of abdication, on February 12, 1912.[1] No one knows what the form of government will ultimately be, but it is interesting to note the reforms which the old dynasty was willing to concede. At the same time, this statement will explain why the radicals, who had learned in infancy some of the principles of democracy, and had later seen how democratic institutions had made the Western nations strong, were not satisfied with what the Throne had conceded.

It is an interesting fact that the new Chinese administration was to be somewhat along the lines of the Japanese constitution. The whole purpose of the new constitution was to consolidate the empire and to deprive the provinces of the virtual autonomy which they had enjoyed. This was to be accomplished by centralizing the administration, nationalizing finance, justice, and education, and bringing the representatives of the people into an advisory position. It was the intention of the Throne, not to transfer its authority to the people, but to retain

[1] "China Mission Year Book, 1910," p. 23 et seq.; Ibid., 1911, p. 30 et seq.

within its own control the rights of sovereignty.
At the same time, it wished to silence the demand
of the people for a greater measure of self-government. Thus, the Emperor was to be the source
of all legislative, administrative, and judicial action, the legislative bodies merely giving their
advice.

The constitution provided four classes of representative assemblies. At the head, the National
Assembly was to contain in germ the two houses
of the future parliament. One-half of the members
were practically nominated by the Emperor, representing the imperial princes, the peerage, the imperial clansmen and elder statesmen, representatives
of the administrative boards, distinguished scholars,
and the large land owners in the provinces. The
other half was composed of representatives from
the provincial assemblies. After discussion, the Assembly could memorialize the Throne but it could
not enact laws that the Emperor had to sign. Each
province was to elect a council with functions
within the province similar to those of the National
Assembly for the empire. One-fifth of the members were to constitute a committee, to act as the
adviser of the governor when the council was not
in session. The members were to be indirectly
chosen by the people, the actual election being by
an electoral college in each *Fu* or prefecture, which,
in turn, was chosen directly by the voters in all the
Hsien. Below this was the local government, of a
higher or lower grade, for the *Hsien*, and for each

city, market town, and village within the district. Here the people were given a share in administration as well as in legislation, and one of the most interesting features was that in villages with a population of less than twenty-five hundred, all the voters were to constitute the village assembly, quite in the spirit of the New England town meeting, which has been regarded as the best instance of pure democracy in all the world.[1]

Such were some of the lines along which China was moving when its leaders decided that the time had come for the most populous nation in the eastern hemisphere to follow the example of the most populous nation in the western hemisphere, and establish republican institutions.

The provisional constitution of China is modelled upon those of the Western democratic states. The bill of rights protects the people against arbitrary arrest and the illegal search of their residences. It guarantees such rights as those of holding property, free discussion, secrecy of letters, and freedom of movement and religion. It gives the rights of petition, of appeal against infringement by officials, and of being examined to become officials. Only by due process of law can the rights be suspended and then only in the public interest or for the maintenance of order and peace.

The National Assembly is representative of the provinces and outlying regions. It has the usual powers and its members are free from arrest during

[1] "China Mission Year Book, 1911," p. 49 et seq.

the sessions, except for flagrant offenses or during times of internal disturbance or foreign invasion.

The Provisional President commands the military and naval forces, appoints and dismisses civil and military officials, and with the minister of justice appoints all judges, who are to be free from interference by higher officials.[1]

These are some of the salient features of the provisional constitution under which China is supposed to be governed, pending the adoption of the real constitution by the National Convention.

In addition to the matters of political reconstruction, the Chinese people, through their government, have been setting their house in order in other respects also. The judicial system has been so corrupt and inefficient that it was impossible to demand that the Western nations give up their rights of extra-territoriality. During the closing days of the first session of the National Assembly of 1910, the new penal code was discussed, and the Assembly sanctioned its adoption.

New courts have been established in certain provinces, and trial by jury has been introduced, though not with entirely satisfactory results. The Manchu Government issued edicts abolishing torture, but it is not certain that justice can yet be secured in China without the use of the bamboo to extort confession. The prisons of China have begun to be reformed. China was represented at the last International Congress on Prison Reform by dele-

[1] "China Mission Year Book, 1912," Appendix, p. 24 *et seq.*

gates who subsequently made a study of European prisons. As long ago as 1908, I was privileged to visit in Tientsin and Paotingfu what might almost be called model prisons, in which the prisoners were well cared for under good sanitary conditions, were given instruction, and were taught useful arts. This movement is spreading wherever want of will and of money do not prevent, and a model prison has been discovered even in distant Yunnan.

The question of economy and that of securing a sound and national, not provincial, currency, have also been taxing the ingenuity of Chinese statesmen, but here the profits from graft and provincial jealousies have been serious obstacles to overcome.

What the outcome of this experiment will be, no one can foretell, but it is to be noted in passing that in this whole movement Christian men have been prominent. Many non-Christian and unworthy men have come to the front, but many of the best leaders have been men actuated by Christian principles. In one of the earlier gatherings in Nanking, it was discovered, so it was reported, that three-fourths were Christians. The leader in Taiku, Shansi, who was made chief of police and who prevented the city from being sacked by troops, was the principal of a Christian school. The need of China to-day is for more men who have Christian principles and who yet have sanity and balance and a grasp of the difficulties inherent in all great political reconstructions. Through the schools maintained by American missionaries and

through the record of the United States, China
has come to look to us for its inspiration as it seeks
to reconstruct its social organization.

One of the most recent and, until the revolution
in China, most surprising overturns resulting in a
political development along Western lines, was the
revolution in Turkey in 1908. Up to that time,
Turkey had been an autocracy. The Sultan,
through the Grand Vizier, or head of the temporal
government, and the Sheik ul Islam, the head of
the ecclesiastical power, exercised all legislative
and executive powers. Through his representatives, his authority extended to the small local
communities and there was no real redress or possibility of obtaining justice against the decree of the
officials. Turkey had never been a nation, but
rather a collection of ecclesiastical nationalities, if
one may use the phrase, each religious community
having its head, who sought to see that justice was
done his followers. Meantime, however, Christian
schools had been teaching the young men of the
country, and leading Turks had studied in Europe,
had imbibed Western ideas, and at the same time
had largely lost their old religious beliefs. The
result was that suddenly, in 1908, the old régime
was overthrown and the Sultan approved of the
restoration of the constitution, which he had himself granted in 1876 and suspended fourteen months
later. The watchwords of the new régime were
Liberty, Justice, Equality, and Fraternity, the use

of any one of which would previously have brought down severe punishment. In temporal matters, the Sultan is now a constitutional monarch, advised by a cabinet, which, in turn, is responsible to the elected Turkish Parliament. All Turkish subjects are supposed to have equal political and juridical rights, and all discriminations as to military service have been abolished. Islam is still the state religion and the Sultan remains its head. While the people of Turkey are hardly prepared for parliamentary institutions, because of their ignorance and the intensity of the racial and religious antagonisms, yet the new régime has promise in it of much that is good, the great obstacle being the attitude of the European powers.

Since this paragraph was first written, the world has seen the Turk all but driven out of Europe by the Balkan states, which for a time sank their age-old racial, religious, and political animosities, and surprised the world by their exhibition of military skill and power. When the victory had been won, its fruits were largely thrown away through the selfishness and overweaning ambitions of the states, and the old bitterness is revived in greater force. All of this goes to show how much hollowness there can be in political reforms unless they are wrought out by people who have been so thoroughly Christianized and educated that they can act a Christian part in international relations. Judged by such standards, however, what nation has yet become truly Christian?

In all these movements in the farther and the nearer East, we find at work the same spirit, namely, the desire to organize society along Western lines, with a view to securing greater efficiency, raising the political if not the social status of the individual, and entering the family of nations on a plane of equality with any Western nation. In the work of preparing for these momentous changes, which portend the reorganization of society on a radically different basis, the work of the missionary has played an honourable part. Western influence has also had a large share, especially in Japan. In all these movements, however, there is one weakness, less acute in Japan than in India, and perhaps less marked in the new republican China than in the old reformed monarchical China. This is the lack of leaders, who possess unimpeachable character, absolute integrity, utter devotion to the welfare of the country, and the balance and sanity that come from a broad and a Christian education. Unless this lack can be supplied, the future of these new political movements will be dark and, in the end, may prove a disaster, not a blessing. It is this that emphasizes the duty of the Christian West. It is a threefold task that lies before the Church : first, so to influence the governments of the West that they will permit these new nations to work out their own problems without undue interference ; secondly, to set their own house in order, so that it cannot be claimed, as it is now claimed, that Christianity has failed to solve the problems of the

West; and, finally, so to develop its work of education and evangelization that it will put a Christian impress upon the leaders of the new Orient and thus ensure that the new developments shall rest upon the solid foundation of the Christian convictions of leaders and followers alike.

VI

CHRISTIANIZING TENDENCIES IN NON-CHRISTIAN RELIGIONS

THE first five chapters have discussed the relation of Christian missions to social progress in mission lands and have shown how social institutions are changing under the influence of the West, religious and secular. Yet, after all, the work of Christian missions is religious. The missionary is more than a philanthropist, educator, reformer. He is engaged in teaching the religion of Christ and in persuading men to forsake their former religious allegiance and become the followers of the Saviour. He thus arrays against himself from the beginning the religious forces in mission lands. Much as the dissatisfied natives may welcome the good news, those who are heartily committed to the old views, and especially those who are financially interested in the maintenance of the old religion, see that this foreigner is engaged in a work that means the overthrow of their old cherished beliefs or of their means of livelihood. What shall be the result of this impact?

In many a field Christianity has met animism and the lower forms of religious belief and has vanquished them completely. The old religion is

gone, with its votaries.   This is true in Fiji and in
certain other islands of the Pacific; it is true in
parts of Sumatra, as well as among certain tribes
of the North American Indians.   But now Christianity is facing the strong religions of the world,
which claim the allegiance of millions, which have
their sacred books and an elaborate philosophy and
theology, and which are entrenched among peoples
with a high degree of civilization.   These are foe-
men worthy of the steel of the Christian warrior.
Islam, Hinduism, Buddhism—these claim the devotion of considerably more than half a billion,
and they are not yielding without a struggle.
With the exception of Islam, these religions have
not become greatly excited over the Christian
propaganda, so far as its teaching of strange doctrines has been concerned.   They have felt secure
in their position and could afford, they fondly believed, to regard with more or less of supercilious-
ness the arrogant attacks by foreigners upon their
very citadel.   Of late years, however, they have
come to recognize in these Christian workers for-
midable foes, who have brought from the West
strange educational and industrial systems and
radical political ideals, all of which have been
steadily undermining their own defenses.   Hence,
they are viewing the outlook with somewhat of
alarm, and are attempting a new disposition of
their forces against the invaders.

One of these old religions, Hinduism, is purely
an ethnic religion, which, according to its tenets,

can never cross the oceans, and which has made no earnest attempt to extend its sway beyond the limits of the Indian peninsula and its adjacent islands. The other two are the great rivals of Christianity as a missionary religion.

Islam began in Arabia, conquered Syria, Mesopotamia, and Egypt; it spread westward through North Africa and eastward through Persia; it invaded Europe and threatened to control the continent, and it was with difficulty expelled from all but one corner. It then spread further eastward to India and China, as well as to the islands to the southeast of Asia, to Asia Minor, and to southeastern Europe, and it is to-day advancing steadily but surely to the conquest of the Dark Continent.

Buddhism, which is older than its younger rivals, Christianity and Islam, began in India, left its impression upon modern Hinduism, and then won its way northward and eastward until its ideas have become dominant in the thoughts and lives of one-third of the human race.

Entrenched in the system of caste, Hinduism is expanding at the bottom by the absorption of aboriginal tribes, even if it is losing control of some at the top.

Yet, secure as these religions may appear to the outsider, they are nevertheless feeling the competition of Christianity. They are unwilling to confess themselves defeated. Rather would they resist the disintegrating tendencies, either by a greater insistence upon their central doctrines or by adaptations to meet the new conditions. Hinduism and Buddhism, in particular, are so flexible, that they have little difficulty in even adopting Christian features in their attempt to drive back Christianity by meeting it on its own ground. These three religions are contending against forces that are inevitably making for their disintegration; but they are seeking to resist this process by incorporating elements stolen bodily from Christianity.

These three great non-Christian religions were developed among peoples whose knowledge was limited and who had no conception of a physical universe governed by natural laws. They took over into their thought and practices the beliefs and customs of that primitive animism which seems to have been almost, if not quite, universally prevalent in Africa, Asia, and the island world, and which has left its marks even upon the thinking of the most advanced peoples. Their ethical ideals reflect views regarding God and man which cannot produce a highly developed and progressive civilization, in which the rights of each individual are fully protected. Their cosmogony is crude and unscientific, and their mythology absurd and often unethical. Woman is given a position quite inferior to that of man. The goal of life is essentially selfish and the spirit either fatalistic or pessimistic.

People with these views of God and the world have now been brought into contact with Western-trained men, who have gained a scientific understanding of the world and an ability to use its natural forces. The resulting efficiency has forced the people of the Orient to respect the learning which has brought many of them under subjection to its possessors, and many of them have come to desire it for themselves. Hence, the great development of education in these Eastern countries. But, with the knowledge of nature derived from the study of Western science, their old cosmogony and mythology become in their eyes nothing more than superstition. They see the absurdity of their old religious beliefs, with the result that the students and educated classes tend to break with the old religion and to become agnostics or atheists.

A religious census of the nearly five thousand students in the University of Tokyo revealed the fact that Shintoism and Buddhism held the allegiance of fewer students than Christianity; that these three religions numbered their followers at hardly more than a hundred; and that the remainder called themselves atheists or agnostics, and in Japan agnostics are of a belligerent type.

To be sure, some persons, chiefly in India, seem to be able to hold their old beliefs with one-half of their mind and accept the teachings of science with the other half; but this anomaly cannot continue. Others in all countries, who are proud of their past, wish to readjust their old beliefs into harmony with the new light. Whichever is done, it means that, so far as these educated people are concerned and those whom they influence, the old religions will lose their hold unless they can be modified. Even among the common people, the introduction of new machinery and the working before their eyes of what appear to be marvels, if not miracles, tend to shake their belief in the powers of the spirits and demons. At the same time, the new sanitary and medical measures for controlling disease break the sense of fear, and thus weaken the hold of the gods through whose malignant power these calamities were supposed to come.

Again, with the introduction of the new industry and the new means of communication, as was shown in a previous chapter, the social organization changes, and this modifies the attitude of the people towards the religion which was the basis and sanction of the old order. Especially in India, where the caste organization is the church of the common people, the old restrictions tend to weaken, and this means the lessening of the hold of Hinduism. The new political ideals of these people and the old religious ideas do not harmonize, and that which is coming to be dearest to them, the political, tends to prevail.

Instances of these tendencies are seen all through Asia. The leaders of the New Turkey are nominally Moslems, but actually Islam has lost its hold over many of them. If they dared, they would declare themselves free from its restraints or even come out openly as agnostics or free thinkers. One of the sources of the strength of Mohammedanism has been its exclusiveness; but in Turkey, under the new régime, intercourse between Christian and

Moslem is increasing to a remarkable degree. The missionaries experience no difficulty in organizing, or in helping to organize, clubs in which they meet Moslems on a footing of equality and discuss with them interesting questions, historical, literary, political, and social. Added to this is the fact that Moslems are reading the Bible as never before. This means the beginning of disintegration.

In India, also, the same process is going on. A generation ago, few village Hindus could be found who failed to defend polytheism and idolatry as essentials of their faith. Now there is coming to be a universal assent to the unity of God, though in a pantheistic sense, and polytheism is explained away. Idolatry is declared to belong to a kindergarten stage of development, and to be good only for the ignorant, or for women and children. Even a prominent orthodox Hindu has been known to declare, " How can we be blind to the greatness, the unrivalled splendour of Jesus Christ ? Behind the British Empire and all European powers lies a single great personality,—the greatest of all known to us,—of Jesus Christ. He lives in Europe and America, in Asia and Africa, as King and Guide and Teacher. He lives in our midst. He seeks to revivify religion in India. We owe everything, even this deep yearning towards our ancient Hinduism, to Christianity." [1] Not a few believe that the tenth, that is, the coming incarnation of Vishnu refers to Christ. A Hindu Saivite priest told an

[1] Jones, J. P., " India's Problem, Krishna or Christ," p. 357.

American missionary that he proposed to place in his temple an image of Christ, as they had placed there one of Vishnu![1] When Hindu leaders begin to take such an attitude towards Christ, it means that their loyalty to their former beliefs is changing. They are admitting into their religious thinking elements that will profoundly modify their former position. A similar process is found elsewhere, and it may be said that, in general, these ancient faiths are gradually losing vitality, and undergoing a process of disintegration, except as they are trying to meet the competition of Christianity by adopting Christian elements.

It is a matter of common knowledge that Islam has been modified in those regions where it has come into close touch with Christianity, and that one must go into isolated regions to see it at its worst. The Mohammedanism of India is very different from that of Turkestan, for instance, and that of Constantinople from that of Kurdistan. Further than this, there have arisen in India certain leaders and sects which have attempted to Westernize Islam and interpret it into harmony with present social and ethical ideals. While the religion of the great prophet has been divided into many schools, and has had its reforming movements, yet there has been a point beyond which it could not seem to get. Grant that the religious system and the political system were alike founded by Mohammed, and that

[1] Jones, J. P., "India's Problem, Krishna or Christ," p. 359.

the records were literally and eternally inspired; admit, also, the fatalistic spirit which has characterized that religion, and one can see that, without the introduction of new principles of interpretation or of new factors, the social system of Islam becomes stationary.[1]

Twenty years and more ago, reform movements began in India among the leaders of the 60,000,000

[1] "The reasons why Islam as a social system has been a complete failure are manifold.

"First and foremost, Islam keeps women in a position of marked inferiority. In the second place, Islam, speaking not so much through the Koran as through the traditions which cluster round the Koran, crystallizes religion and law into one inseparable and immutable whole, with the result that all elasticity is taken away from the social system. If to this day an Egyptian goes to law over a question of testamentary succession, his case is decided according to the antique principles which were laid down as applicable to the primitive society of the Arabian Peninsula in the seventh century. . . .

"The rigidity of the Sacred Law has been at times slightly tempered by well-meaning and learned Moslems who have tortured their brains in devising sophisms to show that the legal principles and social system of the seventh century can, by some strained and intricate process of reasoning, be consistently and logically made to conform with the civilized practices of the twentieth century. But, as a rule, custom based on religious law, coupled with exaggerated reverence for the original lawgiver, holds all those who cling to the faith of Islam with a grip of iron from which there is no escape. 'During the Middle Ages,' it has been truly said, 'man lived enveloped in a cowl.' The true Moslem of the present day is even more tightly enveloped in the Sheriat.

"In the third place Islam does not, indeed, encourage, but it tolerates slavery.

*   *   *   *   *   *

Moslems there.[1] These have in themselves the promise of profound changes.

The leader in one line of work was Sir Sayed Ahmed Khan of Aligarh, who was born in 1817, of a pure-blooded family of lineal descendants of Mohammed. He entered the civil service in 1838 and served England well at the time of the Mutiny. He visited England in 1869–1870, where he was presented to the Queen and Prince of Wales and made a careful study of English life. On his return to India, he came to realize that, although the Moslems had conquered and for centuries had ruled India, yet, since the passing of their political power, they had not maintained their position. He saw that they had been overtaken and passed by the Hindus in education, wealth, and influence. He therefore preached the gospel of self-help, and tried to arouse the Moslems to remedy their condition by education. The chief result of his efforts has already been mentioned, namely, the opening in Aligarh, in 1878, of the Anglo-Mohammedan College. The college has had a useful career, having furnished, during the years 1898–1902, 116 out of the 478 Moslem graduates in India. It is now developing into a university. One object of the col-

---

" Lastly, Islam has the reputation of being an intolerant religion, and the reputation is, from some points of view, well deserved, though the bald sweeping accusation of intolerance requires qualification and explanation. . . ."—Cromer, " Modern Egypt," Vol. II, p. 134 et seq.

[1] Vid. Zwemer, S. M., et al., " The Mohammedan World of To-day," p. 187 et seq.

lege, it has been declared, is the training of a new type of *mulla*. Its principals have been able English educators and they have impressed upon the institution some of the spirit of the English public school and university. At the same time, it must be added that the atmosphere of the college is rather secular. Eight years after the founding of the college, Sir Sayed Ahmed initiated an annual Educational Conference for Mohammedans, which has led the efforts of progressive Moslems.

One of the leaders in the later movements has been the Agha Khan, the leader of the Bora community of Bombay, a wealthy mercantile tribe. He has denounced the seclusion of women as a barrier to the progress of the whole community, has combatted the fatalistic spirit, and has opposed the formalism which supports in idleness fakirs and keepers of spurious Moslem shrines. Quite a controversy has proceeded as to the seclusion of women and polygamy. Polygamy has been defended by *mulvis* of the old school with the crudest and coarsest arguments, while the reformers have vindicated the rights of women in a modern and almost Christian spirit. Progressive Moslems have broken through custom, and gone about with their wives and daughters unveiled; and this usually means in European dress. Even in matters of social intercourse, in which the Moslems followed Hindu customs, the progressive section has broken over the barriers. One of the latest outgrowths of this Educational Conference has been the starting of a training school for female teachers, something hitherto unheard of in Islam.

Sir Sayed Ahmed was not sufficiently educated to take the lead in reconciling modern thought and the religion of Islam. To be sure, he was, to a certain extent, a rationalist. Thus he put forth a modified theory of inspiration, declaring that not every part of the sacred book is equally inspired, and that we may acknowledge in it a human element. He regarded conscience as a condition of man's character, which results from training and reflection. It may rightly be called his true guide. Still, it is liable to mutability and needs to be corrected from time to time by historic prophets. The principles of these prophets must be themselves tested by comparison with the laws of nature. This was as far as he went. Others, however, have attempted a more thorough Westernized interpretation of Islam.

About twenty years ago, two Moslem thinkers [1] announced themselves as Moslem rationalists, and declared that all articles of faith should be tested by reason. Acting upon this principle, they denied the existence of the Koran before creation. They asserted that man creates his own acts, that the ethical nature of acts may be ascertained by reason, and that the future of a man depends, not upon a profession of faith, but upon his past conduct. They accepted the Koran, but regarded the Sheriat, the reported sayings and interpretations

[1] Vid. Contemporary Review, Aug., 1893.

of Mohammed, as merely common law, designed to meet specific needs and not irrevocable. The spirit and not the letter of the Koran, they held, should be regarded, while the civil precepts were merely temporary in their nature. By declaring that even the Koran should be rationally interpreted, they believed that Islam could keep pace with the most rapidly developing civilizations. They also opposed Mohammedan ethics. Polygamy and slavery they denounced, even declaring that neither could be supported by the example and teaching of Mohammed. In the matter of easy divorce, they declared: "As usual, the Fathers of the Church have taken up the temporary permission as a positive rule and ignored the principles of humanity, justice, and equity inculcated by the Master." When one has rejected the civil institutions of the Sheriat and held that the moral teachings are temporary measures, not positive injunctions, it is hard to see how much is left, and yet this is what these men attempted, in their effort to harmonize Islam and modern ethics. They would have agreed with an official of Hyderabad who publicly declared: "To me it seems that as a nation and a religion we are dying out; our day is past and we have little hope of the future. Unless a miracle of reform occurs, we Mohammedans are doomed to extinction, and we shall have deserved our fate. For God's sake, let the reform take place before it is too late."

Other reformers have attempted a middle way between such extremes and the impossible old standards.   One of these was Mirza Ghulam Ahmed of Qadian in the Punjab. He was disquieted by the inroads of Christianity upon the Moslems of the central Punjab, and announced himself as a prophet, to prepare the way for the return of Jesus and the judgment day. He rejected the doctrine of the *Jihad*, or holy war against pagans, which, he declared, is not permissible under present circumstances. Slavery, likewise, he denounced, claiming that the Koran intended it to be abolished gradually. He declared the veiling of women, divorce, and polygamy to be merely permissible, in order to prevent worse evils ;[1] but he availed himself to the full of the permission regarding polygamy. His movement, which gained thousands of adherents, was bitterly anti-Christian and anti-Hindu. After his death in 1908 from cholera, though he had promised his followers immunity from pestilence, the sect declined.

Lucknow and Lahore are the headquarters of societies which seek to promote Moslem education on a modern basis, but with less departure from Moslem orthodoxy than Sir Sayed Ahmed's school. The former has branches in Madras and elsewhere. It claims that the features of Christian civilization which are attracting Moslems towards Christianity have no connection with the Christian religion.

The orthodox Moslem theory was that the Koran, as a sacred and inspired book, could not be translated. In India, a concession had been made to the

[1] Zwemer, S. M., *et al.*, *op. cit.*, p. 199 *et seq.*

rights of those who knew only the vernacular, and a bald translation· produced in Urdu, the language which the Moslems made the *lingua franca* of India. More recently, however, idiomatic translations have been produced, one of them by a well-known novelist. The use of fiction for teaching religious and social ideas has been adopted, while monthly and weekly periodicals and newspapers have been started. The Mohammedan Tract and Book Depot in Lahore is issuing works in English, which defend Islam and try to reconcile its teachings and its history with modern views.

Other reformers have declared that the village *mullas* are degraded, that there are in consequence abuses of marriage rites, and that the Moslems should institute a reformation similar to that in Europe in the sixteenth century.

It cannot be asserted that these movements have yet taken much hold of the Moslem community in India, but they are indications of the way in which those who have received a Western education are seeking to reconcile their new scientific and social views with loyalty to their religion and thus to check the movements which are leading Moslems to abandon the ancestral faith.

There is also a reform party in Egypt, which denounces certain features of Islam with a vigour that would not be tolerated in a Christian.

On passing from Islam to Hinduism, one discovers that the reform movements among the Hindus have gained a greater following, though even here the more progressive movements are either stationary or retrogressive, and the growing ones are those with reactionary tendencies.

The fourth chapter described some of the ethical reforms in India, which have curtailed a few of the worst excesses adhering to Hinduism, and the opening paragraphs of this showed that the general attitude towards some of the tenets has been modified. It remains only to discuss the reforming Hindu sects, the Brahma-Samaj and the Arya-Samaj.

The movement known as the Brahma-Samaj has, during its existence of a century, gone through many vicissitudes under four great leaders, Raja Ram Mohan Roy, Debendra Nath Tagore, Keshub Chunder Sen, and Protab Chandra Mazumdar.[1]

The first of these was a Brahman who was born near Calcutta about the time of the opening of the Revolutionary War in America. As we were closing our second war with Great Britain, he went to Calcutta to fight against the evil social conditions then prevailing, namely, immorality, caste, *sati*, infanticide, and the position of women. He advocated the unity of God, learned Greek and Hebrew in order to study the Bible in the original, and later declared, "I have found the doctrines of Christ more conducive to moral principles and better adapted for the use of rational beings than

---

[1] *Vid.* Murdoch, J., "Papers on Indian Religious Reform"; "Encyc. Brit.," Vol. IV, p. 388; Vol. XXII, p. 877; Vol. XV, p. 759.

any other which has come to my knowledge." He assisted Carey and his associates at Serampore in the translation of the Scriptures; at times he attended Christian worship; he secured for Dr. Duff the house in which he opened the Scottish Missionary Institution; and he recommended that the day's work be begun with the Lord's Prayer.

Just before 1830, he and his friends began to meet every Saturday evening for public worship and united prayer, the first time that this had ever been done by Hindus. In 1830, the first theistic church was opened in Calcutta. It was called the Society of Believers in Brahama (neuter), the one self-existent god of Hinduism. No image, statue, or picture was to be admitted to the building, no sacrifices were to be offered, and nothing that was recognized by others as an object of worship was to be spoken of with contempt. Every sermon was to promote piety, morality, charity, benevolence, virtue, and union between men of all religious creeds, or to assist in the contemplation of the author and preserver of the universe. Raja Ram Mohan Roy believed in the unity and personality of God and in the individual immortality of the soul. He called Christ Redeemer, Mediator, and Intercessor. On the other hand, he rejected the Christian doctrines of the trinity and the atonement, the day of judgment and miracles, as well as the Hindu belief in transmigration. He was also prominent in social reform and he rendered one of his greatest social services in England, where he died in 1833. That

service, as already described, was leadership in the
agitation which prevented the British Government
from annulling the order of 1829 against *sati*.
Though he broke the rules of caste, he never did
this openly lest he forfeit his property. Yet, in
spite of this moral weakness, he was a spiritually
earnest man and very nearly a Christian.

The next leader in this theistic movement was
Debendra Nath Tagore. After several years spent
in satisfying his sensuous and sensual desires, he had
a wonderful spiritual experience in which he says,
" The world lost its attractions and God became
my only comfort and delight in this world of sorrow and sin." Since the death, in 1833, of its
founder, the Samaj had become little more than a
platform for discussion. The new leader joined the
society in 1842, at the age of twenty-eight, and revived it. The principal duties he taught were the
worship through love and good deeds of the one
God, the avoidance of the worship of any created
object, the abstention from vicious deeds, and, in
the case of falling into vice, added caution to prevent a recurrence of the sin. He sought his moral
precepts, not in the New Testament, but in the
Upanishads, the second division of the Vedas, which
contain the beginnings of Hindu philosophy. His
sense of sin was weak. To him sinfulness and car-
nality were the private concerns of individual men,
and ought to be conquered by resolute determina-
tion. Yet his writings and teachings breathed a
spirit very different from that of orthodox Hindu-

ism. As an example, take this prayer with which he concluded one of his sermons:

"O Thou supreme Soul, as Thou hast made us independent, do not leave us alone—our entire dependence is upon Thee. Thou art our help and wealth; Thou art our Father and Friend; we take shelter in Thee; do Thou show us Thy beautiful and complacent face. Purify me with Thy love and so strengthen my will that I may be able to perform Thy good works for my whole life."[1] He gave a printing-press to the Samaj and established a monthly journal, which did much to give strength and beauty to the Bengali language.

About 1850, the first schism occurred in the body. This was due to the withdrawal of a section which held the greater part of the Vedas to be polytheistic, and claimed nature and intuition as the basis of faith. Between 1847 and 1858 branches were started in different parts of India, especially in Bengal, and the progress was rapid because of the spread of English education and the work of Christian missionaries.

The creed of the Brahmas was formulated as containing fourteen articles:

1. As the basis of religious faith, the book of nature and intuition.

2. The acceptance of any religious truth contained in any book.

3. The progressiveness of the religious condition of man.

[1] Murdoch, *op. cit.*, " Brahma Samaj," etc., p. 21.

4. The fundamental doctrines of every true religion the same.

5. The existence of one supreme, personal, moral, and intelligent God, who is alone to be worshipped, and the rejection of all incarnations.

6. The immortality and progressive state of the soul, and a state of conscious existence succeeding life in this world, and supplementary to it in the matter of the universal moral government.

7. Repentance the only way to salvation and to reconciliation to the offended but loving Father.

8. Belief in the efficacy of prayer for *spiritual* welfare.

9. The providential care of the divine Father.

10. Love towards Him and the performance of the works that He loves as constituting worship.

11. The necessity of public worship, but communion not dependent upon it.

12. Rejection of pilgrimages and the belief that holiness can be secured only by elevating and purifying the mind.

13. Rejection of faith in rites, ceremonies, and penances. Moral righteousness, the gaining of wisdom, divine contemplation, charity, and the cultivation of devotional feelings are their rites and ceremonies.

14. Theoretically, no distinction of caste between those who are children of God and, therefore, brothers and sisters to one another.[1]

The third theistic leader was Keshub Chunder

[1] "Encyc. Brit.," Vol. IV, p. 388.

Sen, whose life, written by his disciple Mazumdar, was the first true biography ever written by a Hindu. He was a native of Calcutta, and early gave promise of the future, being marked by so bright a mind that he was regarded by all as a prodigy. In this judgment he heartily concurred. As a youth he was not religious but he had great purity of moral nature. He became intimate with three missionaries, one of whom was a Unitarian. He started classes for the benefit of his companions, in which Shakespeare was studied and acted. He was an omnivorous reader and spent his days in the Calcutta Public Library, reading poetry and especially the history of philosophy. He had become a member of the Brahma-Samaj in 1857. Three years later he began to publish tracts. He deprecated the willingness of the educated classes to talk reform, but their unwillingness to carry out reforms, and he attributed it to a lack of an active religious principle. A godless education, he held, should be opposed.

In 1862, he became the minister of one branch of the Brahma-Samaj and soon after issued an appeal to young India, in which he took the position that the fundamental evil of Indian society was idolatry, followed by caste, marriage customs, and the zenana system. "Ninety-nine evils out of every hundred in Hindu society are, in my opinion, attributable to idolatry and superstition." "If you wish to regenerate this country, make religion the basis of all your reform movements." In 1866 he electrified missionary circles by an address entitled, "Jesus Christ, Europe and Asia," in which he glorified Jesus. "Was He not above ordinary humanity? Blessed Jesus, immortal Child of God," but five years later he held that all great men are god-men, divine incarnations. The scriptures of the Samaj were a compilation from the sacred books of the Christian, Moslem, Parsee, and Hindu. Their tenets were: "(1) The wide universe is the temple of God. (2) Wisdom is the pure land of pilgrimage. (3) Truth is the everlasting scripture. (4) Faith is the root of all Religion. (5) Love is the true spiritual culture. (6) The destruction of selfishness is the true asceticism." [1]

Keshub Chunder Sen was also a social reformer. In fact, the radical character of his programme led to a rupture in 1865. He and his followers demanded the abandonment of the external signs of caste distinctions. The older leaders were so opposed to his innovations as premaure that, in 1866, he withdrew to form a new branch known as the Brahma-Samaj of India, with God as the head and Keshub as the secretary. The more conservative members called themselves the Adi- (original) Samaj, and declared their aim to be the fulfilling rather than the abrogating of the old religion. The vitality of the movement had left it and the Adi-Samaj became hardly distinguishable from orthodox Hinduism, while Debendra Nath Tagore escaped his difficulties by becoming an ascetic. The new body made rapid

[1] " Encyc. Brit.," Vol. XV, p. 760.

progress until 1878. As a part of his social work, Keshub Chunder Sen was active in securing the passage of the law, mentioned elsewhere, which authorized inter-caste marriages between the Brahmas, and raised the minimum ages to eighteen and fourteen.

About this time his followers began to abase themselves before him and sing praises in his honour as an abode of God. He refused to stop them. His head was evidently turned, and after 1878, when his daughter was married before the age of fourteen and he claimed that in this he but followed the will of God, his course was rather downward, until he died in 1884. As a result of the controversy over this marriage question, another secession occurred, and the seceders, who called themselves the Sadharana (Universal) Brahma-Samaj, became the most popular and progressive section of the movement and are to-day conspicuous in the cause of literary culture, social reform, and female education.

These movements, which were profoundly influenced by Christianity, had in them promise; but because of their break with Hinduism and the lack of a real vital religious principle, they have become little more than another caste. Their numbers hardly exceed four thousand, mostly found in Calcutta and its neighbourhood. Yet they have had an influence upon social reform and are significant of the leaven of Christianity within Hinduism.

The other great movement within Hinduism, the

Arya-Samaj,[1] is nationalistic and anti-Christian in its spirit, and has been called into being by those who would throw off the excrescences of Hinduism, return to the purity of the primitive faith, and, upon this as a basis, reconstruct Hindu thought and organization. They would combine Western political and social ideals with Indian religious thought. This revival has been assisted by the study of Sanscrit, which the British introduced through the universities, and by the application of scientific methods for sifting the old and pure from the new and impure.

The founder of this sect, which has some 100,000 members and is growing in these days of anti-foreign feeling, was a Gujarati Brahman, Dayanand Saraswati. He early became dissatisfied with idolatry and began to study the Vedic philosophy, in the hope of solving the problem of the Buddha, namely, how to alleviate human misery and attain final liberation.

About 1866, when he was some forty years old, he first saw the Bible and about the same time the Rig Veda. The former he assailed, while the latter he extolled. He accepted the four Vedas but rejected all the later sacred writings.

The principal beliefs of this reformer were:[2]

1. The Vedas are eternal. The present edition was taught by God to the first four men created.

[1] "Encyc. Brit.," Vol. II, p. 712.
[2] Murdoch, Rev. J., *op. cit.*, "Account of the Vedas," p. 151 *et seq.*

2. God is one. He opposed an Indian theism to a foreign theism.

3. Souls are eternal. Whatever now exists has always existed and will always exist. A belief in transmigration necessarily follows this.

4. There can be no sacrifice for sin.

In these four truths he brushed away the idolatry of Hinduism and much of its superstition. The remaining truths concern social conditions.

5. He rejected caste. One may eat food from any hand save that of a Christian or Moslem.

6. He denounced child marriage, but rejected second marriages, save temporary ones by which a widow, if she so desired, might secure children. Children were to be taken from their parents, after they were five years old, put into schools eight miles from any village, with the sexes strictly separated, and taught by teachers of the same sex.

The object of the Samaj was declared to be to benefit the world by improving its physical, social, intellectual, and moral conditions. Of late years, this movement has rather compromised on the subject of caste, and thus has secured a larger following.

Dayanand Saraswati read into the Vedas all he wished of his own beliefs and of Western scientific discoveries. Thus, he explained the Vedic sacrificial cult as "the entertainment of the learned in proportion to their worth, the business of manufacture, the experiment and application of chemistry, physics, and the arts of peace; the instruction of the people, the purification of the air, the nourishment of vegetables by the employment of the principles of meteorology." One can imagine the amazement of his first four men when informed that their writings meant all that. He also found in the Vedas the steam engine,—the white horse cannot possibly mean anything else,—railways, steamers, guns, balloons, and the like; and had he lived until our day, he would not have failed to include the aeroplane. With equal convincingness, he argued against the use of animal food, because, in the lifetime of a cow and her descendants, the milk would give enough food for one day for 410,440. Hence, in the interests of economy, it is wrong to kill a cow and eat the meat.

We smile at these evidences of exuberant imagination, but the spirit of the movement appeals to the present social reformers in India. It is believed that many of the members have been active among those agitators against British rule who have used bombs to voice their protests. In 1898, the Arya-Samaj began to carry out the old Vedic system of education, as suggested by their founder. At an early age, the child is entrusted to his *guru* or spiritual teacher, who becomes to him more than a parent. For sixteen years the child is under instruction, practically cut off from the outer world, and is then to be sent forth as a missionary, to propagate the Aryan doctrines throughout India.

The ten articles of the creed of the Arya-Samaj have been summarized as follows:[1]

[1] "Encyc. Brit.," Vol. II, p. 713.

1. The source of all true knowledge is God.

2. God is all truth, all knowledge, all bliss, boundless, almighty, just, merciful, unbegotten, without beginning, incomparable, the support and Lord of all, all-pervading, omniscient, imperishable, immortal, eternal, holy, and the cause of the universe; worship is due to Him alone.

3. The medium of true knowledge is the Vedas.

4 and 5. The truth is to be accepted and to become the guiding principle.

6. The object of the Samaj is to benefit the world by improving its physical, social, intellectual, and moral conditions.

7. Love and justice are the right guides of conduct.

8. Knowledge must be spread.

9. The good of others must be sought.

10. In general interests members must subordinate themselves to the good of others; in personal interests they should retain independence.

Article 6 comprehends a wide programme of reform, and includes abstinence from spirituous liquors and animal food, physical cleanliness and exercise, marriage reform, the promotion of female education, the abolition of caste and idolatry.

Parallel to these movements, which show the marks of contact with Christian thought, must be mentioned in passing the revival in India, under the influence of nationalism, of the worship of the old gods. The worship of the bloody goddess Kali, the cult of Shivaji Maharaj, a Maratha chieftain who humbled the alien conquerors of Hindustan, and the exaltation of the elephant-headed god of learning, Ganesh. These are being revived, and some of the extreme nationalists are even glorifying polytheism and the old social institutions, which have been the cause of so many of India's sorrows. The battle is joined between the old Hinduism, the new reactionary Hinduism, the Westernized Hinduism, the agnosticism and nationalism of the student classes, and the forces of Christianity.

The last of the great religions, the modifications of which, under Christian influences, must be mentioned briefly, is Buddhism. The Buddhists, both in Ceylon and in Japan, have felt the competition of Christianity. Here they have been aroused to a new activity and have sought to embody in Buddhism certain Christian elements. In the other Buddhist countries, religion seems inactive and unable to resist the disintegrating forces at work.

In Ceylon, the propagation of a revived and aggressive Buddhism is making rapid progress. In this the Buddhists are assisted by certain European converts to the religion founded by Gautama, who are standing evidence to the Buddhists of the superiority of Buddhism to Christianity. One of the methods used in this work is education. In Colombo they have a strong school of high grade, which is one of four Buddhist colleges maintained in Ceylon. Throughout the island, with the development of compulsory education, the Buddhists have seen their chance to open schools, claim the government grant, and thus secure the control of the education of thousands of boys and girls. Not only in methods but in doctrines, they are imitating the Christian forces. For instance, the Buddhists speak of the incarnation of Buddha, and even of his immaculate conception. They comfort the dying by saying that, when they have crossed the river of death, the Lord Buddha will receive them to his arms. What would Gautama, who denied the personality of God and the existence of soul, have said to such amazing heresy, and that, too, among those who regard him as God? It testifies to the demand of the soul for those religious elements which Buddhism and the other ethnic religions have denied but which Christianity offers.

In Japan the revival of Buddhism is most interesting. During the days of feudal Japan, Buddhism in its Japanese form was practically the state religion, and its priests were possessed of honours and titles. These latter were done away with at the Restoration. Buddhism then began to feel the competition, both of Shintoism, which sought to become the state religion, and of Christianity. The latter's representatives very quickly attracted the attention of the samurai, who had recently been deprived by the change in government of their former position and duties. Professor Takakusu declares, " The characteristically broadminded nature of the Japanese, the new knowledge brought back by the priests who went to Europe and America, and the methods and attitude taken by the Christians in their missionary work, gave the Buddhists new incentives for the improvement of their organization, doctrines, and philanthropic work."[1] A Buddhist priest, who had invited Dr. DeForest to speak in his temple on religion, said that he was hoping to visit the United States and England to thank these nations, both for the political and civil blessings which had come from them, and also for the influence in Japan of the Christian religion, which had revealed to the priests their faults and forced them to reform their lives. This priest knew the facts. Baron Kato, who himself believes religion to be a superstition useful only for the lower orders of mind, delivered an address some years ago on Buddhist Reformation. He declared, " The men who have the doctrines in charge are indeed so corrupt that they themselves have need of reformation. They are absolutely unable to save the masses, and, moreover, are a peril to society. . . . They stand for the salvation of the people. . . . Yet they actually use the people in carrying on their evil lives. . . . There is not one priest that devotes himself to saving the masses. They are all corrupt." While this was an exaggeration, the Japanese themselves admit that the Buddhist priesthood was rotten to the core, and that men who had taken the vows of

[1] Okuma, Count, "Fifty Years of Modern Japan," Vol. II, p. 73.

celibacy were themselves patrons of brothels. This is now changing and Buddhism is springing into new life.

Buddhism has been one of the three great missionary religions, and the revived Buddhism of Japan has learned that in missions is one secret of prosperity. It is, therefore, sending missionaries to China, to Korea, to Siberia, to the Malay Peninsula, to various Oriental ports, to Hawaii and the Pacific Coast States, and even into Thibet.

The Buddhists in Japan have adopted some of the methods of Christianity. They have stated times for preaching, and these on Sunday. They have pastoral visitation, street preaching, Buddhist Sunday-schools, Young Men's Buddhist Associations, and other organizations for women and children. They have Buddhist chaplains who work in prisons after the best Western methods. They hold services in factories, in the army, and among the poor. They maintain orphan asylums, schools for the deaf and dumb, and charity hospitals. They aid prisoners and have started free lodging houses. Temperance and other lines of reformatory work fall within their programme. They observe the birthday of Shaka, the Japanese name of Gautama, the Buddha, much as Christians do Christmas.

The Buddhists are also developing education. As Professor Takakusu puts it, " Another evidence of the Christian influence upon Buddhism is shown in the establishment of sectarian schools of various kinds, and especially in an eagerness to start schools

for girls and women." [1] These Buddhist schools
teach science and philosophy, as well as their own
doctrines. The students are beginning to handle
Buddhism historically, to submit it to free and
open discussion, and a certain body of young Buddhists even consider this to be the only way to
reach truth. Comparative religion is included in
the curriculum. Christian teachers are employed
and the Bible is actually used as a text book. The
Buddhists are also using the press with vigour, and
it is claimed that half the magazines published in
Japan to-day are Buddhist in tone. If so, it must
be that of the neo-Buddhism, for the ethical tone
of all the literature of the empire to-day is declared to be Christian. The educated Buddhist
entirely rejects the doctrine of transmigration,
which puts him on a level with a snake, a bird,
or a beast, and has substituted the doctrine of
heredity.

No one who has visited the new Japanese temples can fail to be impressed with their beauty
and good taste. There is a new temple of this sort
in Seoul, Korea, which we visited in December,
1908. It reminded one of an artistic Roman
Catholic Church. In the new Buddhism, the Goddess of Mercy takes the place of the other deities
which have been adopted into Buddhism, and in
this temple she is represented in much the same
position as a statue of the Virgin Mary, with a
halo over her head. The air of the place was

[1] Okuma, *op. cit.*, Vol. II, p. 74.

reverential and one instinctively felt almost like worshipping in such a house.

This is characteristic of the new Buddhism. Buddhism has seen the need in Japan of a religion which can solve the moral and social problems of the people. It has recognized in Christianity a force which is efficient in meeting these needs, and which has succeeded in winning the support of thousands of those who were formerly Buddhists. It has thought that by adopting its methods and some of its doctrines it could overcome this new competition and reinstate itself as the dominant religion of the empire. Little does it realize the real source of power in Christianity. A prominent missionary in Japan reported recently that the Buddhists, realizing that their new methods are only partially successful, are now seeking to discover the source of power in Christianity, in order that this, too, may be adopted. If they discover it, we can assure them it will mean the forsaking of Buddhism and the acceptance of Christ. Yet this movement in the Buddhism of Japan both bears a strong testimony to the value and power of Christianity in that empire and gives promise of better things in the ethical life of that people.

When all due allowance has been made for these changes in the other great religions, it yet remains true that they are powerless to meet the needs of the awakening East. A sense of their inadequacy is dimly perceived by the leaders of Japan, who see that, unless that country shall secure a religion which can grapple with and solve the distressing moral problems now before them, the future of the country is gloomy. The earnest, almost frantic, efforts recently made to reëstablish Shintoism as the state religion testify to this fact. The moral condition is so far from what it should be, the old sanctions are so fast being removed, and the students' agnosticism is so patently unable to make them what Japan needs, sane moral leaders, that statesmen are turning to Shintoism, the religion that embodies the highest of all virtues to the Japanese, patriotism, to save them from the dreaded approach of socialism and anarchism. Many of them fear Christianity, because it is from the Christian West that the radical social theories came which inspired the recent base plot against the life of the late Emperor. Those who do not fear Christianity doubt its efficacy, for they know that in the West, where Christianity has had its home for centuries, the social and even the moral conditions are perhaps worse in some respects than those in Japan.

Likewise, the leaders of Indian thought see that a revival of religion must come if their plans for a self-governing India are to be realized, and to this end they are reviving some of the less attractive cults of that congeries of rites which is comprehended under the single term, Hinduism.

Why, then, can it be claimed that in Christianity, and in Christianity alone, these great countries must find their religion? The points to be mentioned are not new; they are old ones, with which all are familiar but which cannot too often be emphasized.

1. The Christians' Father-God is the only god who can fully meet the social and religious needs of humanity. A far-off, cold, impersonal deity cannot satisfy the human heart. Note the way in which the Moslem tends to exalt Mohammed to the position of a mediator or even a deity, or gives allegiance to other incarnations or manifestations of the divine. Note how the Buddhist turns to the Buddha or to the Goddess of Mercy for one to whom he can pray and from whom he can expect the blessings he craves. Hinduism cares little for the great unifying, impersonal neuter Brahama, and gives itself up to the worship of inferior deities like themselves. And what a conglomeration of deities these people have conjured up! Creatures of lust and of passion, monsters of cruelty; or spineless deities who are willing to forgive without repentance, and who are too kind-hearted to punish. These deities are vanishing in the light of science, which takes away the philosophical basis upon which they rest. Yet, unless something else can be found to which the feelings of men can go out in passionate devotion, science or no science, the human heart will go back to these old gods, with their immoral characters, or else will take refuge in blank atheism. Both phenomena are visible upon the mission field to-day.

To people who are thus in dire need of God, the
Christian comes with his conception of a God who
is infinite, and yet a person ; who is justice, and yet
is love ; and who comes into the most intimate fel-
lowship with His children. No one can read the
results of the inquiry that was made of missionaries in 1909–1910 regarding the Christian message
in its relation to the non-Christian religions, without being impressed anew with the power of the
Christian view of God,' and at the same time being
forced to wonder whether, after all, we of the
West are actually letting God mean to us all that
He should mean. To the animist, with his belief
in myriads of hostile spirits, to the Hindu, with his
pantheon of disgusting deities, to the Buddhist, with
his doubt whether there be any personal God, and
to the Moslem, to whom God is an arbitrary

---

[1] " The correspondent who has most minutely discussed the pa-
thology of animistic religion, Dr. Joh. Warneck, . . . lays
much emphasis on the fact that throughout the East Indian Ar-
chipelago the truth in the Christian Gospel which makes the first
and most powerful appeal is that of the unity and omnipotence
of God. His testimony is confirmed in this by other papers from
the same region which expressly corroborate the witness of his
volume ; and also by the independent testimony of Mr. Camp-
bell Moody from Formosa. . . . The same testimony comes
from Herr Hahn, who labours among an aboriginal people in
India, and from other regions. In these cases it seems to be the
monotheism of Christianity that at the first forms its greatest
power of appeal. . . . To the animist the world is peopled by
many unseen beings, who are envious of the living, and who, unless propitiated, strike them with disease or calamity. The whole
life of the animist therefore lies under an incubus of terror. He

Oriental despot, the message of a God who is at once powerful, just, righteous, and loving, comes with an inspiration which we little realize. And it is a God like this who is needed to solve their problems. They need to realize the universal brotherhood of the race. They must understand that a standard of absolute holiness is to be placed before them, and that over these perplexing problems of life there stands a Being of infinite love who wishes His children to become like Him.

2. Christianity has an adequate doctrine of sin. It possesses a means of salvation which, on the one hand, is available for each individual, however weak or ignorant, and which, on the other hand, is yet difficult enough to call out the best efforts of the noblest for its full realization. It is at this point that these other religions, even the best of them,

---

may propitiate some, but he cannot propitiate all. Ancestor worship is at best a palliative but not a full deliverance, and therefore there arises an intolerable division of life.

"Hence the message of one Almighty God comes as good tidings of great joy. Because God is One, it is possible now to escape from the unbearable division of life which polytheism entails, and, because He is Almighty, He can protect the worshippers from every foe and lift them above doubt and fear. Have we not here a clue to the rapid spread of Islam among the animistic peoples?

"The climax of the Christian Gospel, according to Warneck, is that this God is love, He has not only the power but the will to protect His worshippers. The love becomes real, it becomes possible to realize it through Christ."—*Report of World Missionary Conference*, 1910, Vol. IV, p. 218 *et seq.*

"The first thing in missionary preaching which strikes and at-

fail. The Hindu and the Buddhist make a man's lot the result of his deeds in a previous existence. While they recognize the need of punishment for sins,—although these may be merely the violation of ceremonial law,—yet they put so great a burden upon the individual that he throws it off and takes refuge in a blind fatalistic resignation. Unless a religion inculcates a keen sense of sin, for which the individual is personally accountable and from the power of which he may and can escape, it will not secure clean living. And, after all, the great problems of life have their root in wrong relations to God and man which cannot be called anything else than sin. At this point every other religion fails, and it is interesting to note the unanimity with which the missionaries testify that it is only as men come to know Christ that they begin to feel a sense of sin which leads to repentance and reform. Through Christianity, men come to know themselves as they are, to realize their relations to God and man, and to make efforts to realize this ideal.

tracts a Chinese is the doctrine of the unity of God, being in strong contrast with the multitude of gods whom he himself worships. Monotheism appeals to him as being eminently reasonable, and he listens willingly to the statement of God's glorious perfections—His holiness, righteousness, and love. He is interested, perhaps attracted, while the preacher sets forth this all-mighty, all-seeing, and everywhere-present God as the creator and preserver of all things and the giver of all good. The attraction deepens as he hears of God's fatherhood, His love for all, and providence over all. It is this great doctrine of the Divine unity combined with the Divine love which attracts the immense majority of Chinese."—*Ibid.*, p. 58.

3. This leads to a third point, namely, that in Jesus Christ Christianity has the only perfect example of what man should become, and at the same time the only perfect manifestation of God. It is an interesting and noteworthy fact that, next to the Christian doctrine of God, and often taking precedence of it, the missionaries claim that Christ is the greatest asset Christianity possesses. Even if Meredith Townsend did claim years ago that Christ appeals to us because of moral characteristics which we do not possess, and that for this same reason He does not appeal to the Indian, who is strong at the same points as Christ, the fact remains, upon unimpeachable testimony, that Christ does appeal to all, Moslem, Hindu, Confucianist, Buddhist, and Shintoist.[1] If only Christ would not be so exclusive in His claims and would consent merely to occupy a niche in the pantheons of the nations, He would be enthroned everywhere within

[1] From China comes this testimony :

"The beautiful and perfect life of Jesus, His tender forgiving spirit, His love even for His enemies, and His high moral teaching impress all who hear or read the wonderful story. 'Many scholars,' writes the Rev. C. G. Sparham, 'give Him what is from their point of view high honour, and say that He is one of, and perhaps the greatest of, the world's four sages—Socrates, Buddha, Confucius, Christ.' His sufferings, death, and sacrifice for us men make a strong appeal even to the heathen, while to the Christians the loving, suffering Christ is the power that grips them. 'The centre and core, the one unique and supreme element, the Cross,' writes Archdeacon Moule, 'possesses the greatest and overmastering power of appeal.' The Cross, however, is now, as in the early days of Christianity and for the same reasons,

a few years. His ethical teaching and the quality of His life appeal to all men of every race and creed. To Him every one who desires an ideal is inevitably drawn.

In a remarkable address given in December, 1911, in New York, that noble Japanese Christian, Mr. Uyemura, described how the Shinto party in Japan is revising the list of heroes in whose honour shrines are erected. Some are rejected for one reason, others for another, the cause in each case being the fact that their characters do not harmonize with present ethical standards. If this process is carried through to the end, Mr. Uyemura declared most impressively, each one of their heroes, saints, and deities must be rejected, and there will be but one person to whom they can turn, the unique Galilean, the peerless Son of God. As one studies the characters of the holy men of other religions, of Mohammed, of Krishna, and the other unspeakable deities of India, the marvel is, not that the moral conditions are as bad as they are, but that the innate moral sense has kept the mass of the

an offense, yet now as then it is the power of God unto salvation. On the other hand, the Rev. P. J. Maclagan of Swatow says: 'The character of Jesus has not much place in the primary appeal; nor has the Cross of Christ, except as the means of procuring forgiveness and so of Heaven.'

"More attractive, perhaps, is Christ as a present Saviour from sin, not from sin as guilt merely, but from sins, evils, vices, especially those which harm men in body and soul, for most Chinese think more of the power of sin than of its guilt."—*Report of World Missionary Conference*, 1910, Vol. IV, p. 59.

people from falling to the point where they should be with such examples held before them. It is in the comparatively pure character of the Buddha that Buddhism has one secret of its strength, and yet how the Buddha pales before the Christ! In His purity of character, in His hatred of sin, in His utter devotion to men, and in His willingness to go to the utmost that they might be His, we see the only one who can become the exemplar of the nations in these days of transition and growth.

4. Christianity has a social gospel. Here is another point at which all other religions fail. The Moslem, if he is true to his faith, believes that in the Koran and the traditions are embodied the religious and social codes that must endure for all time. The Moslem civilization is what it is because of this belief. Look at Turkey, look at Arabia, look at the countries of North Africa, which once were lighted by Christ and civilization, if one would see how Islam would solve the social problems. It is because the enlightened Moslems realize this fatal weakness in their religion that they are attempting to graft upon their Islamic theology a Christian view of society. This is bound to fail. Hinduism is patently unable to solve its social problems, as enlightened Hindus are forced to admit when, as some of them do, they advise the outcastes to become Christians as the only avenue through which they may pass into manhood. Confucianism is preëminently a social system, and it is as far above Hinduism as Confucius was above Krishna. Yet even

here it is lacking in the positive vital note, and China has discovered to her sorrow that Confucianism cannot make her efficient in these days of competition with the West. The desire to correct these weaknesses is perhaps the chief purpose which lies back of the present overturn in that most ancient and most populous of the nations. Even Japan, which has sought all through the West for the secret of social efficiency and has corrected the most glaring inequalities in her midst, finds, as has been noted, that something is lacking. That something Christianity can supply. In its doctrine of universal brotherhood, in its Golden Rule, and above all in the loving devotion to Christ, who entrusted His disciples with the completion of His own work, Christianity has the only social gospel which can solve these world problems. This leads to the last point.

5. Christianity is the only religion which possesses a sufficient dynamic to make its ethical standards realizable. One of the sad and yet encouraging features in that recent study of the non-Christian religions, to which reference has more than once been made, is the realization that is coming over Moslem, Hindu, Buddhist, and Confucianist alike, namely, that their moral precepts may be most admirable, but they lack power to realize them in their lives. It is because at this point Christianity is strong that it is bound to win. In its new birth, by which man's nature is raised, the centre of his life is changed, and he becomes literally a

new man in Christ Jesus, Christianity has another
unique claim to distinction. Here, too, the testimony is unmistakable. It is the lives of the missionaries and the changed lives of the native Christians that, above everything else, commend Christianity to outsiders and make them willing to in-
vestigate the claims of Christ to their allegiance.
The other religions look for salvation by magic, or
by the performance of impossible tasks, or entrust it
to the working of some transcendent law like *karma*.
Whatever it is, they divorce religion and ethics,
while Christianity makes the Christian into a Christlike man.

Yes, from these five considerations and from
others which could be adduced, there are two inevitable conclusions : these other religions are inade-
quate and insufficient; Christianity is adequate. It
is both sufficient and efficient. This being so, what
is the duty of the Church at this hour? It is nothing less than the immediate propagation and naturalization of Christianity throughout the world.

There have been many crises in history. Doubtless, in all ages, there have been those who have
claimed that their age was the most critical time
that the world had known. It is easy to make this
claim; it is more difficult to justify it. Hence, one
ventures with some hesitation the declaration that
the immediate future is one of the most strategic
periods in history. We have heard for many years
of the crisis of missions. There have been many
such crises, but the present has been characterized

as a crisis of crises. This is no mere fulmination of brainless enthusiasts, but the deliberate opinion of some of the brainiest and sanest men of the world. This is the conclusion to which the members of Commission I of the Edinburgh Conference came after they had completed the most comprehensive study ever made of the situation in the non-Christian world. Great forces, which have been at work for generations, have now united in the production of a situation that has never been equalled.[1]

This book has been a study of some of these forces and their results. It has been shown how education has been undermining ignorance, how industry has transformed the economic situation, how new ethical ideals have found lodgment in the hearts of leaders throughout Asia and in parts of Africa, and how these have all resulted in the simultaneous unrest and political change, the latest phase of which has been the turning of the most populous empire of the world into a republic.

---

[1] "The Commission, after studying the facts and after taking counsel with the leaders of the missionary forces of the Church at home and abroad, expresses its conviction that the present is the time of all times for the Church to undertake with quickened loyalty and sufficient forces to make Christ known to all the non-Christian world.

"It is an opportune time. Never before has the whole world-field been so open and so accessible. Never before has the Christian Church faced such a combination of opportunities among both primitive and cultured peoples.

"It is a critical time. The non-Christian nations are undergoing great changes. Far-reaching movements—national, racial,

Japan, Korea, China, Siam, India, Persia, Turkey, Egypt, North Africa, South Africa,—these are but some of the places in which just now the old is giving place to the new. The Christian missionary has been one of the most prominent factors in producing this change. The Church has been praying for the day when heathenism should be supplanted and when the nations should become brotherhoods. That day is upon us. The whole social and political organization is in the process of transformation. It has been cast into the melting pot. Everything is in a state of flux, but will soon solidify. Shall the new mould be Christian or atheistic? That is the question before the Church to-day, and it is a question that can be answered only by the Church.

Now is the day when the Church can move into this new East, can plant Christian institutions where Christ has never yet been proclaimed, can show how Christianity can solve these problems, can furnish Christian leaders for these new movements, and can put a truly Christian impress

social, economic, religious—are shaking the non-Christian nations to their foundations. These nations are still plastic. Shall they set in Christian or pagan moulds? Their ancient faiths, ethical restraints, and social orders have been weakened or abandoned. Shall our sufficient faith fill the void? The spirit of national independence and racial patriotism is growing. Shall this become antagonistic or friendly to Christianity? There have been times when the Church confronted crises as great as those before it now on certain fields; but never before has there been such a synchronizing of crises in all parts of the world."—*Report of World Missionary Conference*, 1910, Vol. I, p. 362.

upon the China, the India, the Persia, and the Turkey which will soon emerge. The doors are open now. The people are more aware of their need than before. They feel that they are passing through a crisis. A helping hand now is doubly welcome. Take China as an example. The revolution was led by men trained in the West. They have Christian ideals. Some of the most prominent are themselves Christians. The Christian and Western-educated Chinese, who have been waiting for years for their chance, are now stepping to the front. They are favourably disposed towards Christianity. Now is the time, as they are working out their problems, to make certain, for instance, that the new education which China must develop shall not be anti-religious, as is that of Japan. If the Christian forces fail to do this now, the result will be that the younger generation of Chinese will be educated in an irreligious atmosphere, and a Christian education will be so relegated to the background that it will exert a relatively small influence, whereas it will be more needed than ever. The doors are open. How long they will remain so, God only knows.

If, however, the Church is to make its impress upon these countries, it must not go as a foreign body. A foreign religion will never be welcomed by these peoples, in whom the sense of nationality is awaking, and who are very jealous of anything that looks like foreign domination. It is not the Christianity which is propagated primarily by the missionary, but that which has been naturalized and is under native leadership that will prevail. It is because Christianity in Japan has come under Japanese leadership, that the intensely patriotic spirit of Japan, which is as powerful now as it was two decades ago, has almost ceased to be anti-Christian. What has come to pass in Japan and in parts of Turkey is bound to come very soon in China and presently also in India; and unless the Church is willing to pass over into other hands the leadership, she will fail in her duty only one degree less than if she refuses to enter the open doors.

The two greatest obstacles to Christianity in the East to-day are the unworthy lives of many nominal Christians, resident in the East, and the failure of Christianity to solve the social problems at home. The leaders of Japan, of China, and of India know about our red-light districts, about our lynchings, about our strikes, about our bomb outrages, about the industrial injustice that is found all through our country, about our tenement houses, and about our poverty and crime. The outrages upon Japanese residents in our Pacific Coast States a short time ago almost paralyzed the arms of the missionaries, who were working among people who resented these unjust acts. It is true that the churches must Christianize the world in order to save America, for without the world vision they will neglect the task at their doors. It is equally true that they must Christianize the life of America or they cannot save the world. As it is the lives of the Christians abroad which commend Christianity to individuals yonder, so it is the life of the United States and Great Britain which will commend Christianity to Japan, China, and India ; and every step of progress here towards the better realization of the Kingdom of God will make so much easier the realization of the ideals of Jesus for Asia and Africa.

Christians rejoice in the forward movements at home. They take courage because of all those steps abroad which this book has sought to trace. The two are more closely related than is often realized. The task before the Church is the renewed dedication of itself to its Master and to His work of making the nations of the world the nations of our God and His. This study has failed of its purpose if it has not revealed the need of the world, the power of Jesus Christ, and the imperative duty of obedience to His last command. May the Church see the world through the eyes of the crucified and risen Lord, who was Himself a man of the Orient, all of whose active life was passed upon the soil of Asia, and who died that Orient and Occident might alike submit to His sway and be transformed into His likeness.

Bibliography

No attempt has been made to prepare a full bibliography of the subjects treated in this book. It has seemed wise, however, to list a few of the authorities which have been used in its preparation and to which those interested in pursuing the subject further may be referred. As the book concerns itself only with social movements of the last hundred years or so, volumes dealing with the social influence of early and medieval Christianity have been omitted. The books are arranged according to chapters.

General

Dennis, James S., "Christian Missions and Social Progress." 3 vols. New York, 1897–1906.

Dennis, James S., *et al.*, "World Atlas of Christian Missions." New York, 1911.

Chapter I

Eddy, Sherwood, "India Awakening." New York, 1912.

Jones, J. P., "India's Problem, Krishna or Christ." New York, 1903.

Chapter II

"Statesman's Year Book." London, 1913. Macmillan, New York.

"China Mission Year Book, 1911." Shanghai, 1911. M. E. M., New York.

"Japan Year Book, 1912." Tokyo, 1911.

Chapter III

Chintamani, C. Y., "Indian Social Reform." Madras, 1901.

Douglas, R. K., "Society in China." London, 1894.

Fuller, Mrs. M. B., "Wrongs of Indian Womanhood." New York, 1900.

Jones, J. P., *op. cit.*

Murdoch, Rev. John, "Papers on Indian Social Reform." Madras, 1892.

Smith, Arthur H., "Chinese Characteristics." New York, 1894.
  "Village Life in China." New York, 1899.

Wilkins, W. J., "Modern Hinduism." London, 1900.

Chapter IV

Blaikie, W. G., "Personal Life of David Livingstone." New York, 1880.

Fuller, Mrs. M. B., *op. cit.*

Griffis, W. E., "The Mikado's Empire." New York, 1876.

Jones, J. P., *op. cit.*

Chapter V

Bhattacharya, J. N., "Hindu Castes and Sects." Calcutta, 1896.

Chintamani, C. Y., *op. cit.*

Low, Sidney, "A Vision of India." London, 1906.

Morse, H. B., "The Trade and Administration of the Chinese Empire." Shanghai, 1908.

Richard, L., "Comprehensive Geography of the Chinese Empire," trans. M. Kennelly, S. J. Shanghai, 1908.

Smith, A. H., *op. cit.*

"China Mission Year Book," issues for 1910, 1911, 1912. M. E. M., New York.

"Christian Movement in Japan," for 1910. Tokyo, 1910. M. E. M., New York.

"Japan Year Book, 1912." Tokyo, 1911.

"Encyclopædia Britannica," 11th ed. Articles, "Caste," "Japan, Domestic History."

Chapter VI

Murdoch, Rev. John, "Papers on Indian Religious Reform." Madras, 1894.

Okuma, Count, Editor, "Fifty Years of Modern Japan." London, 1909.

World Missionary Conference, 1910. Report of Commission IV. Edinburgh, 1910.

Wherry, E. M., *et al.* editors, "Islam and Missions." New York, 1911.

Zwemer, S. M., *et al.* editors, "The Mohammedan World of To-day." New York, 1906.

Contemporary Review, August, 1893.

"Encyclopædia Britannica," 11th ed. Articles, "Arya Samaj," "Brahma Samaj," "Keshub Chunder Sen," "Ram Mohan Roy."

Index

ADI-SAMAJ, 254
Africa :
    Cannibalism, 149
    Christian leaders, 174
    Education, Industrial, 69
        Missionary, 37, 55
    Human sacrifices, 146 f.
    Legal system, 162
    Medical Missions, 71
    Ordeals, 162
    Polygamy, 97, 119
    Slavery, 164 f.
    Witchcraft, 162
    Woman, 97, 119
Africa, British South :
    Education, Mission :
        Effect of, 63
        Objections to, answered,
          63, 64
Africa, Eastern Central, slave-
    trade suppressed, 167
Agha Khan, 243
Aligarh College, 242
Allahabad Christian College, 67
Amanzimtote Seminary, 63, 70
Amoy, Infanticide, 152 f
Anglo-Mohammedan College,
    242
Animist, 268
Anti-Opium League, 176
Arya Samaj, 256, 258 f.
Assam :
    Human sacrifices, 146
    Slavery, 164
    Temperance, 145
Assiut College, 58
Attainments, limit change, 24
Azariah, Bishop, 174

BABY-TOWERS, 153
Bakin, 182

Balkan War, 230
Baroda women, marriage age, 100
Basel Mission, 65 f.
Bataks, Women of, 116
Batelas, Cannibalism, 149
Bechuanaland, Temperance in,
    143
Beirut, 58, 75
Bentinck, Lord, abolished *sati*,
    126
Blaikie, quoted, *re* Livingstone
    and slave-trade, 166
Blind and Deaf, Missionary
    Schools for, 54
Boarding Schools, Missionary,
    53, 55
Bombay, Plague statistics, 74
Bombay Social Conference, 125
Bose, Miss C. M., 133
Brahman, 192, 196
    Kulin, 103
Brahma-Samaj, 248 ff.
    Marriage age, 126
    Vid. Ram Mohan Roy,
      Debendra Nath Tagore,
      Keshub Chunder Sen
Brahma-Samaj of India, 254
Brown, S. R., 222
Buddhism :
    Ethics of priests, 141, 262
    Pessimism, 23
    Sway of, 235
Buddhism, Reformed, 260 ff.
    Ceylon, 260 f.
    Japan, 261 ff.
Bule women, 97
Bulgaria, Missionary influence
    on, 39
    Robert College, influence of,
      58
Burma, Temperance, 145

Burma, Upper, Human sacrifices, 146
Busoga, Sleeping sickness, 22

CANNIBALISM, 148 f.
Canton, Fight against gambling, 178
Carey, William :
    Educational work, 52
    re female infanticide, 155
    re sati, 126
Caste, 191 ff.
    Brahmans, position of, 196
    Divisions, 192
    Functions of, 193, 199
    Multiplication, 192 f.
    Obstacle to industrial education, 69
    Outcastes, 197, 213
    Relations of castes, 195 ff.
    Results, 198
    Rules, 194 ff., 212 f.
        Penalties for violating, 198, 212
    Spirit of, 194
    Statistics of, 192
    Sudras, 197
    Weakening of, 211
Ceylon, Buddhism, 260 f.
Changes, Social :
    Causes of, 20
    Extent in Orient, 25 ff.
    Limitations, 21
    Slowness of, 24
Character :
    Limits change, 24
    New types under Christianity, 174 ff.
    Relative permanence, 24
Chauhans, Infanticide, 154
Cheh-kiang, Infanticide, 152
China :
    Christians, 171, 174
    Constitution, reformed Manchu, 225
        Provisional republican, 226
    Coöperation, 211

Divorce, 110
Education, government, 57, 85
    Industrial, 70, 86
    Schools provided by decree of 1903, 81 ff.
Education, Missionary, 54 f.
    Government and, 56
    The missionary and, 37
Ethics, 140
Family, character and authority, 209 f.
Family life, 108 ff., 111
Foot-binding, 111, 179, 180 ff.
Fu, 206 f.
Gambling, 178 f.
Girls' orphan asylums, 153
Government, 205 ff.
    Changes in, 223 ff.
Hsien, 205
Individual in, 36
Infanticide, female, 151 ff.
Intemperance suppressed, 176
Marriage customs, 107 f.
    Among Christians, 128
Medical missions, 71, 75
Medical progress and training, 89
Opium, 176 ff.
Polygamy, 109
Railway development, effect of, 27
Reform, constitutional, 223 ff.
    Judicial, 227
    Prison, 228
Religions of, 23
Responsibility, corporate, 210
Revolution, 224
    Women in, 129 f.
Selfishness in, 172
Self-torture, 160
Slavery, 164
Social organization, 204 ff.
Standard of living, 87
Suicide, 158
Unity, increase in, 27

Village, government of, 206
Widows, 110
Woman, 106 ff.
    Christian, 128
    Clubs, 129
    Daily paper, 129
    Foot-binding, 111
    Progress, 128 f.
    Sale of, 107
    Schools for, 129
    The new, 130
    Wives, rights of, 108
    Vid. Foot-binding
Christ :
    Appeal of, 271
    Social influence, 20
Christian community, effects of
  poverty, 49
Christianity :
    Ethics of, 142 f.
    Naturalization of, 278
    Only hope of Orient, 266 ff.
    Strength, elements of, 267 ff.
    vs. advanced religions, 234
        animistic religions, 233 f.
Christians, Native :
    Africa, 174
    China, 174
    India, 133, 174
    Japan, 222
    New types of character, 174 ff.
    Relative immunity from
      plague, 74
    Attitude towards vices :
      Vid. Cannibalism, Infanti-
      cide, Truthfulness, etc.
Chuckerbutty, Miss S., 134
Chū-Gakkō, 77
Church, Duty of, 46, 231, 277
Cilicia, Christians and plague, 74
City problem, 28
Class spirit, 191
Climate effects, 21
Coillard, Pastor, 164, 167
Colleges, Missionary, 53 f.
Combinations, Industrial, 19
Commerce, Social influence of,
  26 f.

Confucianism, 23
Congo Valley :
    Human sacrifices, 146
    Ordeals, 163
Creek Town, *Vid. Old Calabar*
Cromer, Lord, 33, 241 note
Crowther, Bishop, 149

Dayanand Saraswati, 256 f.
Debendra Nath Tagore, 250
    Beliefs, 250 f.
Dependence, 18
Ding Li Mei, 174
Divorce, 110, 113
Doshisha students' record, 59
Du Bose, Dr., 176
Dutt, Miss Toru, 134
Dutt, R. C., 33

Economic Life, Relation to
  soil, 22
Education :
    Effect of, 27, 41
    Relation of missionary to,
      37, 39
Education, Christian, 92 f.
Education, Government, 77 ff.
    China, 81 ff.
    India, 80
    Japan, 77 ff.
Education, Industrial, 86
    Vid. Africa, India, etc.
Education, Mission :
    Elementary, 54, 55
    Government, relation to, 56 f.
    High Schools, 53, 55
    Industrial, 65 ff.
    Medical, 54, 75 f.
    Objections to, answered, 63 f.
    Statistics of, 53 ff.
    Women, 114 f.
Education, Secular, 45, 52
Elgin, Lord, Anti-nautch action,
  187
England, Industrial and social
  changes, 20
Environment, Influence of, 17
Eta, Vid. Japan

Ethical Ideals, *Vid. Ideals, Ethical*

Ethical Standards, 36

Ethics :
Difficulty of comparison, 138
Divorced from religion, 140
Effect of Christianity upon, 142 f.
Vid. China, Japan, India, Islam, etc.

Evils, Social, 30 ff., Chapters II–V
Vid. Ignorance, Poverty, etc.

FAITH, in India and Japan, 142

Family, Importance of, 95 ff.
Progress in Ideals of, Chapter III

Female infanticide act, India, 156

Feudalism, Japan, 200

Fiji Islands :
Cannibalism, 148 f.
Infanticide, 151

Foochow :
Infanticide, female, 152 f.
Baby-tower, 153
Foot-binding, 180

Foot-binding, 111, 179 f.
Missionary and, 38, 180

Formosa :
Temperance, 145
Truthfulness of Christians, 170

GAMBLING, 178 f.

God, Christian Doctrine of, 267

Gold Coast, ordeals, 163

Goreh, Miss, 135

Gospel, effect and appeal, 41 f.

Government, Corruption of, 36

Grants-in-aid, 56

Great Britain and slave trade, 165

Griffis, Dr. W. E., 181

Gujarat, Infanticide, 154

HANKOW, Infanticide, 154

Hausaland slave-trade, 165

Hawaii :
Industrial education, 65
Instructions to missionaries, 42

Health conditions, effect of, 21

Heimin, Vid. Japan

Hervey Islands, *Vid. Raratonga*

Hindu, The, re position of woman, 122

Hinduism :
Change of views *re* polytheism, 239
re idolatry, 239
Expansion, 235
Indebted to Christ, 239
Pessimism, 23

Hinduism, Reformed, 248 ff.
Vid. Brahma Samaj, Arya Samaj

Hinin, Vid. Japan

Holi, festival, 186

Holy men, 141

Home, Christian, 117 f.

Honesty, lack of, 36

Hong Kong, Christians and plague, 74

Honour, Missionary influence on, 40

Hook-swinging, India, 160

Housing, Problem of, 28
Reform in United States, 19

Human sacrifice, 145 ff.

IDEALS, ETHICAL :
Growth and influence, 28
Missionary and, 38

Ideals, Social, Missionary and, 38

Ignorance, 30
Removal of, Chapter II

India :
Ascetics, 159
Caste, 191 ff.
Weakening of, 211
Christian leaders, 174
Christians, poverty, 49
Doctrine of faith, 142

Economic inefficiency, 32
Education, 80
    Hindu, 80
    Moslem, 80
Education, Government, 80
    Christian women teach-
      ers, 62 f.
    Industrial, 86
Education, Missionary, 54 f.,
  56
    Effect of, 60
    Government, relation to,
      56
    Influence of higher
      schools, 60
    Standing of, 61
Education, Missionary In-
  dustrial, 65 ff.
Ethics, 140
Government, 216 f.
    Municipal, 215
    Representation in, 216 f.
Holy men, 141
Human sacrifices, 145, 147
Impurity, 184 ff.
Infanticide, female, 154 ff.
    Act of 1870, 156
    Sacrificial, 155 f.
Islam, *Vid. Islam, India*
Marriage, early, 100 f.
    Raising of age, 125
Medical missions, 71, 90
Ordeals, 161, 164
Outcastes, influence of Chris-
  tianity upon, 175
    Education, 61 f.
Political unrest, 105 f.
Polygamy, 103
Poverty, 33
    Social effects of, 48
Prostitution, 141, 186
    Religious, 187 f.
Purity, new standards, 185
Races, 193
Sati, abolished, 38, 126 f.
Self-torture, 159
Slavery, 164
Suicide, 158

Truthfulness of Christians,
  171
Widows, 103 f.
    Child-, 105
    Marriage of, 127
    Widow Marriage Act,
      127
Woman, 99 ff.
    Christians, 133 ff.
    Conservative force, 96 f.
    Education, 123
    New attitude towards,
      122
    Progress, 121
    Vid. Caste
Indian Social Conference, 187
Indian Social Reformer, 157
Indians, North American, indus-
  trial education, 65
Individual :
    Missionary influence on po-
      sition of, 40
    Position in Japan, 204
    Position of, in Orient, 35,
      189
    Type of, created by Chris-
      tianity, 172
Industrial Training, Missionary,
  53, 55
Industry :
    Influence of new, 28
    Missionary, relation of, to, 38
    New dangers in, 45 f.
Inefficiency, Economic, 31 f., 39,
  Chapter II
Infanticide :
    Female, 151 ff.
    Prevalence of, 150 f.
Influence, Western, 26, 45
    Missionary's relation to, 37
Initiative, lack of, 190
Institutions, Social, 18 f.
Intemperance, 143 f.
Irrigation, 23
Ishii, Mr., 222
Islam :
    Ethics of, 142
    India, 241 ff.

Agha Khan, 243
Educational societies, 246
Mirza Shulam Ahmed, 246
Rational reinterpretations of, 244 f.
Sayed Ahmed Khan, 242
Social reforms, 243
Modifications of, 240
Slavery under, 164
Sway of, 235

JAINS, Infanticide, 155
Jamaica, Slavery, 168
Janes, Capt., 222
Japan:
Adopts achievements of others, 25
Buddhism, *Vid. Buddhism, Reformed*
Christian influence in, 175, 222
Commoners, 202
Concubinage, 131, 181
Daimyos, 202, 218
Divorce, 113
Earthquake construction, 23
Education, Government, 77 ff.
Industrial schools, 70, 87
Education, Mission, 54 f., 57, 59 f.
Missionary and, 37
Eta, 203
Faith, doctrine of, 142
Feudal organization, 200 ff.
Government, 219 ff.
and mission education, 56
Reconstruction of, 217 ff.
Heimin, 202
Hinin, 203
Individual, position of, 204
Industrial changes, 20, 87
Journalism, Christian influence on, 59

Literature:
Ethical tone, 264
Influence of Christian schools upon, 59
Marriage, forms of, 113
Medical progress and training, 87
Monogamy in, 183
Moral tone, 45
Nobility, 201
Orphanages, Christian, 76
Patriotism, 172
Philanthropy, 91
Poverty, effects, 48
Prostitution, 181
Purity, 181 ff.
Revolution of 1869, 217 ff.
Samurai, laws *re*, 201 f., 218
Sanitation, 88
Slavery, 164
Suicide, 157 ff.
Temperance, 145
Truthfulness of Christians, 171
Virtues, retention of, 221
Woman, 112 ff.
Christian influence on, 136
Dangers for, 131 and note
Progress, 130 ff.
Johannesburg, record of mission education, 63 f.
Johnston, Sir Harry H., 167
Justice:
Absence of, 36
Effect of Gospel upon, 41

KENJIRO, TOKUTOMI, 59
Keshub Chunder Sen, 253 ff.
Khama, Chief:
Character, 174
Fight for temperance, 143 f.
Polygamy suppressed, 119
Kindergartens, Missionary, 54
Kinnear, Dr., 75
Koran, New attitude towards, 244 f.

Korea :
    Medical progress, 88
    Slavery, 164
    Vid. Japan
Kois, Ordeals among, 161
Kōtō-Gakkō, 78
Kshatriyas, 192

Le Roy, Rev. W. E., 63
Lewanika :
    Human sacrifices suppressed
        by, 148
    Ordeals under, 164
Life, Estimate upon, 35
Lifu, Cannibalism suppressed, 149
Literature, Western, 27
Little, Mrs. Archibald, 180
Living, Standard of, 33, 39
Livingstone, David and slave-
    trade, 166
Livingstonia Mission, 70
Lovedale, 70

Macgowan, Dr., 180
Madagascar :
    Infanticide, 151
    Ordeals, 162, 164
Madras :
    Infanticide, female, 157
    Marriage age, 126
Madras Christian College, 60
Maebashi, Prostitution in, 182
Malwa, Infanticide, female, 154
Maoris :
    Cannibalism, 149
    Temperance, 144
Mazumdar, 172
Mbau Island, Infanticide, 151
Medical Missions, aim, 51
    Vid. Missions, Medical
Medical Schools, Missionary, 54
Medical work, need, 70
Medicine :
    Development of, 87 ff.
        China, 89
        India, 90
        Japan, 88
        Siam, 89

Missionary and, 39
    Social results of, 41
Men and Religion Movement, 42
Messina earthquake, 20
Mirza Ghulam Ahmed, 246
Missionaries, Medical, 72
Missionary :
    Scope of work of, 43 f.
    Social influence, 37 ff., 40
    Influence on Bulgaria, 39
    Influence *vs.* Foot-binding, 38
        Ignorance, 39
        Obscenity in Hinduism,
            38
        sati, 38
    Influence on Turkey, 39
        in suppressing social
        evils :
        *Vid. Cannibalism, In-
        fanticide, Ordeals, etc.*
Missions :
    Aim of, 42 f.
    Crisis of, 275 f.
    Objections to, 25
Missions, Medical :
    End of, in Japan, 87
    Extent of, 71
    Influence of, 72
    Plague, work against, 73
    Training natives, 75
    Women physicians, 71
Mitter, Miss Mary, 134
Morals, *Vid. Ethical Standards*
Mysore, marriage age, 100, 125

Natural-Foot Association, 180
Nature :
    Aspect of, 22, 41
    Dependence upon, 47
Nautch-girls, 186 f.
Neesima, Joseph H., 59, 222
New Hebrides, Woman, posi-
    tion, 98
New Zealand, Temperance, 144
Nigeria, Slavery, 169
Ningpo, Woman's Club, 129
Nitobe, Dr., 222
Nogi, General Count, 158 f.

Normal Training, Missionary, 53 f.

North-West Province, Infanticide, 157

Nurses' Training, Missionary, 54

Nyasaland :
    Ordeals, 162 f.
    Temperance, 144

OCCIDENT *vs.* ORIENT, 26

Okuma, Count, 222

Old Calabar :
    Cannibalism, 149
    Human sacrifices, 147
    Infanticide, 150
    Ordeals, 162 f.
    Slavery, 168

Opium, *Vid. China*

Opium Conference, International, 177

Ordeals, Cruel, 161 ff.

Orient *vs.* Occident, 26

Orphanages, Christian, 59
    Missionary, 54

Osaka, Prostitution, 182

Outcastes, *Vid. India, Outcastes*

PACIFIC ISLANDS :
    Vid. Infanticide, etc.
    Woman, 98, 119

Panama, Health conditions, 22

Parsees, Marriage law, 126

Patriotism, Lack of, 172

Peking :
    Government schools, 57
    Union Medical school, 76, 89

Persia, Education, 37

Pessimism, 23

Philanthropy, Christian, Chapter II

Philippines :
    Cholera, 22
    Slavery, 164

Plague, Immunity, 73 f.

Political, Ideals, 29
    Missionary, relation of, 38 f.
    Reforms, weakness, 231

Polygamy, 97 f., 103, 109

Population, Density, 22

Poverty, Chapter II, 33, 50 f.

Progress, Chapter I
    Hindered by poverty, 49
    Missionary, relation to, 37 ff.

Prostitution, *Vid. India, Japan, Purity*

Provincialism, 30

Purity, 36, 40
    Vid. India, Japan

RAJPUTS, Infanticide, 154

Ram Mohan Roy, Raja, 127, 248 ff.

Ramabai, Pundita, 134, 136

Raratonga, Cannibalism, 149

Rearing-marriage, 108

Red Cross Society, Japan, 91

Reform, Lack of leaders, 46

Religions, non-Christian :
    Changes in, Chapter VI
    Characteristics of, 236
    Disintegration of, 237
    Weakness of, 265 f.

Responsibility, personal, 189, 210

Rhodesia, Mission education, 56

Robert College, 58

Royal Niger Company, 169

SALVATION, Christian doctrine, 274

Samurai, hara-kiri, 157
    Vid. Japan

Sanitation, 28, 73

Sati, 38, 104, 126

Satthianadhan, Mrs., 134

Sayed Ahmed Khan, Sir, 242 f.

Selfishness, 172

Self-support, 49

Self-torture, 159 ff.

Seoul, temple, 264

Serampore college, 52

Sexes, in India, 155

Shans, Human sacrifices, 146

Shensi, Christians, 171

Shintoism, 266, 272

Shome, Mrs. N., 135

Siam, Slavery, 164
Sin, Christian Doctrine, 269
Singh, Miss L. R., 134
Slavery, 20, 41, 164 ff.
Slave-trade, Work of Livingstone, 166
Sleeping-sickness, 22
Social Ideals, *Vid. Ideals, Social*
Social Organization, Chapter V
Society Islands, Human sacrifices, 146
Soil, Influence of, 22
Sorabji family, 135 f.
Standards, Ethical, compared, 138 ff.
Standard of living, 41, 87
Steam engine, 20
Sudras, 192 f., 196 f.
Suffering, Physical, 31
Suicide, 157 ff.
Syrian Protestant College, 58, 75

Tamil proverbs, 99
Temple-girls, 187 f.
Thakurs, Infanticide, 157
Theological training, 53, 55
Tientsin orphan asylum, 153
Tilak, Rev., 174
Tokyo, Religious census, 237
Torture, Self-, *Vid. Self-torture*
Toson, Shimasaki, 59
Townsend, Meredith, 271
Trade, Relation of missionary to, 37
Transportation, Effect of, 26
Truthfulness, 36, 169 ff.
Tsuda, Miss Ume, quoted, 131 ff., note
Turkey :
    Constitutional reform, 229
    Education, Missionary, 37, 54, 56, 65
    Missionary influence, 39
    Religious disintegration, 238

Uganda :
    Education, 56, 70
    Human sacrifices, 146 f.
    Polygamy, 119
    Slavery, 169
United States, Slave-trade, 165
Universities' Mission to Central Africa, 167
Ushashi, Woman in, 98
Uyemura, Rev., 272

Vaccination, 73
Vaishyas, 192
Verbeck, Dr., 222

Warneck, Dr. J., 148
Watanabe, Judge, 222
West, Need of Christianizing, 231, 279
Widows, *Vid. China, India*
Widow-Marriage Act, 127
Witchcraft, 162
Woman, Chapter III
    Vid. Africa, China, India, etc.
Woman, Education, Christian, 39, 114 ff.
    Influence, 96
Woman, The New, 130 f.
    Vid. China, Japan
Women, Christian, 128, 133 ff., 136
    Vid. China, India, Japan
World's Women's Christian Temperance Union, 145

Yokoi, 222
Yoruba, Human sacrifices, 148
Young Turks, 39, 58

Zanzibar, Slave-trade, 165, 167
Zulu, Preacher, 174
    Homes, 119 f.
Zulu Mission, Temperance, 144

Printed in the United States of America

ROLAND ALLEN, M.A.

Essential Missionary Principles

12mo, cloth, net $1.00.

An author new to American readers has claimed attention of students of missions through his recent thought-compelling book, *Missionary Methods—St. Paul's or Ours?* This latter volume dealing with the *principles* of missions well supplementing the volume on *methods*.

ROLAND ALLEN, M.A.   *Library of Historic Theology*

Missionary Methods : St. Paul's or Ours ?

With Introduction by Rt. Rev. Henry Whitehead, D.D., Lord Bishop of Madras. 8vo, cloth, net $1.50.

Is this book the true answer to the question as to why Christian Missions do not progress to-day as rapidly as we should like to see them doing? Dr. Allen was formerly a missionary in North China and author of "The Siege of Peking Legations", and writes from large experience. His arguments for the application of truly Pauline methods of envangelization in foreign mission fields are startling. The reader may not agree with all of his criticisms and suggestions but the discussion which will be aroused cannot fail to be helpful. It is a vigorous presentation of a profoundly important subject.

MISS MINNA G. COWAN

The Education of the Women of India

Illustrated, 12mo, cloth, net $1.25.

The subject is treated historically, philosophically and suggestively. The contributions made by the government, the East Indians themselves and the missionaries, to solving the educational problems of the country are clearly shown. The book is an important and suggestive addition to the literature of education in foreign lands, being a worthy companion volume to Miss Burton's "The Education of Women in China."

LIVINGSTON F. JONES

A Study of the Thlingets of Alaska

12mo, cloth, illustrated, net $1.50.

For twenty-one years the author has labored as a missionary representing the Presbyterian Board of Home Missions among the people about which he writes. Probably no living man is better qualified to tell about this interesting race. Hon. James Wickersham says: "Contains much that is new and valuable in respect to the social life and ancient customs of the Thlinget Indians. An interesting and valuable contribution to the ethnology of the Pacific Coast."

M. WILMA STUBBS

How Europe Was Won for Christianity

Illustrated. 12mo, cloth, net $1.50.

The story of the first seventeen centuries of Christianity is here told in the lives of the great missionaries of the church beginning with St. Paul. So far as we are aware no single volume containing so complete a collection of the lives of these pioneers in missionary work has before been published. Miss Stubbs has done a very real and important service to the cause of missions in making the lives of these great men live for the inspiration of younger generations of to-day.

R. FLETCHER MOORSHEAD, M.B., F.R.C.S.

The Appeal of Medical Missions

12mo, cloth, net $1.00.

The author is Secretary of the Medical Mission Auxiliary of the British Baptist Mission Society and Baptist Zenana Mission. He gives a general survey of the main considerations upon which the Medical Mission enterprise is based, presenting a true conception of the need, value and importance of this great work in the spread of the Gospel. Dr. Moorehead knows his subject well and he gives a wealth of interesting facts regarding The Character and Purpose of Medical Missions—The Origin and Authority, Justification, Need, Value—The Practice of Medical Missions, Woman's Sphere in Them, Training for, Home Base, Failure, Appeal, etc.

JAMES S. DENNIS, D. D.

The Modern Call of Missions:

Studies In Some of the Larger Aspects of a Great Enterprise. 8vo, cloth, net $1.50.

"This is a magnificent presentation of the call of missions, showing their great and sweeping influence on human life and social progress. It is a logical and searching study of the power of the Gospel as it goes into other lands and there meets the facts and elements that make up the life of the people. Dr. Dennis has had the personal experiences and knowledge which enable him to speak with authority. An exceedingly valuable contribution to the missionary literature of the day."—*Herald and Presbyter.*

ARCHIBALD McLEAN

Epoch Makers of Modern Missions

Illustrated, 12mo, cloth, net $1.00.

The author of "Where the Book Speaks," has given in these "College of Missions Lectures" a series of sketches of modern missionary leaders which for clearness, brevity, directness of style and inspirational value, have rarely been surpassed. Each characterization is truly "much in little," and the book is a distinct and most acceptable addition to missionary biography.

BELLE M. BRAIN

Love Stories of Great Missionaries

Illustrated, 12mo, cloth, net 50c.

Miss Brain has made a distinct place for herself in missionary literature. She is preeminently a story-teller, knowing well how to invest her subject with charm and interest. In these love stories of the World's great missionaries she is at her best. It is evident from these romances of Judson and Gilmour and Livingstone and Moffat and Caillard and Martyn, which she portrays with such fascination, that love, courtship and marriage are very vital factors in the Missionary Enterprise.

JULIA H. JOHNSTON

Fifty Missionary Heroes Every Boy and Girl Should Know

Illustrated, 12mo, cloth, net $1.00.

The author of that popular Mission Study Text Book, INDIAN AND SPANISH NEIGHBORS, has supplied a real need in this volume for Junior readers and leaders. Miss Johnston gives living portraits of a large number of missionary heroes well adapted to interest and inspire young people.

EMILY E. ENTWISTLE

The Steep Ascent

Missionary Talks With Young People. 12mo, cloth, net $1.00.

Martha Tarbell says of the book, "It is exceedingly well and interestingly written, adapted to the Junior and lower Intermediate grades for which so few books of this sort are written."

BASIL MATHEWS, M.A.

The Splendid Quest

Stories of Knights on the Pilgrim Way. 12mo, cloth, net $1.00.

The Prologue, "The Pilgrim's Way," serves as a background for the life stories of famous Knights of the Quest which follow. The stories are suitable for children of from 8 to 15.

REV. W. MUNN

Three Men on a Chinese Houseboat

The Story of a River Voyage Told for Young Folks. Illustrated, 12mo, cloth, net $1.00.

The story of an actual trip up the Yang-tse river taken by three missionaries on the way to their stations. In breezy, easy-flowing narrative one of the three tells the very interesting story of their fifteen hundred mile journey. The book should be a very acceptible addition to missionary stories and side-light reading.

JOHN T. FARIS　　　*Author of "Men Who Made Good"*

The Alaskan Pathfinder

The Story of Sheldon Jackson for Boys. Illustrated, 12mo, cloth, net $1.00.

The story of Sheldon Jackson will appeal irresistibly to every boy. Action from the time he was, as an infant, rescued from a fire to his years' of strenuous rides through the Rockies and his long years' of service in Alaska, permeate every page of the book. Mr. Faris, with a sure hand, tells the story of this apostle of the Western Indians in clear-cut, incisive chapters which will hold the boy's attention from first to last.

G. L. WHARTON

Life of G. L. Wharton

By Mrs. Emma Richardson Wharton. Illustrated, 12mo, gilt top, cloth, net $1.25.

A biography of a pioneer missionary of the F. C. M. S., written by a devoted wife who shared the experiences of her husband in a long service in India and Australia. It is a life of unusual interest and an important addition to the annals of modern missionary effort.

MRS. LAURA DELANY GARST

A West Pointer in the Land of the Mikado

Illustrated, 12mo, cloth, net $1.25.

The story of a great life given unreservedly to the service of God in Japan—a life story representative of the best the West sends the East and typical of that missionary spirit in America which is one of the marvelous things in the growth of the Christ life in man. The Christian world will be proud of and wish to study such a record—coming generations will find here inspiration and incentive for yet greater effort and larger sacrifice.

HENRY OTIS DWIGHT

A Muslim Sir Galahad

A Present Day Story of Islam In Turkey. Net $1.00.

"The author of 'Constantinople and Its Problems,' has written an intensely interesting story of present-day Turkish life. A fascinating picture of the Mohammedan world. Recent events in the Near East make this book of unusual interest, and a better book, throwing sidelights on the Mohammedan question, could not be found."—*Pacific Presbyterian.*

DANIEL McGILVARY, D.D.

A Half Century Among the Siamese and the Lao

An Autobiography of Daniel McGilvary, D.D. With an Introduction by Arthur J. Brown, D.D. Illustrated, 12mo, cloth, net $2.00.

There is no more fascinating story in fiction, or in that truth which is stranger than fiction The years of toil and privation of loneliness and sometimes of danger; how the missionaries persevered with splendid faith and courage until the foundations of a prosperous mission were laid are portrayed with graphic power. It is a book of adventure and human interest and a notable contribution to American foreign missionary literature."—*Presbyterian Banner.*

WILLIAM ELLIOT GRIFFIS, D.D., L.H.D.

A Modern Pioneer in Korea

The Life Story of Henry G. Appenzeller. Illustrated, 12mo, cloth, net $1.25.

This life is another stirring chapter in the record of modern missionary heroism. The author's name is a guarantee of its thoroughness, accuracy and interest. Dr. Griffis has woven a most picturesque and interesting background of Korean landscape, life and history. It is a book that will win interest in missionary effort.

MARGARET E. BURTON

Notable Women of Modern China

Illustrated, 12mo, cloth, net $1.25.

The author's earlier work on the general subject of Women's Education in China, indicates her ability to treat with peculiar interest and discernment the characters making up this volume of striking biographies. If these women are types to be followed by a great company of like aspirations the future of the nation is assured.

ROBERT McCHEYNE MATEER

Character-Building in China

The Life Story of Julia Brown Mateer. Illustrated, 12mo, cloth, net $1.00.

"Gives a vivid, many-sided picture of missionary work. It is, in fact, an answer to such questions as, How is missionary life practically lived? It is of engrossing interest alike to the advocates of missionary work and general readers who enjoy real glimpses of foreign and pagan civilization."—*Presbyterian Advance.*

NEWELL DWIGHT HILLIS, D.D.

Lectures and Orations by Henry Ward Beecher

Collected and with Introduction by Newell Dwight Hillis. 12mo, cloth, net $1.20.

It is fitting that one who is noted for the grace, finish and eloquence of his own addresses should choose those of his predecessor which he deems worthy to be preserved, the most characteristic and the most dynamic utterances of America's greatest pulpit orator.

DAVID SWING

The Message of David Swing to His Generation

Addresses and Papers, together with a Study of David Swing and His Message by Newell D. Hillis

12mo, cloth, net $1.20.

A collection of some of David Swing's greatest orations and addresses, mostly patriotic, none of which have before been published in book form. Dr. Hillis, who has gathered them together, contributes an eloquent tribute to his distinguished confrere in an Introductory "Memorial Address."

WAYNE WHIPPLE

The Story-Life of the Son of Man

8vo, illustrated, net $2.50.

Nearly a thousand stories from sacred and secular sources woven into a continuous and complete chronicle of the life of the Saviour. Story by story, the author has built up from the best that has been written, mosaic like, a vivid and attractive narrative of the life of lives. Mr. Whipple's life stories of Washington and Lincoln in the same unique form, have both been conspicuously successful books.

GAIUS GLENN ATKINS, D. D.

Pilgrims of the Lonely Road

12mo, cloth, net $1.50.

In nine chapters the author presents what he calls the "Great Books of the Spirit". Beginning with the Meditations of Marcus Aurelius, he interprets with spiritual insight and clarity of expression the Confessions of St. Augustine, Thomas a'Kempis' Imitation of Christ, the Theologia Germanica, Bunyan's Pilgrim's Progress, etc.

ROSE PORTER

A Gift of Love   and Loving Greetings for 365 Days

New Popular Edition. Long 16mo, net 50c.

"All the texts chosen present some expressions of God's love to man, and this indicates the significance of the title."—*The Lutheran Observer.*

www.ingramcontent.com/pod-product-compliance
Lightning Source LLC
Chambersburg PA
CBHW081145020726
47504CB00009B/2009